The Release of a Well-Padded Scotswoman

THE BIG
BLUE
JOBBIE #2

BY YVONNE VINCENT

Books by Yvonne Vincent

The Big Blue Jobbie

The Big Blue Jobbie #2

Frock in Hell (coming in 2021)

First published in 2021 by Yvonne Vincent
Copyright © 2021 Yvonne Vincent. All rights reserved

THE CAST

Me:

I'm Mrs V. Fan of cake, wine, gin, cocktails, ice cream, chocolate, presents, pyjama days and men in kilts (yes, I just copied and pasted that bit from the last book, but why meddle with perfection?) You might find a few mentions of Jaffa Cakes as you read. I am very easily distracted by shiny things, yet strangely focused when it comes to purloining other people's Jaffa Cakes. At the grand old age of forty-nine and ten quarters, I am the proud keeper of two young people, one grumpy husband and a couple of utterly perfect Jack Russells.

Mr V:

The aforementioned grumpy person. He is in charge of the sacred garage, where things magically go when I leave them by the front door. Once a year, he organises the sacred garage and shouts things like "IT IS NOT A TARDIS!" at me. His hobbies appear to be photography and preventing me from spending money on things we (allegedly) don't need. Thus far, he has been more successful at the former than the latter. He also keeps saying something about him not being the only one who should put the bins out, but none of us have a clue what he's talking about. I love him heart and soul. And I know that he lovesh me very very mush on the rare occasion he drinks beer and decides that shexy shenanigans might be on the cardsh, what with him being an utter shex god and all.

Cherub 1:

Cherub 1 is my gorgeous daughter who, despite our efforts, has turned into a brilliant young adult. Yes, I'm as surprised as you! We have lovely conversations about boys, fashion and why I never told her that her eyebrows were truly hideous when she was sixteen. She's twenty-one. One day she'll understand. At least she has come out the other end of her teenage years with a healthy appreciation of comfy pyjamas and the healing power of chocolate. For that, she has me to thank. I can only assume she inherited being a bossy-boots from someone else.

Cherub 2:

Nineteen and knows it all. Actually, genuinely knows it all. He likes a good documentary and tells me off for turning up the heating. Jeez! It's like living with two Mr Vs sometimes. He is also possibly the nosiest person I have ever met. As a wee boy, no drawer was safe. As a young adult, he cannot cope with unopened post. He likes to know what's in all the parcels and we will have to wait until he moves out before we can order anything from Ann Summers.

The Wee Hairy Boys (WHBs)

Biggles:

Excitable Jack Russell. Age almost eleven but behaves like a bonkers puppy. Hobbies are barking threateningly at everything and running away, chasing the vacuum cleaner, biting the watering can and standing behind the shed. None of us quite know why behind the shed is his happy place but he goes there when he's happy, sad, scared or just fancies a good old bark. He's terrified of the wind so spends quite a lot of time behind the shed on windy days. Hates surround sound, farts, bathrooms and the mail. Sleeps with Cherub 1 and no alternative will do. Refuses to get up most mornings. Mr V calls Biggles 'FOMO', although he recently confessed that he sometimes gets confused and accidentally calls him 'MOFO.'

Vegas:

Elder statesman Jack Russell. Age fourteen. Smelly, deaf, senile, no teeth and follows me around everywhere. Goes the wrong way at the top of the stairs when he comes to bed with me every night, despite having lived in the same house his entire life. Occasionally gets it right, but carries on walking and can be found in the en-suite, wondering where his bed has gone. Hobbies are sleeping and eating. He used to enjoy licking his balls, but we had to have them removed last year. Since then, his bottom has somewhat expanded and his laziness has reached new heights.

Lovely Granny & Grandad (LG &G):

Very important people and beloved by all. LG makes valiant efforts to crack technology and G ignores the fact that technology exists at all. Somehow, they muddle through together and occasionally get Netflix to work. More importantly, they always have a good selection of biscuits.

Old Ivy Next Door:

Our neighbour. Nice lady. Does things like gets properly dressed in case she has to answer the door to the postman, irons her tea towels and takes her washing in at the first drop of rain. Regards my laissez-faire attitude to wearing matching socks with suspicion. Possibly thinks my children are heathens, due to Cherub 2's loud and repeated use of the eff word since he discovered it at the tender age of seven.

That brings you up to speed with who's who and what's what. As we trundle along, you'll often read references to Wineday. The days of the week are Monday, Tuesday, Wednesday, Almost Wineday, Wineday, More Wineday and Sunday. This is definitely factually correct. The only thing left to mention is Covid Corner. This my name for our dining room, where I have been shielding and working from home during lockdowns. I wisely chose the room where we keep All The Wine. And possibly All The Gin. If I could move the fridge in, I would.

IN THE BEGINNING

Have you ever wondered why there is a dangly red ball under the ironing board? You may not have wondered, but you are probably wondering now. Be still your googling fingers, for I will explain. In my view, it is all the fault of Adam and his inability to appreciate a good cushion.

In the beginning, God was having a nice rest after creating Man. She was rather fed up of working from home and all the spare bits of Man were cluttering up the place. 'What this workshop needs,' She mused, 'is a makeover.' God quickly created online shopping and got down to business.

Man ambled over to see what God was up to. 'Cushions,' She told him. 'We need cushions.' Man had no idea what God was talking about, so She quickly invented cushions and showed him. Man still had no idea what God was talking about. What was the point of these squidgy square things? God assured him that cushions would make beds and chairs look pretty. Man foresaw a future of having to remove cushions from beds and chairs so that he could relax, and a future of being yelled at to put them back again when he had finished relaxing. He tried to tell God that cushions seemed like a waste of…whatever She was going to use to get the cushions. 'Money!' cried God, slapping Herself on the celestial forehead for forgetting to create a means of trade. Quickly, She invented money and immediately the earth started to spin. 'Wow!' God gasped. 'Money makes the world go round.' And that is how God also accidentally created gravity.

Not content with gravity creation via the means of cushion shopping, God got on with the important business of picking out paint. Man looked at Her basket and reminded Her that She didn't need to buy a new roller because there were about fifty of them in the shed from all the other times She'd decided that Heaven needed a makeover. In fact, there were also approximately three billion tins of paint in there from previous makeovers, all with a tablespoon of paint at the bottom and the lids glued firmly shut.

God was becoming rather impatient with Man's attempts to do what he called helping and She called interfering. She told him to go to his shed and stay there until he was ready to discuss new curtains. Man complained that She had no right to banish him to his shed for eternity and, ever since She created spiders, his shed was a bit scary. What he needed was a nice, Manly place to go. A place where there were things to do and no cushions. Somewhere with plants and stuff he could climb and different types of rocks that he could pontificate about. A Man-cave or a den, but an environmental den. 'So, what you want is an e-den?' God asked.

'Ooh, that's a good name for it,' said Man. 'You could fill it with trees and animals. Maybe some of that green stuff that tastes disgusting.'

'Grass?'

'No, vegetables. But grass too. I could use the machine in the shed to cut it.'

'I always wondered what that machine was for,' said God. 'I mean, I know I created it, but I was in a vengeful mood that day and was thinking more along the lines of something to cut your balls off. Then you gave me ice cream and I forgave you and I never really got round to finishing it. Good idea, Man. I'll make a lovely garden for you and we'll call it Eden.'

Distracted from Her divine decorating, God got on with creating Eden. She decided that, as gravity now existed, Earth would be a good place to put Eden. After all, you didn't want to go to all the trouble of creating pretty flowers, only for them to float off. It was quite difficult, though, because the Earth was turning and She kept missing and putting trees in the wrong places. It was also ridiculous that Man would happily live on a diet of chips and sausages, She decided, so She popped in loads of fruit and veg. He really ought to appreciate broccoli more. Perhaps She should put Woman in there to make him eat more fruit and vegetables. It would probably be a lot easier than having to invent clogged arteries and defibrillators. God rang Her friend, Eve.

'Hi Eve. I'm having a spot of bother with Man, so I'm making him a garden on Earth to get him out of my hair for a bit. Trouble is, he'll starve to death down there because I haven't made any sausage trees. You're an outdoorsy type. Could you go with him and help him live off the land. Maybe also explain cushions to him?'

Eve said she was up for the challenge and would even explain scented candles. She suggested that, rather than all of Man living in the garden, perhaps God could send just one man. God agreed to this most excellent of suggestions and said She'd send Adam. He was a reasonably sensible representative of the species, quite kind and God had blessed him with an enormous…At this point, God realised She'd need to make the fig leaves a bit bigger.

God put all of Her creative efforts into making the most beautiful garden. Some hours later, exhausted, She peeled off Her gardening gloves and put the spade back in the shed (because Herself help Her if She left it out – there would be no end of ranting from Man about how, since She was so bent on creating rust and rain, She had to take responsibility for putting things away). Nevertheless, something was nagging at Her. There was something missing. God looked at all the trees and carrots and daffodils and grass and rocks and birds. And the blank space, right in the middle. Yes, what Eden needed was a centrepiece. She popped the gloves back on and got to work.

The next morning, God showed Adam and Eve around Eden and they were truly amazed. As they approached the centre of the garden, God placed a hand on their shoulders and gravely told them, 'I've created the most wonderful place for you to live, but the tree you see before you took me ages. You see those dangly red things. Don't eat them. In fact, don't even touch them.'

'Why? What are they for?' asked Eve, breathless with anticipation.

'I haven't decided yet. I work in mysterious ways,' said God. 'Just know that, if you touch them, there will be consequences.'

They gazed at the tree in wonder, immediately desperate to taste the forbidden fruit. Or at least Eve was, because she liked vitamins and had a sweet tooth. Adam thought the dangly red things looked very tasty, but told God he'd have preferred a sausage tree.

Adam and Eve assured God that they definitely would not go near the dangly red things, no siree. God was not wholly (holy?) convinced, yet She left them to it and went back to Heaven.

Later, as She took her gardening clothes out of the tumble drier, God reflected that it had been quite good fun to mess with Adam and Eve's heads. She shook out Her trousers and wondered what on Earth had possessed Her to create linen. If there were ever a place that was the opposite of Heaven, She would make everyone there wear linen. See how they liked it when a rumpled ball emerged from the drier. What She needed was something to make the wrinkles go away.

With a wave of Her hand, God created irons. Then, realising that Her knees were well and truly buggered from all that gardening, so a towel on the floor wasn't working for Her, She waved Her other hand and created ironing boards. She gazed at Her ironing board and couldn't get rid of the nagging feeling that something was missing. What had She done last time She'd felt like this? Oh yes, dangly red things. That was the answer. That would mess with their heads for millennia.

AUGUST 2020

August was the month of almost normal. I took my first steps out of shielding and into the big, bad world of face masks, social distancing and queues for shops. The Chancellor told us all to Eat Out To Help Out and we took him at his word. Tantalised by cheap pub breakfasts, Mr V and I emerged from our cocoons. And after the Cherubs vociferously complained that we'd somehow forgotten to invite them, we had many a family pub breakfast. Of course, family breakfasts are never straightforward. There are complex trade negotiations over who will have whose food. Every breakfast began with hard bargaining - 'I will swap you one rasher of my bacon for your beans.' Lord help me, at one point I told the waiter not to give me eggs and I swear Mr V almost had a stroke. 'I would have had your eggs,' he hissed, far too polite to look like a greedy git in front of the waiter, yet happy to insist I call the waiter back so I could look like a twat by announcing that I did, after all, like eggs. I am utterly useless at breakfast trading and always end up with four fried tomatoes and no sausages.

In other breakfast news, August was the month when I hit peak middle class by burning brioche and almost setting the house on fire. It was like near death by Waitrose.

Other important things happened in August too; some of them unutterably sad, such as a train derailment in Aberdeenshire and a shockingly huge explosion at a warehouse in Beirut, and some of them utterly bonkers, such as all the flip-flopping around over UK exam results. As kids faced losing their university places due to an algorithm which worked/didn't work/ah-sod-it-we'll-go-with-the-teachers'-recommendations-which-is-what-we-should-have-done-in-the-first-place, the UK had its hottest day in years and actual flip flop sales went through the roof. COVID-19 slipped off the UK news agenda and we all started to relax.

Elsewhere, though, cases were on the rise and Russia announced it had developed a vaccine. All the other countries in the WHO WhatsApp groupchat sent rolling eyes emojis, ignored Russia and went back to wondering why the US had left the group. Belarus erupted in protests and the question on everyone's lips was 'Is Kim Jong Un really in a coma?' Two days later, he strode into a meeting and it turned out he was just joshing with us, the naughty minx.

My own life was a frenzied round of work and finishing off The Big Blue Jobbie. I'd thought that the hard work was done when I finished writing it. The hardest work was in the final edit! August was the month when I got very, very good at commas.

1st August

Queue? What Queue?

Hello shielding people of the UK. Welcome back to the world. How are you feeling?

It has sometimes felt like the shielding people were forgotten in all the kerfuffle over how the rest of the country was getting back to "normal". Unless you've been through it, I think it's difficult for other people to appreciate just how disruptive, lonely and bloody boring shielding can be. So, we need to make a fuss. Have a little celebration of the fact that you've made it through and can finally get in a car with your nearest and dearest, go visiting and eat someone else's biscuits for a change.

You might have all sorts of worries right now or you might be cracking open the champagne. Or you may not be in the least bit bothered. However you're feeling about coming out of shielding, I hope today you finally get all the hugs you deserve for enduring these months of isolation. And if there's nobody there to give you one, then I'm sending a nice, big digital hug your way.

I'm slowly coming to terms with the fact that I am probably the biggest twat in the village right now.

I went to the shop on my own for the first time yesterday. After Cherub 2 put a pause on Wineday with his pilfering of the Pinot, I was forced to go out in search of a replacement bottle.

I parked outside the little supermarket in the village, gave myself a quick high five for remembering to take a mask then confidently strode in, determined to follow All The Rules. Unfortunately, my brain gremlins got so excited by the thought that Mr V wasn't with me (therefore I could buy anything I wanted), that I instantly forgot about All The Rules. It's just as well it wasn't very busy. Half way through, arms full of pizza, wine and chocolate, I suddenly remembered that there was something about arrows and one-way systems in supermarkets. I quickly scanned the floor. Phew! No arrows.

I made my way to the ice cream section and gazed at all the lovely tubs, waving at me through the freezer window. 'Come here,' purred a sexy salted caramel, beguilingly, 'You know you want me.' A large tub of mint choc chip shouldered its way to the front and bellowed, 'No, pick me!' I looked at the forlorn, plain little vanilla, sitting quietly by itself in a corner, and wished I could lick it better. 'I'm sorry,' I told all the delicious ice creams, 'I only came in for wine and now my arms are full of all the other junk food plus some bananas to make me feel less guilty. I'll come back for you another day, I promise.' With that, I turned my back on the freezer of dreams and made my way to the checkout.

I have a new mask. The last one kept sliding down and made a smashing gag. The new one slides up and pokes me in the eyes. It seems there is no happy medium with masks and I felt the need to tell the checkout lady that, even though I couldn't have any ice cream, I wasn't crying. It was just the mask, in its a desperate bid to become a blindfold, making my eyes water. Jeez, there's an idea, if I ever truly want to embarrass Mr V in a shop then I could wear both masks and pretend to be a hostage.

With everything tucked away in my bag, I left the shop and drove home. On the way, I spotted Cherub 2 cycling up the street, headphones on, one hand on the handlebars and the other Snapchatting away on his phone, completely oblivious to the world around him. It is just as well he was cycling on the pavement because I briefly wondered if 'He Ruined Wineday' was sufficient defence for inadvertently losing control of the vehicle and accidentally running the thieving little bugger over.

When I got home I dutifully wiped all the shopping down and put it away in my mouth (except the bananas). Mr V asked how I managed, what with it being my first time out on my own.

'Absolutely fine,' I assured him, 'I stuck to All The Rules, got what I went for and came straight home.'

'Did you have to queue to get into the shop? There's always a queue there, it's sometimes quicker to go to the big supermarket down the road.'

'Erm...there wasn't a queue,' I blustered, picturing myself striding confidently past a few people, who inexplicably seemed to be hanging around the shop entrance. 'As I said, I stuck to All The Rules and everything was absolutely fine, no problems, definitely no queue. Tell you what though, this new mask keeps poking me in the eyes. Couldn't see a thing for my eyes watering!'

***

I know this bit appeared in BBJ but it seemed weird to start the next book on 2nd August.

***

2nd August

I Did the Big Blue Jobbie

I finally got off my well-padded backside and wrote a book! Thank you for all the lovely comments and encouragement.

I finished the book yesterday and submitted it to my editor, Mr V, with a strong suggestion that he keep the constructive criticism to a minimum. He tried to give me constructive criticism about my dishwashing technique the other day. Is it polite to dry the big pan *before* or *after* you batter someone to death with it?

Anyway, The Big Blue Jobbie by Mrs V, age 49 and seven quarters, is complete. I've taken all my lockdown posts and tied them together with narrative and lots of extra bits (including some bits I wrote but never posted, mainly because Mr V said, 'You can't write that, my mum will read it!'). The book will take you on a family journey from 1st March until 1st August, with some reminisces of more normal times and a few diversions along the way. I really hope that readers will recognise themselves in it, but most of all, I hope it makes everyone laugh.

Even if nobody but my family buys it, at least I can tick 'write a book' off my bucket list. Also, if nothing else, I have become very good at punctuation. I'll let you know when it's published and you can check all my brilliant commas.

Having spent several hours a day writing for the last two months, on top of working and being a full-time nuisance, I reckon I'm due a wee break. I'm going to have some non-writing days to recharge my batteries and get some jobs done around the house. I just wanted to share my cock-a-hoopness with you and say thanks.

7th August

Jaffa Cake Wars

Cherub 2 appeared with two boxes of Jaffa cakes yesterday.

'I keep finding these all over the place. Who's leaving them lying around? I even found some in Mount Ironing! I bet it's Cherub 1.'

'It was me,' I admitted. 'I hid all your father's Jaffa cakes.'

'Well, I'm sick of finding them everywhere so I'm giving them back,' said my little traitor.

'Snitches get stitches,' I hissed at him.

It made no difference. He grassed me up anyway. But he hasn't found all the boxes, so I win. Two of them are in Covid Corner, so I fished a packet out today and ate the whole thing during an extremely long online meeting. Completely forgetting that the cameras were on, of course. And now all my colleagues think I'm a greedy cow. Which I am, but they didn't need to know that.

It was a very serious meeting with important bosses, but there was a part which didn't apply to me so, being a teensy bit bored, I decided to play around with the camera settings. To cut a long story short, I ended up superimposing a beach scene behind me and I had no idea how to get rid of it. I had to spend two hours sitting on the effing Copacabana discussing statistics. And now all the bosses think I'm a twat. Which I am, but they didn't need to know that.

Anyway, Cherub 2, who feels he has had to put up with rather a lot from me recently, told Mr V, 'I'm never getting a wife. Not if this is how they behave.'

Thank goodness it's Wineday.

8th August

Housework Is NOT Very Exciting

Today I'm doing Adventure Housework. It will start off with a quick paddle in Lake Dishes, where the big dish, in all its lasagne encrusted glory, lurks beneath the water to surprise unwary dish washers.

This will be followed by a marathon around the house, dragging a vacuum cleaner with two over-excited Jack Russells firmly attached. A feat of both strength and endurance.

Next comes the breath-holding test in the boy bathroom, filled as it is with the delicate whiff of male urinal and crusty towels. I've written to Boris to suggest he adds the boy bathroom to the list of places where wearing a mask is mandatory.

Finally, I'll venture into the Clothes Mountains to scale the highest peak, Mount Washing. There will be a quick rescue mission to pick up any tasty knickers off the floor before Biggles can render them crotchless, followed by a superhuman effort to get All The Washing done. Mount Ironing, a shorter but tougher climb, will not be tackled for at least another three weeks, while the family wait for the ironing fairies to arrive. During that time, the air will be rent by tortured cries of, 'Where is my favourite t-shirt?', as anyone under the age of 21 desperately scans the Clothes Mountain range but doesn't actually move any of the clothes to look properly (on the basis that they didn't put them there, so it's not their responsibility to move them).

In the late afternoon, I'll go for a nice relaxing swim in Loch Gin, with its lovely, clinky ice cubes and pretty glass. Cheers.

10th August

Posties Are Very Exciting

I thought I'd be energetic today and get some steps in by walking to the post office. But I left my fitness tracker upstairs. I couldn't be bothered to go get it and, with no fitness tracker to count the steps, really what was the point?

Mr V is on night shifts at the moment, so we all have to be quiet during the day. None of us are allowed to get excited when the postman visits. There's a new postman and I have to say that he is an improvement on the last one. Our old postie had a face like a bag of spanners and the sparkling personality of Eeyore, so the wee hairy boys and I are always pleased to see the new postie, with his cheery waves, jaunty manner and tasty letters. Tasty if you're canine - unless somebody posted me some cake, in which case I too would probably gnaw my way through the packaging.

Some may say that if I'm so keen on cake then I really should get my lazy backside upstairs and put on my fitness tracker. To those people I say, 'Chill out. Here, have a cocktail and a nice relaxing slice of Victoria sponge.'

11th August

Vegas and His Very Expensive Bum

Vegas has to go to the vet on Saturday, about his warty bum. The only saving grace about him licking his bum all the time is that he's forgotten about his balls and things have calmed down in the gentlemen's department. His cherries are no longer...cherry.

Mr V is at work on Saturday and has made it clear that I'm not to bankrupt us in my efforts to save Vegas' bottom. I'm using as my yardstick the amount Mr V is prepared to pay to get the dishwasher fixed so he doesn't have to wash dishes any more. Then I'll multiply that a few times because, even though he is warty, deaf, toothless and slightly confused, he is worth ten dishwashers. The dog, obviously. Mr V isn't warty.

The dishwasher repairman is coming tomorrow. The best thing about this is that it's Mr V's turn to do the dishes tonight. Yippee! No more dishes for me *does a little mum dance around the kitchen and wonders if she should cook something really complicated that involves lots of pans tonight, just to annoy Mr V*.

I am on a high so far this week. Getting all the things sorted and organised. Mr V is on a low because me being organised means him being nagged. He gave me a list of all the things he doesn't like:

Other people

All drivers

Other people

Messy teenagers

Those incapable of social distancing

Other people

      I suspect I come under the heading of 'other people' right now. Ho hum. He will love me again by Sunday, when he doesn't have to wash the Sunday roast tray and I've lied to him about the vet's bill.

13th August

Mr V Pushes My Buttons

You never really grow out of enjoying spinny chairs and pressing buttons, do you?

Mr V and I stayed up late the other night, trying to fix some stuff on the computer. Well, one of us was fixing. The other spun around so much on his breakfast bar stool that he made himself sick and had to sit quietly, resting his forehead on the kitchen counter top.

He found a €5 note on the counter. It was mine. I told him I'd discovered it in an old coat pocket and kept it to remind me of the good times camping in France. Mr V checked his wallet. £20, €10 and $7.

'If anyone sees my wallet they'll think I'm an international jet setter,' he said.

'Aye, an EasyJet setter,' I replied.

Let's face it, we're neither of us going to pass for the Beckhams. The one and only time I ever got an upgrade on a plane, I was so excited that I pressed all the buttons to see what they did. Then I looked up and all the other passengers were watching me with amusement, as seats and screens went all over the place.

Rich people get far better buttons than we do. When I grow up, I'm going to be rich and press All The Buttons.

14ᵗʰ August

Bursting with News

It is the happiest Wineday in the history of Winedays today. The Big Blue Jobbie has been published and I am so excited that I'm at serious risk of Being A Nuisance to everyone around me.

At the time of writing, it's only available in Amazon's Kindle Store and in Kindle Unlimited. The print version should be available in the next few days. I was holding off telling you in the hopes that the print version would come out, but I can't keep it to myself any longer.

Mr V came through to the kitchen a couple of days ago to tell me the exciting news that I'd sold my first one. 'Yes, it was me who bought it,' I said, bursting his wee bubble. He's delighted because he has a whole new set of charts and graphs to look at. He was quite horrified to discover that I wasn't keeping an eye on sales. 'The best bit about this whole thing is the bar charts!' he exclaimed.

Whether I sell five copies or five million, it is worth all these months of writing for hours after work just to see Mr V's happy wee face bathed in the glow of a 'Units Ordered' bar chart.

Thank you for all your encouragement. If you do buy a copy and enjoy it, I would be so grateful if you could leave a nice review on Amazon.

***

Mr V is appalled by my lackadaisical attitude towards sales. He got up one afternoon (yes, you heard me, AFTERNOON!) and asked, 'How many sales today?'

'No idea,' I replied.

'You mean you haven't looked!' he spluttered, outraged that I don't check the graphs at least six times a day. 'You never look. You're going to be one of those arty-farty airy-fairy writers who say "money is meaningless and I just struggle on in my villa in St Tropez" aren't you?'

I should point out that we actually live in a house with a leaky roof in the North of England. Nevertheless, I admire his optimism.

***

15th August

Wartybum Day

Shh, don't tell Mr V, but I put the heating on last night. And it's not even October! I'd know if it was October because that's my birthday. Also, our wedding anniversary. But, most importantly, it's the month of presents.

It's Wartybum day today. I took Vegas to the vets and he has to have an operation to get all his lumps removed (including his balls). The warts are actually benign tumours associated with hormones in older, uncastrated dogs. If we don't get them and Vegas' baubles removed, they'll just come back. I feel like, in the process, I'm taking away all his hobbies. What is he going to do when he has no cherries to lick?!

I told the vet that I was under orders not to agree to anything expensive, but I was going to agree to it anyway, because my wee hairy boy is worth it and Mr V wasn't there to object. She asked how I was going to break the news to Mr V. 'I'll tell him the operation is going to cost £2000 then I'll say I was only joking, it costs £400. He'll be so relieved, he'll think he's getting a bargain.' Worked like a charm.

So, it's back to the vet for Vegas on Thursday. After which, if he ever goes on holiday and is asked if someone could have interfered with his bags, he'll have to say yes!

16th August

Stay Dangerous

Hooray for all our lovely Welsh shielders today. You've been in isolation for such a long time and it will no doubt feel very strange to be able to go out again. Having been through it myself, I know there will be lots of mixed feelings about being released, particularly as we're not out of the woods yet. Sending you huge Mrs V hugs today and hoping that you're finally getting some real hugs from your nearest and dearest.

Also, hugs for all the readers around the world who are still locked down, in isolation or unable to get out. I should say stay safe, but I'm going to say stay dangerous. Because that sounds far more sexy and exciting. And I think we could all do with a bit of sexy and exciting right now.

Obviously, I don't mean actual dangerous. I'm doing enough cocking up of things at the shops to keep us all covered on that front. Yesterday, I carefully obeyed all the rules in the supermarket, except masks. I'd only got a few steps in the door when I realised I'd forgotten. I was surprised that nobody took out a big stick and chased me around the shop for being an idiot! I carefully checked I had bags, mask, purse and phone, walked the ten metres to the shop and went blank. That feeling where you know something is missing but you can't figure out what. The same feeling that I suspect Vegas will have at the vets on Thursday, when he wakes up after his operation.

I suspect I was having a bout of menopausal brain fog. I apologised to the security guard at the door, but you can't really go about saying to people, 'Sorry, it's "the change". Look! I'm wearing cut off trousers and I haven't shaved my legs. You could braid them and I don't even care! Because I'm hot, itchy, unaccountably grumpy and my brain gremlins appear to have lost the ability to multitask.' That seemed rather a long explanation to give security Steve, who hadn't even noticed my faux pas because he was too busy trying to discreetly pick his nose and wipe the bogies under the hem of his blazer. So, I contented myself with a simple, 'Oh bugger, sorry, forgot the mask.' Security Steve couldn't have cared less. He just rolled a nice crusty bit between his fingers and gave me a cheery smile. Let's hope they never move Security Steve to bakery. Crunchy scones. Yum.

Anyway, to all you lovely people out there who are going to have to deal with shops and rules for the first time - it's not as scary as you expect and, despite the outrage in the newspapers about folk not following all the rules, most people are surprisingly decent if you make a mistake.

Stay dangerous ;-)

17th August

DOODLEOODLEOO...DOO - DOO – DOO

It was a bit cool the other night, so I popped on the shawl that Lovely Granny bought me for Christmas. The shawl that makes me feel like a sophisticated lady, with style and panache. The shawl that I imagine all the other ladies covet and think, 'I wish I had a shawl like that sophisticated lady over there,' whenever they see me in it.

Mr V said, 'Why are you wearing that? Are you going for a gunfight?'

I looked in the mirror and realised that I did indeed resemble a short, plump extra in The Good, The Bad and The Ugly. I'm not sure which one I was, possibly all three.

Anyway, turns out that all this time, rather than strutting my sexy stuff like a swish and stylish supermodel, I've been clomping around like Clint Eastwood after a few too many cakes.

Now, in these situations you can either worry that you've made a complete tit of yourself on many an occasion and die a little on the inside, or you can brazen it out and not give a damn. I considered all my options. Really, as a smart and sophisticated lady who likes online shopping, there was only one option available to me.

And that is why I went straight onto Amazon and ordered a cowboy hat to complete the look. If Mr V thinks I look like I'm going for a gunfight, then he better be prepared to be my pardner next time we mosey on down to the supermarket. If the punk is feeling really lucky, I may also wear a bandana for a mask. Yee haw!

18th August

Yee Haw Indeed

Whoop! My cowboy hat has just arrived. I went for a black hat because my shawl is grey, so wearing a brown cowboy hat would just look ridiculous.

We're off out now. Unfortunately, it's too warm for the shawl, but I feel that the hat is a fashion statement on its own. All the other ladies will be so jealous.

***

At the time of writing (March 2021), I still have the hat. I hung it off the Covid Corner guitar for a bit of country and western ambience and I felt like Dolly Parton. I have the boobs, if not the waistline or the theme park. Maybe someday, when I grow up, I will be famous and someone will name a theme park after me. TwatLand has a nice ring to it.

***

19th August

Hats off to Mrs V

I got into the car yesterday and immediately noticed a problem.

'It's not very comfy, I can't put my head back against the seat.'

Mr V looked round at me and said, 'Oh, you're not actually wearing that, are you?'

'And this is a problem, why?' I asked, innocently twirling the strings of my lovely new cowboy hat.

'Well...it's...erm..um...yes it's ...hmmm...although it's not as bad as the tiara,' muttered the love of my life. I thought he liked my tiara! I mean, he may have asked me to take it off once or six times, but he wasn't serious. Was he?

I should explain that I insisted on wearing a tiara all day on my birthday. Supermarket, shops and posh tearoom; all were graced with a visit from a particularly sparkly, well-padded Scotswoman. And today, Starbucks, the Apple Store and Costco were due to be graced with a visit from a cowgirl with a bottom guaranteed to spill over the sides of any horse.

Mr V looked at my crestfallen expression, sighed and said, 'But if it makes you happy, wear it.' It did indeed make me happy.

Now, I know that in parts of America a lady in a cowboy hat is quite normal. In a rainy car park in England it is...less usual. We moseyed into the shopping mall, me tipping my hat to people and Mr V walking several paces behind in the vain hope that nobody would notice he was with me. I began to suspect that he was getting twitchy about the hat. That possibly he (gasp) didn't like the hat?

It was when I walked up to the Apple Store man and said, 'Howdy stranger, I'm not from around these parts,' that Mr V finally snapped.

'Go and put the hat in the car,' he hissed. I decided that this might not be the best time to point out that I am a delight, cowgirls probably have very strong thighs from all the horseback riding, my Texan accent is brilliant (if a little Welsh) and it was almost his idea to get the hat in the first place i.e. all my best arguments for wearing a cowboy hat. I appeared to have accidentally broken my husband, so I did the decent thing and popped the hat back in the car.

I have had to content myself with wearing the cowboy hat around the house. All the time. And whistling the theme tune to The Good, The Bad and The Ugly to announce my arrival in every room. Mr V says I'm being a nuisance.

As a kind and considerate wife, I have given this some thought and decided that the hat is clearly the problem here. It definitely can't be me.

20th August

And Balls off to Vegas

Okay, it's Vegas' big day at the vets today, so I've stopped messing about with hats. I've dropped him off and I'll spend the rest of the day on tenterhooks.

I thought a bout of housework would distract me from worrying, but then I gave myself a good talking to and opted to sit in the sun with a book instead. Normally I would also administer an antidote of cake, but the doctor rang to congratulate me on my lovely cholesterol levels and I don't want to ruin all the absolutely zero effort I put into magically achieving this.

As you may already know, I have routine monthly blood tests. Nobody has ever asked to speak to me about them before and I always just assume all is well unless I hear otherwise. Well, it seemed that 'otherwise' had finally arrived.

The other week I received a text asking me to make a doctor's appointment and, upon enquiring further, I discovered the doc wanted to talk about my results. Earliest telephone appointment was five days hence. Five days of being convinced I had an awful illness. Five days of asking Mr V to bring me tea in bed because I was determined to enjoy my last moments on earth and was also a lazy cow. Five days of paying for express delivery of online shopping so I could 'make the most of it while I can.' Five days of telling Mr V that I was absolutely not being a drama queen and that I liked biscuits with my tea in bed, thank you very much. On day five my phone rang and, seeing it was the doctor, I steeled myself for the worst.

'Your ABC, DEF, GHI and JKL results are all fine. And you know your MNO?'

'No.'

'Well, it's fine too. Your PQRST and UVWs were a little elevated but still within normal range and the XYZ is good.'

'So, all the letters are okay?' I asked, because my medical degree comes from the university of mum, where I graduated with honours in sticking plasters and paracetamol, so I wasn't sure I'd understood her correctly.

'Yes and well done on your cholesterol. It's lower than last time. What have you been doing to lower it?'

'Ooh..erm..um...healthy diet and exercise,' I said, putting to the back of my mind the many, many Jaffa cakes and concentrating very hard on vegetables.

Mr V asked afterwards if I told the doctor how stressed I'd been, waiting to hear what I'd thought would be bad news. 'No,' I told him. 'She seemed so pleased to be delivering good news that I didn't have the heart to say anything.'

To be fair, although she scared the bejesus out of me, I do appreciate that she took time out of her busy day to ring. They're good people at my local GPs practice.

Now, fingers crossed, Vegas will be fine too. I'm waiting for the vet's call and I'm in a similar state of stress. Which is why I'm distracting myself.

21st August

You Can't Teach an Old Dog New Licks

Vet: Old dogs don't normally bother with wounds.

Me: Give him a cone.

Vet: They don't normally lick.

Me: Give him a cone.

Vet: Yes, but he'll probably be fine.

Me: He's the 2020 ball and bum licking world champion.

Vet: I'll give him a cone.

Vegas is home and he's fine. Mr V popped his cone on at bedtime and, despite a few attempts to lick his own gentleman's area, he had a comfortable night. As did the dog. (Sorry, Mr V)

Cherub 2 drank all my wine late last night. Outraged, I reminded him that today is Wineday. The clever little sod said, 'Yes and, technically, I drank your wine on Wineday.' I'm going to put a bloody cone on him!

This morning, Cherub 2 came downstairs, made chicken nuggets for breakfast and decided to show me a video of the sex museum he visited in Amsterdam in January. I shut that one down pretty quickly. Within ten seconds there was a statue doing exactly what Vegas would like to be doing right now, except the statue was having far more success. Put me right off my cornflakes.

I think I've had enough of boys and their bits for today. (Sorry, Mr V)

23rd August

Visitors and Vegetables

Despite the complete lack of wine in Casa V this weekend, there have been plenty of good things.

On Friday, we visited Lovely Granny. Vegas came with us and bumped into all her furniture. Mr V came with us and ate all her food. I came with us and drank all her wine. Then I started talking wine nonsense and Mr V declared it was time to go home.

Cherub 1 started a new job on Saturday. I texted her all my motherly thoughts, my chief concern being that a new series of sexy Lucifer has started and how was she going to find time to watch it?! I'm a proud mama bear, though. Finding work in the current climate is difficult and I know how much effort she put into it. There is also a new "friend" on the go and he doesn't appear to be a serial killer at all! To be fair, I'm basing this judgement purely on the fact that he was nice about my cowboy hat. But I'm an expert. I've watched Criminal Minds and serial killers don't go around appreciating hats. Fact.

We are having Visitors today, so I'm going to have to shave my legs. You can't have other people sitting around the garden table, watching your leg hair wafting gently in the breeze. Also, vegetables. I'm going to have to poison Mr V by making him eat salad for lunch, because that is what you eat at garden tables when you want other people to think you're a nice, normal family and not heathens at all. Oh, and the downstairs loo. I've cleaned it and told the boys that if they really must use sprinkler attachments, then they're to go in the upstairs loo until the Visitors are gone.

Well, that's legs, vegetables and wee ticked off my list. What else? Nothing! We're good to go

24th August

Puppy Love

You know when you have Visitors coming and you really ought to shave your legs but you're a lazy cow and it's far easier to just wear long trousers and pray for rain so you don't have to sit out in the garden being annoyed with yourself for missing all the sun on your legs because you can't wear shorts? No? Just me then.

I did, however, pluck my chin hair and stick my head upside down under the hairdryer for that beardless yet windswept, Worzel Gummidge look. Never made it as far as plucked eyebrows and makeup but, hey, the stairs were vacuumed. Okay, the lower half of the stairs were vacuumed. They were never going to see the upstairs Armageddon. Never. Not in a million years. Absolutely no chance of that at all. Until the doorbell rang, we opened the front door and their dog ran into the house and straight upstairs. Pursued by his lovely human. I managed to squeak, 'Noooooooooooo!' at such a high pitch that I suspect only the dog heard me.

Napoleon (dog's name, not the Visitor's name - we don't generally entertain dead French emperors) came running back before anyone managed to see the laundry basket full of clean towels and bedding temporarily parked at the waystation in front of the airing cupboard. I say temporarily, I mean weeks. It's like a family Mexican standoff to see who will crack first and put them away. That person won't be Mr V because he created the waystation by dint of carrying the laundry basket upstairs. When that basket touched carpet, his duty was done. People have travelled to the moon in less time than it takes for our pillow cases to make that final metre leap from laundry basket to cupboard. The next time a member of my family sits on the loo screaming, 'We've run out of toilet roll. Pass me a toilet roll!', instead of holding my breath, closing my eyes, opening the door and waving a loo roll at them, I shall place it a metre from the door and tell them it's in the effing waystation.

Sorry, I might have digressed a bit there. Napoleon was the bestest good boy in the world (except my own wee hairy boys, of course). He was such a gorgeous little chap that Mr V got the big camera out. Normally I have to shout at Mr V to get the big camera out. Sometimes I have to shout at him to get other things out too (of course I mean the vacuum cleaner, the pressure washer and other nozzle related items - I have no idea why you're thinking what you're thinking right now!). Anyway, ergo and all that, the Visitors were ignored in favour of taking many, many photographs of Napoleon.

After the Visitors had gone, I said to Mr V, 'It was lovely having Visitors, wasn't it?'

'It was okay,' replied my anti-social butterfly, who was rather miffed that we spent the whole time in the kitchen when I'd made him tidy the living room.

'You seemed quite taken with Napoleon.'

'Oh yes,' said Mr V, his face lighting up, 'I'd have kept him.'

Yep, bugger you lovely people who have travelled miles to see us, but can we keep your dog?

(P.S. we really did love having all the Visitors. Just in case they read this and think we're a bunch of rude, hairy-legged people with an exceptionally clean downstairs loo)

26th August

Cock-ups and Cockwombles

.

***

This one didn't appear in the blog. I've only just discovered it as I was looking through my notes of old posts:

My brain officially hates me. I bumped into an old friend and his wife at the supermarket and called her Elaine throughout the entire conversation. Elaine is his ex-wife's name. Now I'm dying a little on the inside every time I think about it.

My mum always said I lacked diplomacy. She was right. I've had to learn to bite my tongue and not say what I'm actually thinking. However, my face often accidentally says things out loud, which is why I prefer my meetings to be cameras-off. I mean, nobody needs to see my eyebrows shouting TWAT at them first thing of a Monday morning.

I think my most spectacular faux pas was when, post-op and still under the influence of anaesthetic, I kicked off World War Three by calling someone a dysfunctional cockwomble in a group chat. I also promised Cherub 1 my car if I died, promptly fell asleep and woke up with water down my front and a plastic cup stuck to my back. It was not my finest hour, although top marks for creativity and spelling.

***

I don't do very well with coming round from anaesthetic. In 2019, I had a small procedure in the lady garden department. On arrival at the hospital, I was given a gown and told to remove my clothes and jewellery. I could leave my knickers on for the moment but would have to take them off later. This was on the cusp of the number of instructions I could absorb without becoming distracted by shiny things, so I contemplated removing the knickers now in case I forgot later. It's just as well I left them on because the old fandango would have definitely made a guest appearance when the nurse lifted my legs to put the DVT socks on

I waited in a cubicle for four hours and passed the time chatting to nurses, having a snooze and generally making myself at home. I even acquired an extra table and chair. In life, people toady to bosses. I suck up to cleaners and people in charge of furniture and stationery - they have the real power. The boss may get paid more than me, but does she have full lumbar support and a spotless keyboard? Anyway, I digress. Eventually, I was woken up by an anaesthetist so he could tell me all about how he was going to put me to sleep.

On the way to theatre, I mentioned to the nurse that I'd forgotten to take my knickers off. She cheerily told me, 'We do some complex operations in this hospital, but knicker removal isn't one of them,' and very kindly made a detour past the ladies. I duly stashed my knickers under the operating table and lay back while they injected me with a very strong painkiller. I have no idea what it was, but I've never felt so drunk and relaxed in my life. The doctors and nurses were asking me questions and all I could think was that I ought to answer yet, somehow, I really couldn't be arsed. Instead, I worried they'd lose my knickers and wondered why nobody had invented square potatoes yet.

When I woke up in recovery a nurse was by my bed, reassuring me that my knickers were fine. She told me, 'You seemed very worried about your knickers.' I had a vague memory of waking up post-op and mumbling, 'Do not lose my knickers.' Someone said, 'What?' and I recall thinking that I also had to ask about the second thing. What was the second thing? I struggled to remember because my brain was like soup. Oh yes, it was farting. I wasn't sure what it was about farting, but I knew I had to ask them about it. However, there was something over my mouth and I couldn't get my words out properly. So, I just said 'Knickers and

37

farting' as loudly as possible then, satisfied that I had clearly communicated all my concerns, I went back to sleep.

Once I'd properly woken up and the nurse had addressed my knicker worries (wisely ignoring the farting), I was told that they'd struggled to get the tube down my throat because I have a very small mouth. I removed the oxygen mask and croaked through my sore throat that Mr V would beg to differ. Then they said it was important that if I had an op in future, the anaesthetist was told about my small mouth, so here was a letter all about it. I kid you not, they actually gave me a letter which says I have a very small mouth. It was like having a letter from your mum saying that the dog really did eat your homework! Utterly delighted, I presented it to Mr V as soon as he arrived to take me home and gave him the good news that it's now medically certified, I don't have a big mouth. I doubted this letter would ever make it as far as any future doctor because I was going to have the bugger framed.

Mr V did his best curmudgeonly driving all the way home, occasionally shaking his head in disbelief. As soon as we clattered into the house, my loving family asked how it all went. Before I could say anything, Mr V announced, 'It was fine. Your mother didn't lose her knickers and, you'll never believe this, she has a letter saying she doesn't have a big gob!'

Sadly, the letter has since disappeared. Far be it from me to point the finger in the direction of Mr V...

***

28th August

Cone-an the Barbarian

Mr V has decided I have a magic bottom. I can't remember how this came about but his solution to everything this week has been 'You can fix that with your magic bottom.' I wish I did have a magic bottom. I could fart my troubles away.

Also, some air freshener has mysteriously appeared in the downstairs loo and I think it might be directly linked to me and my magic bottom emerging from there on Wednesday night, announcing, 'You might want to light a bonfire.' Because a match was simply not up to the task of dealing with my magic bottom fairy dust.

I took Vegas to the vet for his distinctly un-magic bottom check-up yesterday. All is healing nicely. Other than he started doing a funny walk and I leapt out of my seat, shouting at the receptionist, 'Dog doing a poo walk. Quick! Do you have any poo bags?'

I managed to get him outside before he decorated the vet's floor and he did his business on a traffic cone instead. I have no idea why, but he likes to leave brown presents in prominent places. Anyway, when the vet arrived to see him, she asked if everything was okay in the number two department. I cheerfully handed over the bag of poo that I'd scraped off the traffic cone and said she could check for herself. Both reassuring for the vet and an excellent way of disposing of the offending item.

I was going to stop off at the shop for some chocolate on the way home, but for some strange reason I'd gone off the idea. Instead, I just said a quick prayer for a good shower of rain before some poor sod came along to put away that traffic cone.

30th August

TART!

Masks are great, aren't they. Nobody can see your lips move. You can say stuff, then just look at the person next to you as if they're the big weirdo who said it.

I amused myself at Costco yesterday by loudly declaring the names of things I saw that I liked. Don't worry, Mr V was with me. I wasn't just wandering about the shop on my own, shouting 'SOFA' like a weird randomer. I did all my declaring in what I imagined to be a manly voice, then I'd look at Mr V in shock and tell him to be quiet.

I quite enjoyed announcing the presence of things I liked, and I even threw in a few extras because I could see it was starting to annoy Mr V. I saw a giant wine glass and declared, 'WINE.' I saw some beautiful fluffy towels and declared, 'TOWEL.' I saw some kettlebells. I'm not even sure what they are but I declared 'BELL' anyway and moved on. I could see Mr V rolling his eyes, deciding to say nothing as we passed 'BOOKSHELF', 'ORANGE' and 'CROISSANT.' He pressed his lips firmly together at 'MUFFIN' and 'SHORTBREAD' (by this time we were in the baked goods section so there was rather a lot of loud declaring going on). However, he finally broke when we got to the Portuguese custard tarts

'I knew I shouldn't have brought you!' he cried. I can scarcely believe that, once more, I was forced to remind him that I'm a delight.

31st August

Tech Tantrums

The computer (or the effing machine, as it's now known) has nearly led to blows in our house.

Yesterday, a certain Mrs V had the whizzy idea of backing it up and installing a new operating system. Eight hours, one phone call to Apple for help and a phone call to family for a good swear later, a certain Mrs V looked at the screen, which, for the past two hours, had been promising that the installation would take 38 minutes. She immediately pronounced the computer to be a lying bastard.

There may also have been a late-night rant on Facebook about how I was going to go back in time and kick the shit out of the Tomorrow's World presenters from the 1980s for encouraging all this nonsense.

All of this was done because I wanted to download one piece of software which would, ironically, make my life easier. This morning, Mr V made the mistake of questioning how much I was going to pay for the software and suggesting ways of getting it cheaper. I assured him that I'd thoroughly researched it and if he wanted to avoid a trip to A&E, now would be a good time to STFU.

Really, I'm not surprised that a lot of older people don't use computers. I've grown up with this stuff and my brain was fried yesterday. I think this sort of thing would have Lovely Granny and Grandad hospitalised! Alongside Mr V! Two accidental brain explosions and the forceful insertion of a computer mouse. How much tragedy can befall one family?!

Now, all that remains is to download the software. In the interests of health and safety, Mr V has beaten a hasty retreat to work and I have eaten Cherub 1's chocolate bar. I've heard that the brain needs glucose...or at least that's what I told Cherub 1. I suspect that in the next couple of hours the brain will also need wine.

P.S. Apologies for the amount of language in this post. Believe me, in the real world, I have found to my delight that the number of possible combinations of swear words is infinite. And I didn't even need the computer to calculate this!

***

There was indeed a late night rant. My personal Facebook status on the evening of 30th August was "Use technology they said. It'll make things fast and efficient they said. I want to go back in time and kick the living shit out of everyone on Tomorrow's World. Eight hours of my life, a phone call to Apple for help and a phone call to my sister for a good swear. I hate my effing computer. So how was everyone else's Sunday?"

***

SEPTEMBER 2020

After the heady days of eating out to help out, along came September and students, who were all, allegedly, Covid-ridden party animals. The Covid numbers did start to rise and there was a lot of it in some student communities, however cases were also increasing in the general population. From mid-September, there were dire warnings of a second wave. We were restricted to social gatherings of six and Baroness Dido Someone-or-Other claimed the Test and Trace system was absolutely fine, nothing to see here, now move along. I was disappointed to learn that she is not the same person as the Dido who featured on Eminem's Stan. Almost as disappointed as I was to learn that (England's Deputy Chief Medical Officer) Professor Van Tam's forename isn't Jean-Claude.

My personal triumph of September was the Hands, Face, Space banner on Boris' podium. You could almost hear my squeal of delight on 9th September as I posted this to my friends:

"Look at Boris' podium today!!

My post of 31st July:

Watching with amusement earlier when Boris said Hands, Face...then added Space...then thought 'Ooh that's a good one. I'm a freaking genius!'...then repeated it 50 times so we would also know he was a genius. You could almost see the process happening. I bet he strode back into Number 10 shouting, 'Dominic, Hands Face Space, get the posters done. And a banner thingy for the front of the podium. I'm off to order one of those "Genius At Work" signs off Amazon for m'desk.'"

Despite me being like an actual corona-prophet and people with excellent names warning us about impending catastrophe, we managed to enjoy a last gasp of summer before the PM said, 'Right, that's it, you little tinkers. I'm slapping a 10pm curfew on pubs.' However, he hadn't reckoned on the utter determination of the British people to drink themselves into a virusy grave. They duly poured out of the pubs at 10pm and carried on the party in the streets. 'Something Must Be Done About This!' cried the media. The rest of us just bought a bottle of supermarket wine and shook our collective heads, realising that while there may yet be a cure for Covid, there was unlikely to ever be a cure for stupid. Once again, we were advised to work from home and, on September 24th, the highest ever daily number of cases was recorded; 6,634. Peanuts compared with what was to come.

1st September

Wine, Jeeves!

Quick! Bring me my fainting couch, for I appear to have turned into a Victorian. For the past few days, I've had pleurisy and, forsooth, I'm fed up.

I've googled some other Victorian things and suggested to Mr V that we adopt them. For example, Victorians had different outfits for dinners, walks and carriage rides. Now, that's a shopportunity right there. However, Mr V has pointed out that marriages were made for financial stability and my shopportunities are likely to lead to divorce. I countered with divorce being frowned upon, but he raised the stakes by threatening to send me to a workhouse.

The bad news is that Victorian ladies were never to let anyone see them adjusting their outfit. I don't know about you modern ladies, but the Marks and Spencer scaffolding department is yet to invent a bra where the straps stay on my shoulders. I'm permanently hauling up bra straps, readjusting underwires or sometimes just having a good rummage in case there's a stray biscuit in there. And don't get me started on knickers! I've yet to find a biscuit in my M&S stalwarts but I did once sit on a packet of chocolate buttons when drunk and woke up the next morning to a sticky brown surprise.

The good news is that Victorians had butlers. I'd quite like a butler. Mainly because there would always be someone there to answer the door to the Amazon man and bring my wine on a little silver tray. I think butlers do a lot of looking after of wine. This would be good because I have cherubs who do a lot of pilfering of wine.

Unfortunately, Mr V has pointed out that butlers are right

up there with shopportunities and that, if I'm to avoid the workhouse, there also needs to be fewer gentlemen callers from Amazon. However, he hasn't said anything about wine and I'm fairly sure the Victorians considered it a cure for pleurisy. Bottoms up.

3rd September

Bra Shopping for the Well-Endowed

"Hey, you there, with your sexy straps,

And lacy bits for ladies' baps,

I'm looking for a bra like you,

Do you come in a 42?"

"You poor, deluded, big-boobed twit,

I'd barely cover half a tit,

You see that corner over there,

With giant, droopy underwear,

That corner is your special place,

Big straps and not a hint of lace.

Your choice of colours, black or white,

Three hooks to squeeze your flesh in tight,

So now you have a triple rack,

One up front and two in back.

Forget that sexy bedroom feeling,

Resign yourself to 'unappealing'.

These matronly monstrosities,

Will keep your knockers off your knees.

But don't despair, these tents have features,

In common with their smaller creatures,

The hooks will poke, the straps will slip,

The underwires will pop and nip.

In the bra department, you cannot win,

Your massive hooters have boxed you in."

"Well, thanks for that, you saucy lass,

I think that I will have to pass,

Instead, I'll let the girls roam free,

As long as no one else can see.

And if I need to jump or dance,

I'll tuck them in my underpants."

4th September

Right! Wrong.

When I was writing the poem yesterday, I considered a line where I compared big boobs to giant cylindrical objects. Only I couldn't think of any giant cylindrical objects. Can I just recommend never innocently googling 'large balls'?

I'm in the pub having dinner with Mr V and Cherub 2. Mr V tried to do his usual thing of declaring it time to go as soon as he'd finished, never mind that the rest of us were settled in for the long haul. He's currently in a huff. Cherub 2 and I declared that it was not time to go because we wanted another drink. At the last count, Mr V had asked five times, 'Right, are you nearly ready?'

Saying 'Right' (often accompanied by slapping both hands onto your knees) is the British way of saying, 'Brace yourself, I'm going to stand up and possibly go somewhere now.' I suspect I do it quite often because when the dogs hear me say, 'Right,' they assume they're going somewhere too and run to the door.

I'm going to wait 5 minutes and say, 'Right.' I'll watch Mr V's wee face light up as he thinks we're finally going. Then I'll add 'anyone want another drink?'

I'm evil today. But it *is* Wineday!

7th September

My Opus

Well, I've started writing book 2. Sorry, in advance, to all the midwives. I may have accidentally called one of your number a fanny nurse once or ten times. To be fair, she is based on a particularly unsympathetic midwife I once encountered. But I know that you are wonderful, professional people and I hope you will forgive me.

The book is also a wee bit more rude than you might be used to from me. However, when you think of a marvellous story about a gas explosion in the middle of a sex act, it kinda has to go in there.

I'm using Frock in Hell as the working title, but don't know if it will stick. If anyone has any better suggestions, have at it. Here's the storyline:

Have you ever been on a train and wondered what would happen if you didn't get off at your stop? Just kept going to the end of the line and didn't go home? Well, my heroine, Katie Frock, the once lovely, feisty girl - now a middle-aged woman worn down by the demands of her family - does just that. Katie disappears, much to the consternation of her family, who are most confused as to why windows don't clean themselves and piles of clean washing haven't magically appeared in their bedrooms. In the meantime, Katie has made some new friends and starts to build the life she once dreamed of having. However, little does she know that her world is about to spectacularly explode and that sometimes you really do have to be careful what you wish for.

The book will, I hope, be funny, warm and upbeat. I don't know about you, but I read for entertainment and I love a book that makes me laugh.

By the way, I finally got my hands on my own paperback of The Big Blue Jobbie. It's weird seeing your own book, although there appears to now be a wine bottle shaped stain on the cover. I have no idea how that happened. Loads of you have posted or sent me pictures of yourselves with it, so it's finally my turn [*I posted a pic of myself holding BBJ*]. Apologies for the post-lockdown hair. And the chins. I need to do something about all of those things, but I keep finding excuses to Jaffa Cake. Jaffa Caking is surprisingly time consuming!

Thank you to the lovely people who have taken a few minutes of their day to leave a review on Amazon. It really is much appreciated. If anyone else is able to pop a few words on there, I'd be incredibly grateful.

Most importantly, thank you to everyone who has bought The Big Blue Jobbie. Cross fingers you all like Frock In Hell

8th September

Losing It

Mr V's tray is missing. It's the tray with a beanbag bit on the bottom for when he eats his dinner in front of the telly. He has been tray hunting for three days now; wandering around the house saying, 'I can't understand how a tray can disappear.' I can. The reasons are age 18 and 20 and they eat all our food, steal my wine and leave damp towels on the floor.

Having told Mr V for the billionth time that I don't know where it is, I have eventually had to put my foot down with a firm hand and plead with the cherubs, 'If either of you have your father's tray, for the love of Netflix, will you please give it back.' Because if I find it first, I'm going to insert it in a certain Mr V orifice. Sideways.

I don't cope well with other people losing things. Mainly because it is my job to lose my stuff and their job to find my stuff. When other people step outside their roles and start losing their own stuff...well, it's just not on.

I'm also a tiny bit worried that, as well as his tray, Mr V is losing his marbles. He got home from work last night and pointed to some artificial flowers.

'They're nice. When did you get them?'

'We've had them for ages.'

He eyed me sceptically. 'Really?'

'Yes! And I mean proper ages. Not the ages I tell you when I've bought something and don't want you to know I wasted money, so I pretend we've always owned it. Actual real ages!'

I'm going to suggest he looks for his tray in the garage.

With any luck there will also be an old coffee jar (among the many hoarded for storing screws) containing his marbles.

9th September

Found It

Frock In Hell is coming along. I had to do some research on bruised testicles last night, which involved google and the boys of the house. Never thought I'd be asking Cherub 2 "If someone head butted you full force in the testicles..." Unfortunately, he wanted to know why I was asking. I didn't want to explain that it was to do with sexy shenanigans going wrong. Talking about this exact type of sexy shenanigans with Cherub 2 would be exceedingly awkward, so I just said, tartly, 'You'll have to read the book.' He'll never read the book, so at least he will never know half the filth that is in his mother's mind.

Tray-gate update. Mr V has found the lost tray and the rest of us are very relieved to be free of the incessant insinuations that we are to blame. All delivered in a hurt and confused tone that was supposed to somehow make us give the tray back. Which would have been impossible because, as it turns out, the person who stole Mr V's tray was Mr V.

Cherub 1 called him into the study to help with the computer last night and he came downstairs ten minutes later to announce, 'Computer's buggered, but on the bright side, I found my tray. Must've taken it in there when I was working from home last week. But hang on, I've had loads of meals in front of the telly since then, I'm sure I had the tray, maybe it wasn't me who lost it...'

So, it is Mr V's fault, but also not his fault. Which is somewhat better than one of his theories - 'Could a burglar have broken in and just taken the tray? But why wouldn't he have taken other things. Mind you, it's a very nice tray...'

Honestly, there are some days when head butting your

husband in the balls shouldn't just be confined to fiction.

11th September

Proudly Imperfect

With the rise in Covid cases, Mr V is a wee bit worried about me. I can tell he'd be happy if I confined myself to Covid Corner again. I told him, 'Not before I get my hair done on Saturday.' Brace yourselves for tomorrow, my lovelies, because I will be my sexiest me. Of course, I won't share the pic of the finished article. I'll share the pic of me with the foils in. Chosen on the basis that it's the mirror selfie that makes my hands look least fat. Never mind the fact that I'm sitting there with no make-up on, looking like a big eejit who's trying to block signals from space. Does anyone else get obsessed with the chunkiness of their fingers when they take a selfie in a mirror?

I was going to write a bulletin from Covid Corner, but sometimes when you start writing, you don't know where you'll end up. Seems it's chunky fingers today. But it's not just the chunky fingers. If I take a pic of me holding a wine glass, I have to tuck my fingernails out of sight because, although they look normal in real life, the minute they're in front of a camera they say, 'I know what would enhance this photo, the appearance of a fungal nail infection. Now, forefinger, if you turn a nice shade of smokers yellow, I'll go a bit ridged and manky.'

I swear my fingers are also conspiring with my chins. I look in the mirror - one chin. Lovely. Get the camera out - six chins. Where the eff did they come from? It's like someone rushed in and hung lard baskets off my face!

I think I may have the opposite of body dysmorphia. I firmly believe I look great, until I'm on camera. I also imagine I'm thinner than I am. Sometimes my brain thinks I'm a size 10. I should walk around with a big "Mind The Gap" sign because I see small spaces and my brain confidently tells me, 'Oh, you can fit in there.' This is little comfort when you're making your way through the car park and become wedged between a Ford Escort and a Porsche.

Wow. I did not expect that stream of consciousness to come out today. All my well-padded worries in a few paragraphs. Never mind, it'll soon be the season of the larger lass. Big jumpers and gloves. Finding that you can't get the zip up on last year's boots because the lockdown snacking appears to have inexplicably made your legs expand.

Happy Wineday and have a lovely weekend.

***

Sometimes I start to do things and the brain gremlins take over. In this post, I was going to talk about getting your hair done. Clearly, the brain gremlins decided otherwise and said, 'Tell them about your fat, manky fingers.' I also have perimenopausal brain gremlins, who growl at the normal ones and fill my head with candy floss. The pbgs make me ask my boss daft questions about all the stuff she has already told me. They're the ones who make me post stuff on a Tuesday, saying what a lovely Monday I'm having.

Somewhere deep inside my brain,

The hairy little creatures reign,

Naughty twisted tiny manikins,

Bent on twattery and shenanigans.

Sometimes I walk into a room,

And wonder with a sense of doom,

As I hover vaguely by the door,

WTF did I come in here for?

The gremlins can't contain their glee,

At tricking and confusing me.

As neurones all around misfire,

They plot together, scheme, conspire,

A new game - oh this will be a riot -

Called 'craving sugar when on a diet.'

High on chocolate, cream and jellies,

They rub their hairy little bellies,

And plan their next hilarious joke,

Called "shopping even though she's broke."

I spot The Dress, The Shoes, The Bag,

The gremlins cry, 'Ignore the tag!

You need that thing. It looks so fine!

And while you're at it, have a wine!'

So, when I lose my keys or purse,

Mix up words and loudly curse,

Or instantly forget your name,

T'was the gremlins, they're to blame!

12th September

Getting Something off My Chest

In my mind, all the men at the shops definitely fancied me today. I could tell they were all thinking, 'Who is that sexy lady with the fabulous hair?' I left the hairdressers full of swagger, with a lovely blonde bob, feeling like a glamorous princess. I told the hairdresser that I was so inspired by this bout of personal grooming that I might even shave my legs. Baby steps, though. Don't want to set myself unrealistic goals. Might want to start with filing my nails.

Although I was very happy with my hair, I have to say that going to the hairdresser feels a bit sterile these days. Not the masks and screens - I don't mind those. It's the lack of pampering. No magazines or coffee with little biscuits or people helping you put your coat back on, like when you lost your hair, you also lost the ability to put your arms into sleeves. A 21st century Samson, if you will. I never questioned why hairdressers helped me into my coat before. Now that I had to navigate the complex world of sleeves on my own, I kinda missed having a nice Delilah to mother me.

Anyway, off I went for coffee, all bouffant and beautiful, imagining I was the sexiest lady in the shopping centre. The queue for Costa coffee was a whole five people deep and it took half an hour to be served, so by the time I got to the front, I was also the most bad-tempered lady in the shopping centre. But still sexy. I couldn't see a thing because I had to take my glasses off so I could hang them on the front of my top to hide the gravy stain from last night's dinner. Mucky, half-blind but still sexy.

I did a bit of shopping. New tweezers because, in a fit of mad grooming optimism, I decided to pluck my own eyebrows - knowing full well that I'll probably find the tweezers at the bottom of my handbag in December. At least this gives me enough time to remember my brief, misguided enthusiasm for shaving my legs. Hairy but still sexy.

I went to the card shop to buy a thank you card for a lovely lady who sent me some glasses strings so that I'd never lose my specs again. Yes, I was aware of the irony that I wasn't using the strings for gravy related reasons. But I was still very grateful. And very sexy.

Eventually I returned to my car, giving myself a quick high five along the way for remembering where I'd parked it. As I flumped into the seat, I caught sight of someone in the mirror. Myra Hindley with a distinct hint of Nicola Sturgeon around the sides. Who was this frumpy lady with the frightful hair?

All the sexy had gone. And, to make things worse, a load of hair had stuck to my chest (not just a few strands, we're talking clumps). The glasses may have hidden the gravy stains, but nothing could hide the forest poking up from my cleavage. So, all the men didn't fancy me at all! They were just in awe of my fabulous hairy chest.

Well, at least it's More Wineday. Cheers

13th September

I AM OFFICIALLY A DELIGHT

Mr V has bought me a new t-shirt which says "I am a delight" on it, so I need never again remind him (I will anyway). He gets 1000 husband points today. I tried to take a selfie, but unfortunately my phone doesn't have a wide angled boob lens, so I asked Mr V to take the photo. Then take it again from slightly higher up, so that only five of my chins were visible. Mr V interpreted this as "pretend you're conducting a dandruff inspection". Hence, the result looks like it was taken by a drone.

Cherub 2 gets son points for telling Mr V, 'She doesn't need a t-shirt to say it, she is a delight.' I deducted 500 points for stealing my wine, but I gave him 500 for some excellent sucking up. Then I ate his secret Mars Bar stash because no amount of ass kissing will absolve the thieving little fecker.

At least I now know why Mr V measured my chest the other day. I just assumed he was doing something interesting on the internet, like calculating how many Mrs V boobs it would take to circle the planet. I was quite looking forward to finding out that the moon is 3 million chesticles from Earth. He measured me over my big, fluffy dressing gown so the t-shirt is a tad massive. But as I'm a massive delight, it fits.

What a brilliant weekend I'm having.

16th September

Read All About Tit

Covid Corner News - bringing the important events to you whenever Mrs V gets a notion.

A Covid Corner resident is in recovery today after surviving an online job interview. An unfortunate camera angle rendered Mrs V's head tiny and boobs enormous. A spokesperson for Mrs V has said that, while she appreciates employers may be looking for other skills, if anyone has vacancies for triangle-shaped people with giant knockers, she's your woman.

In health news, a local man has been self-diagnosed with severe man flu. When our reporter caught up with Mr V, he explained that he'd initially convinced himself it was Covid, until nurse Mrs V helpfully pointed out, 'Do you have a temperature? No. Do you have a cough? No. Here, pull my finger. Nothing wrong with your sense of smell.' Professor Norma Snipples, the person in charge of worldwide efforts to develop a man flu vaccine, has recommended sufferers try two weeks of lying on the sofa, moaning and sneezing as loudly as possible, just in case any family members or people three streets away weren't aware of their illness. A handy reminder to our readers that the key to a successful man flu recovery lies in the sufferer's ability to clearly communicate just how ill he is.

There has been a spate of burglaries in Covid Corner recently and the Covid Corner police have taken the unusual step of publicly naming Cherub 2 as the suspect. Several bottles of wine have been stolen over the last few weeks. In the face of Cherub 2's denials and his claims that the number of bottles must have been miscounted, Chief Constable Mrs V took to discreetly numbering the bottles then screaming, '3 and 6 are missing, you thieving little git!'

In politics, Chief Constable Mrs V has submitted a request for increased resources to fight the War on Teenagerism. Unfortunately, the Chancellor, Mr V, has told her that there is no money in the budget for the pretty, lockable wine cabinet she spotted on Wayfair and that she either has to stop buying wine or carry on screaming - both of which are cost neutral. Chief Constable Mrs V told the Chancellor to stop being such a clever dick and ate a packet of his Jaffa cakes to teach him a lesson.

This just in - there has been a serious accident in Mrs V's bedroom. A wee hairy boy fell off the bed in the middle of the night. He was unhurt, but decided that he would leave a little brown surprise on the floor for Mrs V to find in the morning. Then he lay down on Mr V's coat and adopted a 'not guilty, it definitely wasn't me' expression. Mrs V later reported that there had been a narrow miss when she jumped out of bed around 8am, resulting in some swearing and the naked pursuit of a small, unrepentant hairy thing down the stairs.

And finally, the weather. Cooler with a distinct possibility of having to put the heating on. A thunder cloud will hover over the thermostat tonight, as its staunchest defender, Mr V, declares, 'It's only September!' Readers are advised to seek shelter from the hail of swear words, as Mrs V insists on putting the heating on and Mr V insists on...being Mr V.

P.S. Mr V is going to explode when he reads the bit about man flu. He's actually not been nearly as bad as usual and I do feel sorry for him.

17th September

5318008

Me: Ooh, a phone number I don't recognise...Hello, you're through to the fraud department. Can I take your reference number?

Caller: Hello madam. I have information that you have recently been involved in a car accident.

Me: Oh, you'll want the accident department. Hold the line, I'll put you through. Beep boop boop beep...[sings a bit of Stevie Wonder 'on hold' music] I just called to say I looooooooove you...

Still me: Hello, accident department. Can I take your reference number?

Caller: I have information that you have recently been involved in a car accident.

Me: Okay, you're calling about a car accident. Can I take your reference number?

Caller: No, you've been in a car accident!

Me: So, you're calling to report an accident. Can you provide details so I can allocate a reference number?

Caller (determined to stick to his script): I don't have details. I have information that you have recently been involved in a car accident.

Me: That's okay. I don't need details right now. Have you got a pen? Write this down. Your reference number is 5318008. Did you get that? Have you written it down?

Caller: Okay. I've written it down.

Me: Are you sure you've got it? Do you need me to repeat it?

Caller: I've written in down. 5318008. Now, I'd like to talk to you about your car accident.

Me: That's fine. Do you have the reference number?

Caller: [big sigh] Never mind. Goodbye.

Somewhere in Mumbai a man is clutching a bit of paper that says BOOBIES upside down. My work here is done.

***

A few days after this post, I answered a call from an unknown number with a cheery 'Hello, fraud department.' It was a member of my family. I could hear her rolling her eyes at the other end of the phone as I asked her for her reference number. Happily, she had actually phoned to report a fraud – someone had reposted my post as if they'd written it themselves and my family member was going to Do Something About This (i.e. give the person a good telling off). I was genuinely grateful for her loyalty, yet secretly a teensy bit flattered that my work was good enough to plagiarise. I thanked my family member for the information, but advised that, as she didn't have a reference number, I was unable to discuss the matter further. Then I hung up on her.

***

19th September

Driving Me Round The Bend

Say a prayer for me this weekend as I take Cherub 2 out for a driving lesson. I've already been through this with Cherub 1, so I'm questioning my own sanity here.

Mr V had to be banned from taking Cherub 1 out driving because he tends to offer rather too much "constructive criticism". He doesn't just criticise the person driving him, he keeps up a steady critique of all the other drivers too. Which is quite stressful, sets a bad example and is the reason why, at the tender age of 4, Cherub 2 insisted on calling everyone a dickhead.

I'm more laid back in my approach. I gently scream, 'Stay on your own side of the road!' as we drift into the path of oncoming vehicles and give motherly hints and tips on how to, 'Watch out for the effing cyclist, you big maniac.' I favour intermittent death wails over ongoing critique and sometimes I'm distracted by shiny things and forget to offer any directions, so we end up getting lost. Cherub 1 was directionally challenged and when we bought her car, I insisted that it have a sat nav, lest we never see our daughter again.

Cherub 1 pronounced me a terrible teacher, until she went out with her father and realised that I was the lesser of the two evils. Cherub 2 is even less patient than Cherub 1 and it will be interesting to find out whether our relationship can survive me saying, 'Ooh, that's a pretty house!' while he cheerfully drives the wrong way up a one-way street.

Wish me luck!

21ˢᵗ September

Nobody Does Nothing

It is anarchy here, people! If I interpret Mr V's latest rant correctly, someone called Nobody has moved into our house and is taking responsibility for all the housework. Apparently, Nobody cleaned the kitchen, Nobody did the vacuuming and Nobody dusted the telly. Nobody appears to have had a very busy weekend, which is just as well because I sat on my arse watching Netflix.

The only thing that stands between me and divorce is the fact that I can always say I cleaned the bathroom. Because I am the only one who ever cleans the effing bathroom. My family don't notice whether the bathroom is clean or not. Sometimes, just to sound impressive, I lie and say I did it twice. They will never be able to prove a thing.

Mr V is very grumpy about it being his turn to do the dishwasher today, but it's okay, I have assured him that Nobody cares.

23rd September

The Second Wave

I don't know why everyone is so up in arms about the latest coronavirus restrictions. Basically, Boris is encouraging us to stay at home and do day drinking. What more do you want people? The only thing he could do to top this is have Ben & Jerry's make the vaccine!

Yes, I'm making light of a serious situation. Please don't be annoyed. Making light got me through months of shielding. That and chocolate raisins, wine and ice cream. My family are currently less worried about the risk of catching coronavirus than they are about having to put up with me whining for ice cream if I'm made to shield again.

I don't think Mr V would be able to withstand another full lockdown. He's already considering the cost of having a window removed to get my coffin out if I eat myself into an early grave.

Someone offered me a place on their five a side football team yesterday and I suggested that, given the size of my lockdown bottom, they put me in goal. I could just bend over and wedge myself in there. Probably stand up and find myself accidentally wearing it as a skirt afterwards. Then Boris put the kibosh on five a side football. It's like Stay Home, Day Drink, Don't Exercise. Okay, if I really must.

I live in an area where we're currently not allowed to visit people. Halloween without trick or treaters is just around the corner. The wee hairy boys will be gutted. Halloween is their Christmas! Doorbell going every five minutes - they bark themselves hoarse. As for myself, I'll miss tidying up the leftover Drumstick lollies and Refreshers with my mouth. Maybe I should buy some anyway, just in case everything is okay by 31st Oct.

And if it's not...well, every cloud.

On a serious note, I'm genuinely sorry for all the people and businesses that are struggling right now. My own family is not untouched. Keep buggering on, folks. It feels endless but we all know it's not.

Now, I'm off to take a precautionary dose of Ben & Jerry's, de-flea Biggles and cleanse my house. Honestly, we told him we aren't allowed visitors, but he's brought hundreds of the buggers!

25th September

Mum's Done

It has been a manic week. I was going to take Cherub 2 for a driving lesson last weekend, but that never happened because the little beggar got man flu, took my suggestion of a wee whisky toddy a bit too far and, over the space of two days, drank an entire bottle of Johnnie Walker. By Sunday night I'd had enough and texted Mr V at work to ask if he could come home and take over as Cherub 2's sober BFF. Mr V said he'd suddenly realised he might have to stay and do a double shift.

We've spent the week washing every bit of dog bedding we possess at 90 degrees, thanks to Biggles and his fleas. Also thank to Biggles, I have realised that the dogs own approximately 1000 luxury throws and I own none. How did that happen?

I've been working long hours then doing a few hours writing every evening. I sent Mr V the latest chapters of Frock In Hell, with strict instructions to read them now and not eventually get round to it. He came back a couple of days later to tell me it had made him proper laugh out loud, but it was a bit raunchy. I thought that living with me would have desensitised him to raunchy years ago. Maybe I've taken things too far and reached the next level of raunch? When it's eventually published, we will all have a vote. Mrs V filthy cow or Mr V a bit of a prude. The winner gets a fancy cocktail and a box of shiny things. Or if it's Mr V, a sensible man cardigan and a copy of the Radio Times.

I had to wear my headphones and pretend to be in lots of meetings today, due to Cherub World War 3 breaking out over various missing items, all of which had been stolen by him/her/the effing house poltergeist and all of which were duly found exactly where they'd been left. Somehow everything became my fault and by 3pm I was sitting there in fake meetings, eating Mr V's Jaffa cakes and using my calculator to work out exactly how long before I could reasonably ask the little darlings to leave home.

Anyway, it is now the weekend. My Cherubs are off doing their own weekendy things and I intend to throw some alcohol down my throat, so they can't phone me to pick them up later. Mum has had a helluva week, so she's closed for the next two days. Happy Wineday.

***

I did eventually take Cherub 2 for a driving lesson. I'm not going to go into detail. Suffice to say, we have agreed that it must never happen again. He has since bought a motorbike. Motherly objections that this is an effing disaster in the making have been raised. However, he's determined, so, like any good parent, I've had to content myself with roping in other people who own motorbikes to tell him horror stories and scare the shit out of him. I hope and pray this will instil some caution, but like all nineteen-year-old lads, he's immortal and knows everything. Every fibre of my being is screaming, 'Nooooooo!' and there's not a darn thing I can do about it.

***

28th September

The Power of Wine

I shared a pic of my "share size" bag of sweets yesterday. I didn't share the actual sweets, of course, just the picture. I once had a bar of chocolate which said "4 pieces = 1 portion". I decided this must be like one of those click-bait things, like "Lose 5lbs of belly fat with one simple trick", that you see on the internet and immediately ignore.

The U.K. might be heading for another lockdown. I'm trying to look on the bright side. This could possibly be the first Christmas where I haven't turned up at the post office shuffling a full deck of "Sorry we tried to deliver your parcel but you weren't home" cards.

I'm quite worried about my brain. Yesterday, while rummaging around in the freezer for something to cook for dinner, I found a full tub of ice cream that I bought over a week ago and forgot about. Delighted, I exclaimed, 'Ooh, that's pudding sorted!' Then I forgot about it again! At time of writing, it is early morning and I'm wondering if it would be okay to have ice cream for breakfast, just in case I make the same mistake a third time. Also, if Cherub 2 spots it...well, let's just say, in this house, it's survival of the fattest.

I had a busy weekend being mum, counsellor, cleaner, writer and cook. The mothering/counselling mainly involved offering wine (which obviously has restorative powers. Fact.). The cleaning needed wine to get over the burst of activity. The writing was lubricated by wine. Cooking is always improved by wine - one for the pot and one for the cook. Somehow, despite all of the above, I only got through one bottle, so I decided that this must be a magic bottle. Therefore, when Cherub 1 texted last night that she was going to the shop and did I want some wine, I sent her a photo of my magic bottle and said, 'This please.' Sadly, she came home with an inferior, non-magic bottle, but I shall somehow soldier on and drink it anyway.

The struggle is real, folks.

***

This was also the weekend I downloaded the NHS contact tracing app. I was either keeping folk safe or allowing the government to track my every movement, depending on which side of the conspiracy line you're on. I decided that if it was the latter then I could expect a letter from GCHQ, querying whether the app was working because it was showing fifty movements a day between my armchair and the fridge.

Mind you, I do love an ice cream. It's up there with cake as one of the most versatile food groups. Nevertheless, perhaps I was taking things a little too far when I wrote this:

An Ode To Ice Cream

Whoever thought of freezing cream,

And sugar to create this dream,

Of sweet concoctions, lush and pure,

Deserves a medal, that's for sure!

Oh, ice cream what a friend indeed,

You are when I'm in throes of greed,

In sickness and in health, I swear,

The faithful friend that's always there.

When times are good, for making merry,

I turn to Messrs Ben and Jerry.

When times are bad, I'm down and blue,

Then only Haagen Dazs will do.

(And maybe add a wine or six,

To make a good self-soothing mix)

Come tub, come wafer, cone and flake,

Come sprinkles, chocolate, stick and cake,

Your fatty joy may fill my heart,

(And clog my arteries and make me fart),

But this will be my epitaph:

Ate All the Ice Cream, Had a Laugh.

***

30th September

Winning at Life

Today's question - What would you do if you won the lottery?

Also, does anyone else put off reading their "congratulations you have won a prize" email from the National Lottery, just so you can hold on to the hope that it's £28,000,000 rather than £2.80?

I suspect that if we did win the lottery, Mr V and I would buy an enormous amount of nonsense. We went to the Lego shop yesterday and had a serious debate over whether the Harry Potter Diagon Alley set would look good on our mantelpiece.

I've never been a big Lego fan before, yet I enjoyed building my SS Willie so much during lockdown that I'd love to do another one (model, I mean - not sure what I'd do with two Willies). However, it has to be the right thing. I have vetoed all Star Wars models on the basis that they're not pretty. I adopt the same policy with cars. Cuteness and colour - top of the list. Next comes 'does it have loads of lovely buttons to press?' (I will accept touch screens in lieu of actual buttons). Mr V strides into car places and does manly talk with salespeople about engine size and mechanical stuff. Then he does hard negotiating for discounts and free stuff. Then I ruin everything by announcing I want the cute red one and nothing else will do. I have received many, many lectures from Mr V on my rubbish negotiation tactics. I don't understand why, because if I howl 'I want the red one' for long enough, he always gives in. I'd say my negotiation tactics are brilliant!

Anyway, back to the Lego shop. Mr V quizzed the Lego assistant on their display models. Who builds them? What do they do with them afterwards? What if they make a mistake? What if a customer accidentally wrecks a display model? Mr V would now very much like a job in the Lego shop. I wouldn't, mainly because I can't go back for a long time. Their hand sanitiser was far too runny and I spilt it everywhere. I slunk over to Mr V, telling him, 'They don't have enough pretty rivers in Star Wars anyway and at least we now know the answer to your last question.'

By the time we left the shop, we'd agreed that what we need is a Lego room in our house. In addition to the Christmas room and the cake room. Honestly, if we do win the lottery, someone is going to have to look after our money because I don't think we can be trusted.

OCTOBER 2020

October was a very Covidy month. Boris introduced a new three Tier alert system. It started at medium. There was no suggestion of low, probably because all the coronanumpties would interpret 'low' as 'go out and rub yourself on other people and all will be well.' The people in Tier 2 (high) were slightly confused and mildly outraged. I seem to recall that we couldn't visit people indoors, but we could go to shops, pubs and restaurants. Meanwhile, up in Scotland, Nicola told Boris, 'I will take your three Tiers and raise you.' Five Tiers! Who knows what Wales was doing. As far as I can tell, the lovely Welsh people spent more time locked down in some form or another than anyone else. I'm sorry, good people of Norn Iron. It was hard enough to keep track of England – all I know is you were pretty much doing the same as the rest of us. Hoping desperately that we weren't having a second wave and you wouldn't be doomed to a life of home-schooling and no pubs again. Big up the people of the UK, though. Halloween was not lost. We popped pictures in our windows and carved pumpkins to create trick or treat trails for the kids and ate all the sweets on their behalf. It was tough, but we needed to support the Drumstick lolly business in these difficult times.

The news was once more almost exclusively Covid. Does anyone even remember that on 25th October an oil tanker off the Isle of Wight was hijacked by Nigerian stowaways? During normal times, the storming of a ship by the Special Boat Service would have had us on the edge of our seats, yet I can barely recall it. In other news, 80s telly legend Bobby Ball sadly passed away and someone at work made the mistake of pressing 'reply all' to an email sent in error to hundreds of people. I don't know whether you've ever been involved in a 'reply all' incident, but it essentially involves one person replying to all that they don't understand why they've been included in this message, followed by several hours of twats a) replying to all in order to shout at the original replier for replying to all and b) shouting at each other to stop replying to all. Then, two days later, someone who has just come back from leave makes the mistake of replying to all that he doesn't know why he's been included in this message and the whole thing kicks off again. As my inbox rapidly filled with people telling each other to stop replying to all, I fervently prayed that these were the same people as the ones who wore masks under their noses because I simply could not cope with multiple groups of stupid that day. On the upside, one of my friends posted some x-ray pics of weird things people had stuck up their bums and it's a universal truth that, while we may not share bum x-rays, we all look.

On 31st October, Boris killed Bonfire Night by announcing a four-week circuit breaker from 5th November until 2nd December. Hopes were high that, even if we couldn't stand freezing our collective bollocks off in a muddy park while the local council turned thousands of pounds of taxpayers' money into pretty sparkly things, we could still have Christmas. Couldn't we?

P.S. There should be more taxpayers' money spent on sparkly things. How cheery would it be if we made all the binmen wear tiaras?

1st October

Full of Excellent Ideas

I want to start today's post with a thank you to the lovely lady who sent me a reed diffuser to thank me for sending her a signed copy of my book. Also thank you to another lovely lady, who sent me some chains so I need never lose my glasses again. I didn't get into this for presents, but I do like presents. Now, if someone can chase the good folks at Marks and Spencer for the year's supply of free knickers I reckon I'm due for all the free advertising...size BBL (big bottomed lady) please.

I went for my monthly blood test with Nurse Lisa this morning. I'm fairly sure my blood tests take about ten times longer than everyone else's due to the essential exchange of gossip and putting the world to rights. The medical world does not set enough time aside for these services. There should be whole hospitals dedicated to it, with departments called Pleasant Chat, Passing the Time of Day and I'll Put the Kettle On. If you're having a chat emergency (like you're really lonely or have run out of things to say) you could pop into A&E (Anecdotes and Entertainment).

Anyway, I am home with a fine array of sticking plasters, which I will promptly forget about until they fall off and block the shower in three days' time. I console myself with the thought that they will give Mr V a little bonus extra to add to his usual rant about "why am I the only one who ever unclogs the shower drain. It's full of hair and I have the least hair in this house!" I once helpfully suggested that he save all the hair and make himself a toupee. He said he did not find this suggestion helpful at all! I feel like I'm always the one making the effort to keep this marriage alive by adding new and interesting things to the mix and he really doesn't appreciate me enough. I shall raise this with Nurse Lisa!

4Th October

Happy Car Service Day

I couldn't post anything yesterday because it was a day of celebration. A day that happens once a year. The big day when Mr V renews his vow that it will always be this good. That this happy state of perfection shall last forever.

Yes, we are talking about the day Mr V gets his car serviced and has to clear it out so he can get the most out of the free valet afterwards. Because god forbid they miss a spot!

He spends 364 days a year roaring at his family not to leave rubbish in his car, then on day 365 he spends an hour removing all the rubbish that we accidentally left in his car. Yesterday morning, the air was rent with cries of 'Half an effing sausage roll!' (Cherub 2), 'An effing kite!' (me) and '3000 face masks - they're effing disposable - that means you put them in the bin not the floor!' (everyone, including him).

The day started off badly for Mr V. I was unbearably cheerful and warbled my way around the house, singing the theme tune from Balamory. He didn't get his morning coffee because he didn't have time. Then I lingered. I was supposed to be following him to the garage in my car. Why wasn't I ready? Could I please stop lingering?!

He duly went to drop his tidy car off at the garage and I followed in my car ten minutes later to pick him up. As we had a few hours to kill before his car was ready, I suggested we go for a posh lunch in a nearby castle. Mr V does not like unplanned eating in new places, particularly expensive new places.

'I thought we could treat ourselves to an early anniversary meal out. What with lockdown restrictions being tightened, we might not be able to go out at all on our actual anniversary,' I reasoned.

'But we haven't booked. Surely, we would need to book,' said Mr V, starting to feel himself backed into a corner by my excellent emotional blackmail.

'I have this thing called a telephone. Quite new-fangled. Lets you speak to people in other places.'

Mr V realised he needed to take a different tack. Think of somewhere even better than a castle to tempt me away from my expensive notion. He racked his brains, trying to think of the absolute best places that he loves going to.

'I know! I really have to go to Costco. Then we could go to Ikea for meatballs afterwards.' Mr V was delighted with himself for being able to combine his need for a giant multi-pack of crunchy nut cornflakes with my need for lunch. He felt sure I'd leap at the chance.

'Right, so on this rare occasion where we have no Cherubs and it is about to be our silver wedding anniversary, you want to take me to Costco and Ikea?'

'Technically you're taking me,' he said, pointing out that I was driving.

'Well, if I'm taking you, we're going to the bloody castle then!'

We ended up compromising with a really good pub lunch near the castle, where we spent a happy couple of hours ignoring each other. Mr V got sent a video of his car being fixed ('Did you know they even send you a video?! Fascinating stuff!') and I got to be accidentally rude to a waiter. I was doing online shopping for a silver wedding anniversary present for myself and had gone temporarily deaf to all sound other than "why yes, Mrs V, you can spend a ridiculous amount of money on shiny things." Then we had a row over me leaving an enormous tip to overcompensate for the fact that the waiter had had to repeat the specials three times before the information made it past the shiny things in my brain.

But at least we agreed on something. We both agreed that it had been a lovely lunch and we'd come back on Car Service Day next year.

6th October

The Good Old Days?

All the IT is down at work so I'm taking advantage of a free minute to write a post. What did they do for a skive before computers? Set the filing cabinets on fire?

I sometimes miss the old days of memos and fax machines. The slower pace. I caught the tail end of the old ways when I started working in an office as a teenager. We had a telex machine and you needed permission from God to use it. A manager had to approve your message, just in case you sent too many words and cost the department an extra 50p. To get the manager's approval, you first had to figure out which pub he was in. They were mostly 'he'. I got engaged in the early nineties and my manager asked when I was leaving to have babies. I laughed, thinking he was joking. He wasn't. Come to think of it, maybe I don't really miss the 'good' old days.

9ᵗʰ October

There's No Business Like Snow Business

Oh my, what a week. Where are we with the lockdown hokey-cokey? Are we still at shake it all about? All the poor Scottish people. Nicola said sit in beer gardens in October! I'm sorry, Nicola, but are you even Scottish? There is a reason why lots of Scottish pubs don't even have beer gardens. I'm from Aberdeenshire and have memories of snow in June! I'm slightly hoping that an Aberdonian will come on and say, 'That's nothing! We snowboarded doon Union Street in August.'

If there's one thing we're good at in Scotland, it's being better than everyone else when it comes to snow. Snow one-upmanship is our national sport. I know we do well in the curling at the Winter Olympics, but what we really excel at is phoning each other to check "How much snow have you got? Only three feet!" We devote the winter months to complaining that the moment there's a light dusting in London, it's all over the news. Yet here's the giraffes at Edinburgh zoo with their wee heads poking above a snow drift - not even a single mention on the BBC. If it helps, Scotland, England devotes its winter months to complaining about how shit they are at dealing with snow and "why can't we be more like Scotland?" Personally, I feel that England should be asking itself that every day, but I'm biased.

Mind you, most of England's probably not far behind on the pub front. The big coat industry will be booming this winter. Poor bloomin' pubs, cafes and restaurants and all the other businesses that rely on people going out. I'm so sorry for all the people affected. Seeing your job and your business going down the tubes is just devastating.

Here in the North of England we're not allowed to mix with other households, so it's back to Face Timing Lovely Granny and shouting at her to move the phone because, while we think her new curtains are super, we want to see a bit more than the top of her head and several metres of fine damask. Mr V is making noises about me not going out anymore. I know he's serious because he came home with a giant tub of chocolate raisins yesterday. Those have been banned on the grounds of expense since I came out of shielding. I can see he's planning on keeping me contained by throwing lots of treats at me, which I have to say is an excellent idea. Although if I do end up having to shield again, Boris may have to impose some social distancing rules between me and my fridge, for my own good.

Wherever you are, chins up my lovelies. We may all be thoroughly confused/frustrated about lockdown restrictions but at least we know one thing - it's Wineday today and nobody has said you can't buy a bottle to take home.

10th October

A Job Well Done

I just did the government careers advice questionnaire and discovered that I'm creative, sociable and a bit of a bossy boots (yes, yes, oh okay yes) so would make an excellent...hotel porter?! Because the world of suitcase transport needs more arthritic 50-year-old women with a fondness for cake. I have no idea why we are so underrepresented.

The alternatives were holiday resort rep and sports contract negotiator. Mr V has voted for resort rep. The money isn't great, but (see above for bossy boots) he says he could do with the respite. As for sports contract negotiator - if you ever see on the news that Man U have bought some top player from Real Madrid for £1, be prepared for an interview with a very confused Spanish football manager. 'I don't know what happened. She came in, made us all eat something called Victoria Sponge then howled "I want the handsome one who scores lots of goals" until we gave in.' I may have missed my calling.

Sadly, there were no jobs for personal online shopper, sommelier and chocolate checker. Whole industries are missing my expertise!

For the moment, though, I'm quite content with dog warmer. It seems I'm doing a good job there, at least.

11th October

Going Downie Undero

If it looks like I'm liking my own posts, I'm not. I gave Mr V the keys to the social media castle and he's merrily hahaing everything, thinking it's him that's hahaing it. I tried shouting at him to stop making me look like I find myself hilarious, but he's still there, clicking away.

I spent yesterday talking like an Australian, with the odd unintentional segue into cockney. This is because I've introduced an Australian character into my book and I'm writing her dialogue. I don't normally go around randomly talking in accents. Okay, I sometimes burst into Welsh Geordie and I do an excellent Scouse Brummie. But that's it. I think.

Anyway, I had a lovely day yesterday, wandering around the house putting o or ie on the end of everything. I washed the dog's beddo after he did a sickie on it and I made beef stewie with dumplingos for tea. Mr V-o said he hoped the Aussie dialogue in the book is a lot better than the garbage coming out of my mouth. I told him it wasn't garbage, it was garbie.

Cherub 1 wasn't very impressed by my accent. I think her exact words were, 'Can you stop talking like that?' Then her little face went all frowny and scrunched up in disgust. I know she was worried that I'd do the accent in public. Of course I'll do the accent in public! It is such a shame that all her friends can't come round to hear it. Damn you, lockdown!

The character is in the book for a while, so we all have to put up with another few weeks of this. Everyone at work will hear me in online meetings and wonder who the new girl is. 'G'day colleagues. It is me, same person, same day pyjamas, no bra, trying to eat biscuits as quietly as possible because I'm not on mute-o.

Now chuck another sausage on the barbie and let's get this meetingie started.'

I think I might need to find an Australian to read my manuscript, in case I accidentally offend everyone. I've googled Australian words, but you never know with t'internet. It might be telling me that avo means avacado, when it actually means willy. Perhaps I'll edit out the bit about ripe avacado, just to be on the safe side.

12th October

Post Haste

Mr V is very excited. He has discovered postal services that aren't the post office. I have been regaled with in-depth explanations of courier services and international post. I have had to resort to telling him to bugger off, because rolling my eyes and turning the volume up on the telly have failed to adequately convey the rapidly decreasing number of fucks given. Still he wanders about the house waxing lyrical about effing Hermes.

It's like when I introduced him to the Wetherspoons app. He could not believe that if you selected 'full English' on a phone, ten minutes later a man bearing sausages would appear at the table. You'd have thought I'd pulled a unicorn out of my bum, such was the wonder. We are now firmly in the midst of the courier equivalent. Mr V pays £4 and, like magic, the parcel disappears from the porch.

He's just had his first go with our nephew's birthday present. He carefully wrapped the present in brown paper, putting extra sticky tape on the corners, printed out the label and attached it. Should he put sticky tape all over the label in case it rained and the ink ran? He waved a sheet of A4 at me and I calculated that it would probably cost more than the postage to cover the label. No, I told him, the label would be fine. The Hermes man could come any time tomorrow. Should he leave the parcel in the porch now? Might it get stolen? No, I'd get up early and pop it out. He phoned me from work. Had I put the parcel out? Yes, I had. He phoned me from work. Had the parcel been collected? No, it was still there. He took a deep, calming breath and I could hear him assuring himself that they said it would be collected by 8pm. He got home from work. The parcel was still there. They only had three hours left in which to collect it! If it wasn't collected by 8 then it would surely be a calamity. At 8pm we looked in the porch and breathed a sigh of relief. The Hermes elves had visited. The parcel was gone.

It was only at this point that I thought to ask him, 'Did you use birthday paper before you wrapped the present in brown paper?'

'Ah, no. I didn't think of that.'

14ᵗʰ October

You'd Get Less For Murder

Mr V: At least two people at my work…their wives make their packed lunch every day.

Me: Well, they're effing stupid then.

Mr V: I just thought I'd test the water.

Me:

Mr V: I thought there was half a percent chance.

Me:

Happy silver wedding anniversary to us. Twenty-five years of keeping it real.

***

We put the celebrations on hold until post-Covid or our kids are mature enough that we can go away for the weekend without them creating havoc, whichever comes first. Ditto our 50ᵗʰ birthdays. We have learned the hard way. And here, all I will say is imagine sitting in Le Starbucks in France, watching home security camera footage of the police arriving at your house to break up a party.

***

16th October

Going Out Out

We went out for a posh anniversary meal on Wednesday night. The place must have heard about me because they sent an email saying they have a smart casual dress code. Mr V said no, I couldn't wear my pyjamas, and no, not even the new ones that Biggles hasn't had a chance to eat crotchless yet. Then, just before we left, he asked, 'Were you planning on wearing that?' I did my best big sigh and removed my pink dressing gown.

I finished work early so that I had plenty of time to get ready. I even shaved my legs as a wee treat. Mind you, I'm not sure who the treat was for. Mr V has got so used to my Chewbacca legs since lockdown that I think he's desensitised. I've cunningly saved myself lots of hairy hassle for the future. By now, he probably has the same reaction to hairless legs as most of us do to hairless cats (wtf is that?!). Sorry to anyone with a hairless cat. I'm sure your pussy is lovely.

Anyway, it was wonderful just to go out. Cherub 2 had declined to come on the grounds that he is a teenager. Cherub 1 came. I should mention that she gave us the most thoughtful present, so I'm fairly sure she loves us and wasn't just motivated by the free food and the fact that we filled up her tank as a thank you for driving.

Yes, Cherub 1 was driving. This meant banning Mr V from talking for the entire journey. There was a momentary lapse when he offered constructive criticism about the route taken, but he was roundly shouted down and the words 'maniac' and 'carsick' only left his mouth when Cherub 1 was out of earshot. It is just as well he didn't hear my conversation with her before we left:

'I could have just one drink.'

'No, your father will have a fit.'

'But I wouldn't be over the limit.'

'You know your father's driving policy - absolutely no alcohol.'

'But'

'No'

'But'

'No'

'But'

'Really, do either of us want to deal with the lecture you'd get from him?'

'Okay.'

So, it was water for Cherub 1 and booze for the grown-ups. I use the term 'grown-up' loosely because, while we were waiting for the food to be served, I was suspiciously quiet and Mr V asked what I was doing. The answer was, 'I've discovered some buttons on my phone that I've never pressed before, so I'm pressing them all.' I then proceeded to read the menu using my phone torch.

Before Cherub 1 gets annoyed with me, I should point out that she's officially a grown-up now. I've given her the code for the central heating because I feel she can at last be trusted not to whack it up to full blast then leave the house five minutes later. Rite of passage and all that. Now two of us know the code. Technically, it should be three of us, but the code is Mr V's mother's birthday, so of course he doesn't have a clue.

I digress (again). Great time had by all. I let Mr V sit in the front on the way home so he could get the full Mario Kart experience (sorry Cherub 1, you and I both know your dad could get a second job driving a hearse) and I sat in the back, cheerfully singing all the wrong words to Cherub 1's new-fangled music to annoy them both.

***

I miss a good night out. This was our last one. I was going to say 'our last one until...' but there hasn't been another. I popped in an Ode to Ice Cream earlier and I thought this would be a good place to write an Ode to Wine. Except when I started to write it, it turned into an Ode to a Good Night Out on the Wine:

O lovely, grapey, drinky stuff,

I don't know when I've had enough.

I'm warm and merry, chatty, great,

Then I stand up and can't see straight.

In the taxi, windows down,

Don't throw up, you drunken clown.

Lie in bed, the world is spinning,

Next morning I'm not hashtag winning.

The texts start: 'OMG you twat!

You said this thing then you did that!'

Yet, Wine, despite the shame and pain,

We know I'll do it all again.

I don't think we've even had a night out with friends since we went axe throwing in January 2020. According to the instructor, I was "a little menace." The thing about chucking axes at a target is that, unless you are someone who listens properly to the instructions, the axes tend to bounce off the target. Or in my case, walls and, once, the ceiling.

Being a left-handed person in a right-handed world, I am so used to right-handed things that I often get confused about which handed I am. So, the instruction *"if you are left-handed then put your right leg forward"* somehow got muddled and I ended up throwing right-handed with the wrong leg forward. To be honest, I just lack any coordination whatsoever. It's why I can't do aerobics or anything dancey. I go in the opposite direction to everyone else. I also have to think before I use revolving doors and struggle to screw lids on things. Throwing in a straight line is not my forte. Nor is planning ahead, it seems.

I hadn't thought through that I'd have to pick the damn things up off the ground. When you have sciatica, the ground is something that other people do. I developed a method of semi squatting with my legs apart then reaching to the side. The instructor, probably fearing I was about to either give birth or do a poo, asked if everything was okay. *'I'm just old!'* I wailed. He was so kind, rushing forward to pick up my axes for me, that I half wondered how long I could use sciatica as an excuse to get out of doing things. The NHS website said it takes 4 to 6 weeks to heal. Our dishwasher was very low. I feared my sciatica would go on for months.

After a few practice rounds, it was time for a competition. There were nine of us and I knew I didn't stand a chance of winning the actual competition. However, the real competition was between myself and Mr V. He was ahead in the first three rounds, although I did manage to score a few points. Then in the last round, admittedly by sheer luck, I managed to hit the inner ring of the target. It's just as well he loves me because I'm not magnanimous in victory. I'm more about whooping, dancing and never letting him forget it.

Afterwards we went to the pub. I asked the barman if they did cocktails. *'I'll get you the cocktail menu,'* he offered. *'Oh no* *you won't,' I told him. 'We're playing cocktail roulette. Just make me a cocktail. Any cocktail!' I have no idea what I drank, but it was all lovely and for a brief while the sciatica was forgotten. Maybe I should have had cocktails <u>before</u> I went axe throwing?*

***

17th October

#definitelynotadramaqueen

Good morning. I can't believe that my marriage has come to this. Mr V no longer trusts my assurances that I didn't eat his Jaffa Cakes. He actually patted me down for crinkles. Sure enough I crinkled and he extracted an empty packet from my dressing gown pocket. But that is not the point. It's a matter of trust. Our marriage is built on a solid foundation of me stealing his Jaffa Cakes, hiding his Jaffa Cakes and accidentally tidying up his Jaffa Cakes with my mouth, then lying my face off about it! How am I supposed to function in this new world where I can't plausibly blame the children or otherwise dispose of Jaffa Cakes unmolested?

Take a moment to imagine this world. Whole boxes of 180 discs of deliciousness arrive from Costco and sit there, cluttering the place up for weeks. Nay, months - because we all know that Mr V is a big weirdo who hoards sweet stuff for months before he goes to eat it and discovers that the children (and definitely not me) got there first. Everyone has to reach past an enormous box of Jaffa Cakes to get things. It lurks there, waiting for unwary people like me to come along, then it suddenly jumps out and screams, 'Eat me!' I will be so frightened, I may accidentally eat some.

No, I think it's far better that Mr V accepts the status quo of me lying than I be psychologically damaged by Jaffa Cakes.

18th October

When We Means Me

Mr V has suggested that "we" ought to start our Christmas shopping. Let's take a moment to examine what "we" means.

For me, it means searching high and low for lovely things that my nearest and dearest will want, making several trips to shops and keeping track of multiple Amazon orders. There may be some sternly worded emails when things don't arrive and some consternation that I appear to have ordered 18 pairs of bed socks for Lovely Granny. Then I will give myself an RSI by hand stamping recyclable brown paper, glue my tongue to the roof of my mouth by licking recyclable sticky tape and get tangled in metres of paper raffia as I try to make (crappy) bows and be all eco-friendly. There will be lots of swearing and quite a few glasses of wine. I will then wrap the lot in more brown paper, take it to the post office and administer smelling salts to Mr V when he finds out how much the postage cost. Somewhere in all of this, I will do battle with the cherubs, whose idea of a present budget is around ten times higher than mine. I will eventually scream that I am giving it all to charity and they'll get nothing because they are selfish, spoiled little feckers who have forgotten that the meaning of Christmas is effing peace and buggering goodwill.

For Mr V, "we" means that he has approximately two months to think of a Christmas present for me.

Hang on...I'm missing something...oh yes, I forgot to include Mr V's panicked phone call on 23rd December, where he'll shout that he is at the shops, it's very busy, it's too hot, he doesn't like other people and I have to tell him what to buy me.

***

You may be wondering why I'm tying myself in knots, hand-

stamping paper and licking gluey tape. Well, pour yourself a glass of something and I will tell you a story.

Once upon a time in 2019, a well-padded Princess (with good intentions of going on a diet after Christmas but that was ages away so she wasn't going to think about it) was munching her way through a few (packets of) Jaffa cakes when she decided that, this Christmas, she would single-handedly save the planet. This would be an eco-Christmas! She proclaimed to her subjects (Cherub 1 the Duchess of Vodka, Cherub 2 the Earl of Underpants-on-the-Floor, the sexy knight in tartan lounge pants Sir Mr V and the two wee hairy princes) that, this year, there would be less plastic and all gift wrapping would be recyclable. Sir Mr V pretended he hadn't heard the proclamation because it contained the word Christmas and someone might expect him to do something. He decided that now would be a good time to declare a national screwdriver emergency and hide in the garage.

Princess Mrs V sent a royal command to the House of Amazon to deliver a stamp kit (to stamp "Merry Christmas" on brown paper), some brown paper tags, colourful string, some paper sticky tape and a make your own crackers kit, so that she could fill crackers with useful things, such as chocolate.

One cold December night the princess plonked her royal rump on the floor of the grand hall and began to wrap presents. This involved stamping "Merry Christmas" hundreds of times onto wrapping paper and tags. Princess Mrs V was full of enthusiasm, good cheer and not a little Sauvignon Blanc. 'Merry Christmas!' she declared each time she stamped.

Two hours later Princess Mrs V felt slightly less enthusiastic. In fact the neat rows of stamps now looked distinctly wobbly (nothing to do with wine, of course) and the princess was muttering, 'Merry f#%*ing Christmas,' rather a lot. She would have muttered it more, but her tongue kept sticking to the roof of her mouth from licking the sticky tape. Sticky tape which was effing useless anyway. The princess' knees were aching and *testament to her vacuuming skills. Embedded in the fleshy imprint of the carpet were a thousand bits of grit, glitter and sequins. How on earth did she comfortably sit like this as a child? At what point had the evil knee fairy sneaked in and replaced her lovely, limber knees with these gritty, creaky old things?*

Princess Mrs V surveyed progress so far and decided it was time for a royal text to Sir Mr V (who was still in hiding lest he be sent on a quest to do Christmas things). She decreed, 'If you come home and ask if I've done anything at all today, I will have to kill you. It has taken me hours to wrap 2 presents. Eff going green and making all your own wrapping. Eff it all. Bring on the shiny stuff that stays in landfill for a thousand years. WTF was I thinking when I decided that stamping Merry Christmas all over brown paper was a good idea?!' Sir Mr V briefly considered gallantly dashing to her side and offering a knightly shoulder on which to cry. Then he remembered his policy of non-intervention and just replied, 'Ha ha.'

And so it was that Princess Mrs V returned to the House of Amazon and said, 'Send me something vaguely recyclable and lashings of your stickiest plastic tape immediately! Also, more wine.' And through the auspices of Prime Now the princess' wish was granted.

Sir Mr V returned to the (very untidy) palace to find the princess snoring gently on the sofa, dreaming filthy dreams of His Highness Brad of Pitt and a giant chocolate pillow.

And they all lived happily ever after. The end

I was still left with oodles of eco-bits and bobs, so with the ghost of my mother whispering, 'Waste not, want not,' in my ear, I persisted with the brown paper and the infernal stamp. I got better at it, mainly by dint of not bothering to try to stamp "Merry Christmas" in neat rows and shoving extra gluey paper tape on any gaps. By Christmas 2020, all our presents looked like they'd been wrapped by a monkey on crack, but I don't care. There was love in them there presents.

21st October

Definitely Not Being a Nuisance

I woke up yesterday morning with the best hair ever. By best, I mean wildest. I looked like Mr V had plugged me in to charge overnight. Mr V was woken up by a delighted me poking him with his glasses and shouting, 'Look at my hair. Here, put these on and look at my hair. It's brilliant.' He is not a morning person so was not best pleased with me.

It was his birthday so, what with him being awake and all, I took him out for breakfast. Then I took him shopping. You know, it's so annoying when you do your best to make someone's day special by taking them to all your favourite clothes shops and they just don't appreciate it. I had to take him to the Lego shop to cheer him up!

Can I just take a moment to moan about the Apple store? The bouncers refused us entry and said if we wanted to browse, we'd need to make an appointment online. It was 1pm on a Tuesday afternoon. There were two people in the store. Crowd control was not a problem. Mr V dragged me away to the nearest cake shop before I went full Karen.

Eventually we went home so that Mr V could have his afternoon nap. I went for a wee in the downstairs loo and annoyed myself by putting the toilet roll on the holder back to front. I couldn't be bothered turning it round. But it vexed me. I woke Mr V to tell him and, apparently not being an afternoon person either, he unsympathetically told me to bugger off and just turn it round. Part of me agrees that I really should turn it round. The rest of me has been going upstairs for a wee instead.

24th October

The Meeting About the Meeting

Still working from home and doing online meetings. There was a nightmare moment this week when someone unexpectedly suggested we all switch our cameras on.

The suggestion was followed by a horrified silence, as we wondered whether our pyjama tops could pass as t-shirts, before the only one among us wearing clothes eventually switched her camera on. The rest of us stayed resolute, cameras off, transfixed by the woman on our screens. Her hair was perfect. She was wearing lipstick. Before 11am! In her house! What sort of person does that? I bet she was even wearing a bra!!

The silence went on, becoming more awkward, as we all checked ourselves out in the nearest mirror and decided that we were definitely not camera ready.

I worried that I hadn't even issued an underpants warning to Cherub 2 and Mr V. If Mr V made an accidental appearance looking like a total sex god in his morning uniform of boxers and socks, all the ladies would get the vapours!

Could you still get the vapours, I wondered, or was it a Victorian thing? I didn't think I'd like being a Victorian. It seemed to me that there was a lot of fainting involved (and illness and things made of whales). Also, if Mr V gave someone the vapours, then I'd be technically responsible for an accident at work. And that meant form filling. I liked form filling even less than being a Victorian.

The silence stretched to breaking point.

'Well, is anyone else going to switch their cameras on?' demanded the man who had made the original suggestion.

I wondered how to explain that I was wearing Disney pyjamas, my hair looked like I'd brushed it with the arse end of a hedgehog, what sort of psychopath suggests cameras on without at least a week's notice anyway and I really couldn't be bothered filling in the accident forms because they only had quills or something in Victorian times. Just as my brain was scrambling for a summary of this highly important information, I was saved by the bell. The man said, rather grumpily, 'Fuck it. If nobody's turning their cameras on, I'm turning mine off.'

Then we moved onto item 1 on the agenda. Behaviour in meetings - the impact of remote working.

***

I put myself in charge of the meeting from that point. I love being in charge of things and organising stuff. Which is odd because, by nature, I'm quite a disorganised person. I have no idea why and no desire to find out. In this world of "me, me, me" and inspirational quotes, I sometimes wonder if my impatience with the seemingly constant need to self-analyse makes me the odd one out. How can anyone find themselves that interesting?

Don't get me wrong, I'm not talking about mental health – that's a whole different thing. I mean the "truths" dosed out by influencers and celebrities who are "on a journey", infecting others with their narcissism through a drip feed of bon mots on social media.

Ooh, I'm very cynical today. I think it's because I read a quote attributed to the musician Sheryl Crow in Reader's Digest; "If you just keep putting one foot in front of the other, fantastical things can happen." Really, Sheryl? Let's look at the Cambridge dictionary definition of fantastical; "strange and wonderful, like something out of a story." I have been putting one foot in front of another for fifty-one effing years and not once have I been a princess or uncovered a conspiracy involving a big corporation, a politician and a truckload of lube. No, I don't know what they were going to do with the lube. It was just what sprung to mind. Point is, Sheryl, the chances of me snogging the face off a prince by sheer dint of the ability to keep buggering on are very low.

Sorry. I'm not above finding the odd quote quite helpful in encapsulating how I feel about something, but I worry that this sort of introspective celebrity drivel is just fuelling a sense of entitlement and a society that increasingly accepts "I need to work on myself" as an excuse for bad behaviour.

Perhaps age is making me intolerant. Maybe I need to take a long, hard look at myself ;-)

***

26ᵗʰ October

A Life in the Day of...

I need a holiday! This has been my typical day over the past few weeks:

07:00: Get up

07:30: Decide I will definitely shower and change out of my pyjamas later. Start work.

09:00 - 17:00: Either actually be in meetings or wear headphones and pretend to be in meetings so that nobody talks to me and I can get some actual work done. Frantically wave cup at Cherub 1 to demand refills. Put myself on mute to answer at least fifty of Cherub 2's most important questions (It's in the cupboard. The other cupboard. No, I don't know when the Romans invaded Germany. Morgan Freeman. Have you looked under your bed?). Phone Mr V at 10am, when I've heard the alarm go off every 9 minutes for the past hour, and yell at him to get up. Make a snap decision about whether five minutes before a meeting is enough time for a poo. Swear at work phone because someone has noticed I have five minutes between meetings and called me. Put poo on hold and answer phone like a swear word has never passed my lips, ever. Put meeting on loudspeaker so I can let dog out for poo. Lucky dog. It is now my 4pm meeting and I haven't eaten all day. Very quietly suck a packet of crisps. One packet of crisps is not enough. Put self on mute and quickly eat some of Mr V's Jaffa cakes, all the while praying that I don't have to unmute to answer important questions as have managed to fit three Jaffa cakes in mouth and am hashtag winning at life.

17:30 Look up from work computer and realise I'm alone in the house. Have absolutely no idea when everyone left or where they've gone. Do dishes and decide against dinner as am now too full of Jaffa cakes.

18:30 to midnight: Attempt to write book. Cherub 2 wants me to watch a movie with him. It's a zombie movie. It's in Norwegian. Cherub 2 agrees we can watch something else. It's about Romans invading Germany. It's in German. Try not to look at subtitles, while testing self to see how much German I can remember from school. As absolutely nobody is trying to book a hotel room, find their way to the town hall or talk about a dog called Lumpi, the answer is none. Attempt to write book. Cherub 1 wants a chat. This is not going to be a short chat because she has come equipped with a glass of (my) wine. Attempt to write book. Cherub 2 is hungry. Can I show him how to cook mac and cheese? Yes, he knows it is late, but he is very, very hungry and I never do anything with him.

Midnight: Mr V comes home from work. Wonders why I am still in my pyjamas and smell funny. What have I been doing all day? Go to bed. Body informs brain that I still haven't gone for that poo and brain insists I go for it now, otherwise it will refuse to let me sleep and make me do German grammar until 3am.

7:00: Is it nearly Wineday yet?

31st October

A Mrs V Is Not Just for Christmas

Happy Halloween and, most importantly, happy More Wineday.

I held off posting today just in case Boris announced another lockdown and my kitchen clock is no longer the freakiest thing in my life. I should explain that, for the past seven months, my brain has been trained to fast forward the kitchen clock an hour, so has been slow to accept this daylight-saving state of affairs. I keep having my lunch an hour early. Or premature mastication, as I call it.

Innuendo has been the order of the day in our house. I amused Mr V by asking him to fix the patio door in Covid Corner. Or, as he told everyone at work, 'Mrs V wants me to oil her back door.'

The onset of cold weather has meant man must make fire. Mr V was struggling to buy logs from his usual place. Or, as I told everyone at work, 'Mr V can't get wood.'

Cherub 1 has been practicing her cocktail making on me. I objected vociferously. Okay, weakly. Okay, I asked her not to put mint in my next mojito. She's off out for what will probably be the last time in a month. She was asked for ID when buying a Halloween costume the other day, on the basis that it was erotic (the short skirt, not the ID - Cherub 1's driving licence photo is more resting bitch face than Playboy Bunny). It all sounded a bit weird until she texted to say she was in Ann Summers (purveyors of things far more erotic than sexy vampire costumes). I texted her back "tell them your mum sent you out for a loaf of bread, a pint of milk and a giant dildo." Phew. It's just as well I was on hand to give wise motherly advice.

In other text news, Mr V has been ignoring my texts about

Christmas shopping, claiming his phone isn't working, so I've taken to WhatsApping him. He has also been pretending he can't hear me talking, so I've taken to WhatsApping him, even if he's in the next room. Experiments have shown that sending the word "ping" at least fifty times is both amusing and elicits a response. Amusing because I can hear my "pings" actually going ping, ping, ping in the next room. A response in that he has threatened to divorce me if I don't stop. I've been forced to remind him that a Mrs V is for life.

I apologise for being far ruder than normal today. I blame the mojitos. I'm going to just post this now because Boris is running late and the BBC has given us all the lockdown spoilers. Sounds like we're in for a month of it. Stay safe you lovely people. This is going to be tough on us all and I'm sending you big digital hugs.

***

There was an absolute flap on about the leaking of lockdown news. Six months later, there was a media storm around why an investigation had failed to find the source of the leak. However, the best part is that the leaker was branded a "chatty rat." I quite liked this idea. It sounded like a character in a children's book, so I wrote a story:

Once upon a time, there was a Chatty Rat. He would not stop blabbing. Mummy Rat said, 'Stop talking, Chatty Rat. One day you'll get into trouble.' Daddy Rat said, 'Stop talking, Chatty Rat. One day you might accidentally say the wrong thing.' His teacher, Mrs Whiskers, wrote on his report card, 'Chatty Rat needs to pay more attention to his schoolwork and less time telling the headmaster about me going through other teachers' bins for scraps.'

But Chatty Rat did not stop talking. He just got sneakier

about it, until one day, when he had grown up to be a person with power and influence, the Prime Minister told him some secret stuff and he blabbed it all to the newspapers.

The Prime Minister launched an investigation and Chatty Rat was scared. He cried to his family, 'I promise I will never blab again!' and, disguised as a mouse, he ran away, never to be seen again.

Some months later, the Prime Minister was decorating his flat when he lifted a carpet, only to find the Chatty Rat Investigation folder beneath. 'I wonder how that got there,' he mused, as an employee with a very large broom walked by. 'Never mind,' he said to himself, 'I'm fairly sure everyone has forgotten about it.'

***

NOVEMBER 2020

What they called a 'circuit-breaker' lockdown started, redundancies rocketed, the terror threat level was raised and the world's longest running political soap opera looked like it might be coming to an end, with Joe Biden being elected president. It hadn't actually ended, of course. There were multiple legal challenges and a particularly shocking, yet sad, season finale at the Capitol. However, I will make no political comment, other than to say it was a relief to no longer have the American election dominating the BBC news. Honestly, the Beeb, I swear that, at one point, eleven of your top ten stories were about the US election. I was momentarily distracted by the vote count in Arizona, where counties were reported to be working tirelessly. I actually thought they called the vote counters 'counties'. 'How cute is that?' I said. Until Mr V told me to stop being a twat and use my brain for once.

The 5th November brought more fireworks than I've heard in my life. A taste of what life would be like if we weren't normally told to stop blowing ourselves up in our back gardens and go to the state-sponsored Bonfire nights.

Around mid-November, I removed a particularly irritating chin hair and Dominic Cummings resigned. Sky News clearly couldn't decide which momentous event to report on, but disappointingly opted for the departure of Dominic. As he left Downing Street in the full glare of the cameras, clutching the wee cardboard box containing his career, I really wanted him to have a Malcolm Tucker* moment and shout 'Fuckity Bye' at everyone.

There was *some* good news. The UK ordered loads of vaccine and our glorious leaders agreed that we could all meet up at Christmas. They called it a Christmas Bubble. A missed an opportunity there – surely it should have been a Christmas Bauble? Even more exciting was the new series of The Crown. The royal family, the cast and the media kept saying something about it being a drama and "lots of it is made up." The nation put its hands over its ears and said, 'La, la, la, not listening.' We all enjoyed a salacious peep behind the palace curtains and pronounced The Crown our favourite absolutely true-to-life documentary.

At the end of November, more Tiers and tantrums. Many areas, including mine, would be going into Tier 3, which was virtually lockdown, from 2nd December. But Christmas was definitely still on.

*Peter Capaldi plays Malcolm Tucker, Director of Communications and chief enforcer, in the political satire The Thick of It. He is wonderfully ruthless and exceptionally sweary (Malcolm, not Peter).

1st November

Gazebo-Gate

How are we doing with all the tiers, lockdowns, quarantines and isolations? I realise some of us will be fine with it and for others it's a struggle. Some of us in England might actually be relieved that we're going back into lockdown, because we've been feeling increasingly worried. I think I might be in that last category.

We're going to visit Lovely Granny and Grandad today so we can freeze our tits off in their garden and tell them how much we'll miss them. I only hope things improve enough so that we can see them at Christmas.

I've been trying to persuade Mr V to buy a gazebo, in case we're allowed visitors in our garden post lockdown. Mr V has vetoed the idea because "it is very expensive", "anyway where would we put a gazebo", "nobody will use it" and "did I mention that it is very expensive?" Of course, this is Mr V speak for "you'll make me build it and I don't want to build it." I would build it myself, but we have been down the road of Mrs V's best efforts before.

You know how some people deliberately mess up a job so they're never asked to do it again? I'm the opposite. I enthusiastically tackle jobs that I know I'll mess up, in the hope that this one time I'll get it right. This is why I'm not allowed near hand rolling tobacco. I love having a go at making rollies, but apparently people don't appreciate their entire supply of tobacco being turned into a pile of misshapen lumps. I'm told that no, it is not a nice surprise.

I am also the queen of flat pack. I love putting together flat pack furniture, although I have a limited attention span when it comes to instructions. Our wobbly bathroom shelves defied the laws of physics for years!

On second thoughts, maybe I should just get the gazebo and call it my lockdown hobby. After all, I built a Lego Steamboat Willie during last lockdown and I only had ten unidentifiable bits left over. How hard can a gazebo be?

3rd November

Star Witness

Once upon a time a beautiful princess called Mrs V had to go to court to give evidence.

She got everything ready and off she went in the royal carriage, stopping on the way at the palace kitchen known as Greggs to pick up a sandwich. And maybe a cake. Ooh and a donut because they looked very nice and she might need snacks. Make that six, because they were on special offer. The royal chef, whom we shall call Linda from Greggs, kindly offered the princess a bag but, in a move she would later regret, the princess said she could squeeze everything into her handbag.

Princess Mrs V was very pleased with herself. She had managed to arrive at the court on time, with all the correct paperwork and snacks. She went into the building, where some security footmen told her to empty the contents of her bulging handbag into a tray for inspection. Princess Mrs V duly unloaded half a bakery into the tray and felt the need to explain to the footmen that she may be well padded but, honest guvnor, the donuts weren't all for her.

Having established that, unless she was planning to carb everyone to death, Princess Mrs V was not a menace to society, the security footmen allowed her to proceed to the front desk. The keeper of the front desk was a kindly gentleman who had no record of Princess Mrs V being expected in court at all. Princess Mrs V tried waving her phone at anyone who would listen, crying, 'But I have an email!' No knight in shining armour appeared, so Princess Mrs V had to go back outside and phone the solicitors. The solicitors assured the princess that she was definitely in the right place and she should tell the keeper of the front desk to check again.

Once more, the princess emptied half a bakery into the security tray and had a lovely conversation with the footman about why she kept setting the scanner off. Back and forth she went, swearing blind that her pockets were definitely empty. Eventually, her baked goods were returned to her and she was allowed to proceed.

The keeper of the front desk was once more adamant that Princess Mrs V was not on the list. He did, however, suggest she try a different court on the other side of the kingdom.

Princess Mrs V went back outside and called the solicitor. The solicitor said yes, she did appear to have sent the princess to entirely the wrong place and the princess now had half an hour to get to the other side of the kingdom. The princess was starting to feel almost as grumpy as her husband, the Grumpy Prince. She phoned the Grumpy Prince to tell him that she was in the wrong place and he helpfully pointed out 'this could only happen to you.'

The princess knew there was no parking at the other side of the kingdom, so she was going to have to take a bus. Princess Mrs V isn't very good at taking strange buses because she has no sense of direction and doesn't know where to get off. The princess always solves this problem by making friends with strangers at bus stops and getting them to look after her. On this occasion, she became instant BFFs with a man who knew all about buses and the local area. He assumed that the princess was from another place far away and was most pleased to tell her all about the kingdom. In great detail. So enthusiastic was he, that the princess didn't have the heart to correct him and had to spend 10 minutes listening to a monologue on the topography of her own kingdom, all the while wondering how she could get her new BFF to STFU, yet still ensure he told her to get off at the correct stop.

Princess Mrs V was very unhappy about having to take a bus. The bus was full. She wanted to shout at everyone for coming too near her royal person, but had to content herself with texting the Grumpy Prince to moan about ye olde social distancing and declare that she was not touching anything ever again. Also, she needed a pee.

And so it was that a stressed and slightly tearful princess managed to turn up to the right court in the nick of time. She and her handbag of baked goods once again navigated security. She explained that she appeared to have acquired the ability to set scanners off for no reason and she tried not to have a meltdown when the keeper of the front desk told her she was in the wrong building and needed the building next door. There, she was met by a barrister who told her not to be worried when the defence asked her difficult questions. Princess Mrs V was not worried. Compared to her morning so far, being asked difficult questions would be a breeze.

The defence did ask difficult questions and nobody was happy that the princess couldn't remember much. The princess explained that it was three years ago. She wondered if she should explain that she was menopausal, so remembering yesterday was cause for celebration. Also, she had anticipated hanging around for hours eating baked goods and hadn't yet had so much as a sniff of a carb. The princess decided that the judge would not be interested in the menopause and how all she could think about was donuts so there was no room left in her brain for other things. And how she needed a pee. The judge made some comments to the effect that Princess Mrs V had somehow managed to be extremely unhelpful whilst trying to be extremely helpful. Princess Mrs V was delighted that he had recognised her special talents because it had taken the Grumpy Prince years to figure that one out.

When Princess Mrs V was finished giving evidence, she texted a royal pronouncement to the Grumpy Prince that she was going to find a toilet. The Grumpy Prince suggested she also do some shopping to cheer herself up and she agreed that, for once, the Grumpy Prince was right. However, on seeing the queues outside shops, she decided to hotfoot it back to the royal carriage and pray she didn't pee herself on the way home.

Lo, it was with great relief that the beautiful princess ran through the front door, advised the two overjoyed wee hairy footmen that she would be with them shortly and dashed straight to the porcelain throne room. Royal business done, she finally got to eat All The Carbs and take her bad temper out on the royal children, who had lounged around all day doing bugger all. This made the princess live happily ever after.

4th November

Just Testing

After all the fuss of gazebo-gate (remember that Mr V told me how expensive a gazebo would be so we couldn't possibly get one?), we were watching Bake Off last night and a wee voice pipes up, 'You can get ice cream machines?' I glanced across the room and there was Mr V, looking most interested in Hermine's mango masterpiece. And the idea of getting an ice cream machine.

Now, I saw this as the ideal time to experiment on my husband. Worry ye not. No husbands have been harmed in the making of this post.

The question to be answered was - did Mr V just object to spending money on a gazebo because it was something he didn't want, even though it would make his Mrs V happy? I wondered what would happen when he was presented with an expensive item he did want.

Thanks to the power of Messrs Google and Bezos, I was able to find the most whizzy ice cream maker on the market. A steal at almost £300 (which I agree is a ridiculous sum of money). I armed myself with a full business case (it is the equivalent of about 60 tubs of Ben & Jerry's if they're not on special offer) and set about trying to persuade him. Could self-interest and a love of ice cream sway him? What about a sneaky suggestion that this could be our Christmas present to ourselves?

I am disappointed to report that the whole idea totally backfired on me. Mr V told me to go off and write more books, so I could make the family fortune and buy us fancy ice cream makers. He was very interested and accepted all my arguments, but ultimately his short arms and deep pockets triumphed.

This is a shame because, having done the research, I think I now want an ice cream machine more than a gazebo.

5th November

Lockdown 2.0 and Pudding

Day 1 of lockdown 2.0 in England. Of course, the lovely people of Norn Irn and Wales have already been locked down for a wee while and Nicola's still battling away up there in Scotland, where they've all painted themselves blue and are running through the streets of Glasgow shouting, 'You may take our non-essential items, but you'll never take our freedom!' Oh, my lovely Scotland, I wish I was there with you. I'd be like a blue whale wheezing its way down Sauchiehall Street.

If I'm honest with myself, I'm finding the whole thing a bit...well, it feels like it will never end. This is coming from someone with the emotional resilience of Tigger, who generally finds the world a fascinating soap opera and can't bear the thought of dying because she wants to find out what happens next. Fortunately, I'm married to Eeyore, who helpfully advised me, 'Go to bed. That's what I do when I'm finding everyone annoying.' This explains so much of our marriage.

As all the Brits know, it's bonfire night. Our centuries old nod to the foiling of a nefarious plot and our excuse to stand in freezing public parks in front of massive bonfires, wondering how long before the fireworks start because you can't feel your toes and you really need a pee. Biggles, who is so noise sensitive that he's scared of his own farts, is surprisingly unaffected by fireworks. Vegas is deaf as a post and needs a firework lit under him to get him out of bed of a morning. A bit like one of his humans (the Eeyore one). It's a shame we won't have the big public displays this year.

Cross fingers we get Christmas, though. I shall be very annoyed with Boris if he gets up on his little podium and says, 'Lovely Granny and Grandad have to stay at home and here is a chart to explain why.' I will launch a petition to make parliament debate whether my human rights were breached because I bought a massive eff off turkey and now we are doomed to turkey sandwiches for every meal until the 5th of January.

Mr V reminded me the other day that we need to order the Christmas food. I told him I already had. 'I should have been consulted!' he declared. Had I ordered vegetables? No. This was good because I always get vegetables he doesn't like (I was quite surprised, as this implies that there are vegetables he does like - in twenty-five years of marriage I've only managed to narrow it down as far as peas). Had I ordered pigs in blankets? Yes. Lots of them? Yes. Had I ordered stuffing? Yes. This was all good. As long as I hadn't spent a fortune on expensive puddings, it was okay that I didn't consult him. I avoided providing any information on that last point.

This gave me pause for thought. If Boris does cancel Christmas, I shall be stuck eating posh puddings until the 5th of January. That's not such a bad thing. Maybe I won't bother with the petition after all. And, what with Christmas being the season of peace and all, when he finds out that I've bought posh puddings, old Eeyore can go for a lie down in a darkened room.

Ooh, I've cheered myself right up.

6th November

Lady Flu and Farting

Cherub 1 has the lurgy. Not the coronalurgy. Just normal lurgy. The kind where, during the night, the snot fairy creeps into your bedroom and replaces your brain with a big ball of green slime. And while she's at it, she takes an emery board to the back of your throat. I'd feel sorry for Cherub 1 if she didn't keep getting her size zero washboard stomach out to howl, 'Look how bloated I am.' Honestly, I have fatter chin hairs than that.

Also, on the subject of bloating, I've had to be nice through two conversations about her being scared to fart in front of boys. I gave her my best motherly advice, which is that you know you've got a keeper when you accidentally let one rip and your other half says, 'Good one.' Sorry, I know many of you ladies out there will be maintaining an air of feminine mystique but, let's face it, we've all bent over at the wrong moment. The best thing you can do in that situation is own it. Follow it up with an even bigger one and ask for marks out of ten. Get a bit of competition going. There you go, a great suggestion for some family lockdown entertainment. You could probably do it on the work Zoom as well. Bit of a change from the weekly team quiz. You can thank me later.

And on that rather juvenile note, I shall bid you happy Wineday. I'm off to tidy up Covid Corner. I've lost my tablets, my car keys and a notebook, so I'm taking it as a sign from the gods that I need to declutter. Mr V suggested it two weeks ago, but he is not a god (unless thinking you're a total sex god after a few pints counts), so I lied and said everything was essential. Including the bottle of Prosecco. I may start by tidying that up then see how I get on from there

7th November

Flogging My Wares

Thanks to everyone who has asked about book two. Frock In Hell is almost written, but it won't be out by Christmas. Boo! Hiss! It's not like the last one. It's a funny novel this time.

After Frock In Hell, I might get on with Big Blue Jobbie - Number 2. You see what I did there? Sorry, I can't seem to be a proper grown up this week. I've just been given a massive telling off by Cherub 2 for stealing his Appletiser and Mr V said he'd had enough of me today after I tripped over the dog's water dish and sat on his giant box of Jaffa cakes. Or Jaffa crepes, as they are now known. I wouldn't mind, but I'm wearing my 'I am a delight' t-shirt!

If you'd like to buy an 'I am a delight' t-shirt or even some Wineday coasters, Mr V made them for me and has put them in his MrVPhotography shop on Red Bubble. I'm not trying to make the family fortune or do a big plug. He has been putting designs and photographs on there for years and I didn't make a fuss about it because I blog to entertain people, not sell stuff. But as we're all probably doing a bit more online Christmas shopping this year, I thought you might be interested.

8th November

Lest We Forget

Hello from the dull, damp North of England. I didn't get out to buy a poppy this year for Remembrance Sunday, so I bought a digital one. The Royal British Legion have a thing where you can take a selfie wearing your digital poppy, but I looked like a troll and even I have standards, so I bribed Biggles to be my stand in. No disrespect was intended. Just a love of my dog and a desire to display my poppy on something far nicer than a middle-aged lady in a tea-stained dressing gown, sporting a rather marvellous unwashed Elvis quiff that she isn't sure how she'd acquired. In the grand scheme of things, though, my vanity and how I choose to wear my poppy don't matter. What matters is the human beings and animals who were taken from us.

Over a hundred years ago, my grandfather endured horrendous conditions, marching through muddy fields in a kilt in winter. My dad said he never spoke about what he'd seen, except to say that the chafing from the frozen, muddy kilt on the back of his legs was awful. I had two grandparents who served in the Second World War. My granny had good memories of friendships made while doing her bit. Sadly, I never had the chance to ask grandad as he died when I was six. I know I am lucky that my grandparents made it through. So many didn't. And it is for them and their families that I said a prayer at 11am. Lest we forget.

Somethingth of November

Remembrance

I wrote this with a note to self to post it on Remembrance Sunday 2021. The irony being that, a year later, there was no way I would remember writing it. However, since I have found it whilst trawling through my notes for this book, I will include it.

"We have so much to thank those brave, brave people for. In all the hurly burly of the modern world, it is good to stand still for a moment and remember them. It is good to be thankful for what we have and know that, but for those who went before us, how easily the world could have been a very different place. They sacrificed their lives to right wrongs and, in my humble opinion, it's incumbent on every one of us today to be grateful and make the world a kinder place. I'm glad we have a day to remind us of their sacrifice and our duty."

13th November

Dickery on the Drinkery

I have a new lockdown hobby. Cherub 1 bought me a wine set of...well, let's just say they're plastic men whose enormous appendages form a corkscrew, stopper and bottle opener. It's almost Elf On The Shelf season, so every morning when he gets up, Mr V finds a new formation of plastic men on top of the coffee machine. I call them Cocks On The Box. They're currently doing the Beatles Abbey Road pose, if there were only three Beatles and they were all gloriously excited about whatever was on the other side of that pedestrian crossing.

In other news, Covid corner stinks and I'm almost sure it's not me. A wee hairy boy is currently sound asleep, blissfully unaware that he and teddy are destined for a bath. His lockdown bottom has expanded somewhat and we're trying to take him on more walks. However, he's thirteen, which is like a thousand in dog years, so he's not very keen on all this walking business.

In Cherub 2 news, I think I may have created a monster. He threw my own words back at me during an argument the other day. It was a daft argument about the way he'd spoken to me, which ended with him announcing, 'Anyway, I'm a delight,' and flouncing off, leaving me screaming up the stairs at him, 'You are not a delight. I am a delight and I have a t-shirt which says so.' I feel I was the grown up there.

I went for blood tests yesterday. I got one of those texts from the doctor a couple of weeks ago – "Please ring urgently." They really need to preface those with "Don't worry. You're not dying and you don't have a terrible disease." Every time I get one of those texts, I panic. I'm convinced that when I phone, the young receptionist is going to say, 'I'm sorry to break this to you, but you've got nipple rot, ear worms and a raging dose of athletes armpit.' Because this is what happens when you have monthly blood tests - they look at the blood and find stuff. Then they make you wait weeks to find out it was all a fuss over nothing (this time, at least). Anyway, they just wanted me to repeat the test. Nobody knows why. At least I got to have a good gossip with lovely nurse Lisa and you'll be pleased to hear we have sorted all the problems of the world.

I shall toddle off and do something useful now. Mr V bought me a gin advent calendar and I'm wondering if I can pretend that today is the 1st, 2nd and 3rd of December.

14ᵗʰ November

Guess How Sore Mr V's Back Is

Mr V has a sore back. It's the sorest back in the world. In the history of backs, nobody has ever had such a sore one. I genuinely feel sorry for him, but I also want to kill him. Lovely nurse Lisa and I have agreed that if our husbands got Covid, it would be long Covid. Neither of us could possibly catch Covid off our husbands because the virus would look at us and say, 'Aw, she's suffered enough.'

I think I'm such an unsympathetic cow because my mum was a member of the two paracetamols for everything brigade. She was lovely if you were proper ill, but she had no time for malingering or stupidity. When I was twelve, myself and a load of other kids piled onto a car bonnet and sledged down a hill. I broke my finger. This came under the heading of Stupidity, therefore the cure was two paracetamols and an early night. I'm not suggesting that Mr V's sore back is malingering, but there's an invisible malingering line that's quite easy to cross and I'm giving him an awful lot of paracetamol right now.

In other "Mr V being annoying" news, he keeps coming home from work and making me guess stuff. I think it's because his work is much quieter than usual, with lockdown, and he's finding the lack of things to do bizarrely interesting. And he clearly thinks I do too. "Guess how many of these things we did today. Guess how many people I saw today. Guess how long this or that took." Honestly, every evening I just sit there throwing random numbers back at him, only for him to smugly correct me. I say, 'Four,' and he lords it over me with, 'Noooo, sixteen.' I cracked on Wednesday and asked why he was making me play the world's shittest guessing game every day. Apparently, I'm supposed to take an interest, it's what people who love each other do.

I just read what I've written and realised I'm a bit of a grumpy cow today. So, I will leave you with something that made me smile. Last night I broached the subject of Cherub 1 paying digs (not sure what they call it in other places - board money?) now she's working again. She made some "yeah, yeah, whatever" noises and quickly left the room. 'That didn't go well,' I said to Mr V, 'although, on the upside, at least we now know how to get rid of her.'

15th November

Bricking It

Dear Prime Minister,

Please can Mr V and Cherub 2 be first in the queue for the vaccine? This is necessary for the preservation of my sanity, the ongoing safety of Royal Mail staff and protecting our NHS.

Mr V and Cherub 2 have taken to building Lego and plans are afoot for a whole Lego street along my lovely mantelpiece, which currently has tasteful things like an antique clock on it. The whole living room has turned into a Lego man cave and there is nowhere to sit. It is ruining Bake Off viewing and even the dog's bed is full of Lego. Mr V has spent weeks building a massive jeep, only to discover that the back wheels spin in opposite directions. I have to say I'm not surprised. This is entirely consistent with his DIY skills. In our house, if you want to switch the hall light on, you have to switch it off.

The steady arrival of boxes also means the steady ringing of the doorbell. The wee hairy boys don't mind because they get to bark and bark to tell us, 'That bastard the postie is here again!' Time and time again, I end up doing the dance of catching a dog and shutting him in another room (the other one is too lazy to get up, so lies in his bed woofing loudly). All this so that I can open the door without the postie becoming breakfast for a Jack Russell. I retrieve the package and cheerily wave to the postie to let him know I've got it. He does not realise how narrowly he escaped being mauled to slight injury. Then a cherub or Mr V appear downstairs, wondering why the dogs are going ballistic. I glare at all of them, humans and dogs, before going back to my online meeting. Vegas, the lazy, deaf one, is not sure the danger has passed, so he continues to woof until I give him the agreed signal that he can stop now. The agreed signal is a bottle top thrown in his direction. Heavy enough to fly across the room, light enough to do no damage in the unlikely event that I score a direct hit. I have my mother's throwing skills. If I aim for the dog, I will definitely hit the bookcase. However, it's enough to distract him from his wee hairy mission to alert the world to the fact that something is happening. He's not sure what. But it's definitely something.

To top all of this off, last night Mr V complained that hours of leaning over to build Lego has made his back worse. Well, there's a surprise! So now I have to put up with extra weeks of Man Back. It's like man flu but potentially goes on for months. One of us is going to end up with a Lego Eiffel Tower up his backside and we better all pray he built it properly this time because it's the difference between a smooth extraction and shitting bricks.

So, Prime Minister, the sooner we get Mr V and Cherub 2 back out into the community and fully engaged, the better. I rest my case.

Lots of love,

Mrs V xxx

18ᵗʰ November

Tits in a Tin

Cherub 2 has broken all teenage records by sleeping for 16 hours. Mr V, who is a secret teenager, came a close second at 13 hours. Both of them asked the same question when they eventually got up. 'Why didn't you wake me up?!' They were both given the same answer. 'You're a big boy now - set an alarm and actually get up when it goes off.' LIKE EFFING NORMAL PEOPLE. Of course, the real answer was that I was rather enjoying the peace and quiet.

I've abandoned everything this week because The Crown is on Netflix. However, I made an exception for the Bake Off semi-final. It was patisserie week. Or boob cake week, as it's known in our house. They made cakes that looked like boobs a couple of years ago and Mr V got a bit obsessed. I can't remember what the cakes were actually called, but it all culminated in me wandering around Waitrose with a grown man chuntering on about boob cakes. 'Why are there no boob cakes? I want boob cakes. Where do you think they keep the boob cakes? You'd think if anyone had boob cakes, it would be Waitrose.' Although this wasn't nearly as bad as wheeling a trolley around Asda with a two-year-old cherub who, having spotted the bra section, was howling, 'I want a boob nest!'

Sadly, or perhaps happily, there were no boob cakes this week. They were cube cakes. I can't think why, but Mr V isn't nearly as interested in cubes.

19th November

Light of My Life

That's me done with work for the day, now I get to play. Mr V has been to Costco and he bought me a lamp for Covid Corner. It's not the glittery lamppost I threatened to buy, which I thought would look truly fab next to my ancient armchair - give it a touch of class. But it's still a very nice lamp and a sign of his forgiveness.

I was in trouble earlier because I made the mistake of being sympathetic to someone about their illness and Mr V came storming through to tell me, 'I heard you, you know. Being all "ooh sorry you're not well". But when I have a sore back, I'm a moaning git!!' I helpfully confirmed that he is indeed a moaning git and went about my day.

Now I'm off to go and enjoy my evening. By that, I mean nag Mr V to build the lamp. Before anyone gets on their high horse about me making him do jobs I could do myself - he offered. I'm just in charge of nagging. While I'm on the subject of nagging...note to self...remind Mr V that ice maker in fridge is still broken and needs fixed otherwise I shall have to declare a national G&T emergency. A woman's work is never truly done.

20th November

DCI Mr V and the Special Chocolate Place – Part One

Once upon a Friday, a curmudgeonly, middle-aged man, whom we shall call Mr V, noticed that his chocolate bar, which he'd been carefully hoarding for months in a place that his family definitely didn't know about, was missing. He was both outraged and delighted. Outraged because his special chocolate place had been violated and delighted because he rather liked conducting investigations.

In an ideal world Mr V would be a policeman. However, the world was very far from ideal, so he considered doing a Mr Benn. Remember Mr Benn? Unfortunately, it was lockdown and all the fancy dress shops run by moustachioed men in fezzes were closed, which seemed very unfair because surely fancy dress during lockdown was essential for cheering everyone up! So, instead, he imagined very, very hard that he was not a sex god after six pints, the harassed father of two young people and the husband of a failed domestic goddess. He imagined very, very hard that he was a policeman, with nice, shiny boots, a fresh notebook and a special pocket for his detective pens.

Detective Chief Inspector Mr V went to the kitchen Drawer of All Things. The drawer where he stored all the important items that might come in handy one day. Like the back door key for the house he owned in 1995, four McDonalds happy meal toys and approximately five thousand hair bands. He rummaged around and there it was - his detective pen.

Armed with his trusty pen and notebook, he began questioning his suspects.

'So, Cherub 1, do you know where I hide my chocolate?'

Cherub 1 denied any knowledge and pointed out that she is allergic to dairy, except when she goes to Pizza Hut and eats her own weight in mozzarella. Oh, and when she has that one day a month where it's either eat chocolate or murder your entire family for breathing too loudly. Other than that, definitely allergic to dairy.

'So, Cherub 2, have you discovered my hiding place?'

Cherub 2, who was still traumatised from drinking all his mother's tonic water and the resulting fallout from what is now known as Gin-gate, declared that he had learned his lesson and was no longer, as per his mother's words, "a thieving little sod who deserves to be fed to lions and not head-first because that would be too kind, oh no, you will be eaten from the feet up." His mother may have been a tiny bit upset when her plans for a nice G&T were derailed.

On to suspect 3, Mrs V, mother of Cherubs, failed domestic goddess and well-padded supermodel.

'So, Mrs V, have you violated my special chocolate place?'

Mrs V was very busy stirring a pot of soup and told DCI Mr V that she didn't have time for such nonsense and if he persisted in asking stupid questions then she would violate his special chocolate place with this wooden spoon.

DCI Mr V knew when he was being fobbed off. Also, it was an offence to threaten police officers with wooden spoons. Even if they were pretend police officers. However, DCI Mr V was a man of wit, cunning and exceptional patience. He could bide his time.

Sure enough, a couple of hours later, Mrs V announced she was going for a shower. While she was in there, loudly singing the wrong words to all the songs, DCI Mr V conducted a search of her dressing gown.

What did he find? Did he discover the culprit? And why was Mrs V singing a Sister Sledge song about making love in a femidom? We will find out tomorrow in DCI Mr V and The Special Chocolate Place - Part Two.

(Except we didn't find out tomorrow because a certain Mrs V suddenly remembered two days later that she'd forgotten to post part two)

22nd November

DCI Mr V and the Special Chocolate Place - Part Two

DCI Mr V listened to the joyous warbling emanating from the bathroom. Mrs V had moved on from Sister Sledge and their love in a femidom and was now loudly dreaming a dream of times gone by, when soap was gone and bums were minging. DCI Mr V reckoned he had plenty of time to search her dressing gown for wrappers. She hadn't even done any vintage Madonna yet.

With one ear cocked for "When you call my name, I'm gonna shave my hair, The hair on my knees, It's like a grizzly bear," DCI Mr V reached into Mrs V's dressing gown pocket. There was a definite crinkle. He could feel a wrapper. He pulled the wrapper out. Aha! Gotcha! Oh no, that wasn't the chocolate bar wrapper, although she'd clearly been pilfering his Jaffa cakes again. He tried the other pocket. Hmm. Dog biscuit, £10, phone charger, lipstick, orange, indigestion tablet. How much stuff could one woman keep in a pocket? Hang on...another crinkle. Carefully, he pulled the wrapper from Mrs V's pocket and saw, with satisfaction, that it belonged to his chocolate bar. Aha! Definitely gotcha this time!

DCI Mr V knocked on the bathroom door. The happy warbling stopped and a voice shouted, 'No, I don't know where it is, yes, it's all very terrible, don't fight with your brother, be kind to your sister, sort it out for yourself. Now, I'm in the shower, so please bugger off.'

DCI Mr V poked his head around the bathroom door. 'You've been in my special chocolate place. I found the chocolate wrapper in your pocket.'

'No, I haven't.'

'Yes, you have. You violated my special chocolate place!'

Mrs V emerged from the bathroom and said, 'Shut up, you

big eejit with your special chocolate place. I didn't go near your special chocolate place.'

'You did so. And I have the evidence to prove it.'

The argument carried on for some time, only reaching a head when DCI Mr V roared, 'You are charged with theft and the unauthorised touching of my special chocolate place.'

Mrs V stopped threatening to batter him to death with a pillow, drew herself up and, with all the dignity she could muster, told him where he could shove his special chocolate place.

DCI Mr V went downstairs to collect witness statements from the Cherubs. However, the Cherubs were hostile witnesses. They refused to give evidence against their mother. He tried bribing them with takeaways, but they remained unmoved, insisting that Mrs V had not stolen his chocolate. He eventually came to the conclusion that she must have bribed them with something far better than chicken chow mein, so DCI Mr V took the only course of action left to him. He phoned Lovely Granny to tell her all about his rotten family.

That night, as DCI Mr V lay in the spare room bed, he mentally retraced his steps. He definitely recalled putting the chocolate in the special place. Ah well, tomorrow was another day. Tomorrow he would let his family know that he forgave them, even though they were thieving sods.

Once upon a Saturday, a curmudgeonly pretend policeman came downstairs for breakfast. As he sat down at the kitchen counter, preparing to tuck into his cornflakes, a piece of paper caught his eye. He pulled it towards him and couldn't believe what he was seeing. It was the wrapper from his chocolate bar! He checked his pocket. The wrapper he'd found in Mrs V's pocket was there. Perhaps he'd been a bit hasty in blaming Mrs V.

DCI Mr V once more tackled the Cherubs. 'Who left this chocolate wrapper in the kitchen?'

'That was me,' said Cherub 2.

'You ate my chocolate!' shouted DCI Mr V.

Cherub 2, who had barely made it through Gin-gate uninjured and did not want another monumental telling off, hastened to assure DCI Mr V that he'd found the chocolate bar in the vegetable drawer in the fridge. He'd accidentally opened the drawer when looking for cheese.

DCI Mr V had a lightbulb moment. He remembered being about to eat his chocolate. He had heard someone coming and had quickly hidden his chocolate in the vegetable drawer because, well, what sort of person ever voluntarily seeks out vegetables?! Certainly not him! He had reckoned it would be an excellent temporary hiding place.

DCI Mr V felt deflated. He was the thief. Mrs V would never let this one go. Sighing, he opened the Drawer of All Things and put away his detective pen. Then he went upstairs to break the news to Mrs V that she was right and he was wrong.

Epilogue

Eight hours later, the doorbell rang and Mr V answered the door. A man passed over a bag of Chinese food and Mr V paid him. The man was about to leave when he stopped, straining to listen to a voice floating down from the shower upstairs. It sounded exactly like the marvellous songstress, Whitney Houston, and the Greatest Love of All. Except...

'I decided long ago

Never to look in vegetable drawers

If I fail, if I succeed

At least I can blame my family

No matter what they take from me

They can't take away my Galaxy.'

24th November

Covid Corner News

Mrs V, local author and self-proclaimed freakin' genius, joyfully announced on Sunday that she had finished writing her latest book. There was a mixed reaction to the exciting news, with Mr V asking, 'What are you making for tea?' Publication may be delayed, pending the recovery of Mr V's testicles.

A middle-aged man has been auctioning off the contents of his sacred garage. An enormous parcel is currently blocking the entrance to Covid Corner and the man in question has been proudly boasting about his big package. What he is doing with the proceeds from the sale remains a mystery but, in an exclusive interview with Covid Corner News, his wife said she expected a very shiny Christmas present, at least one carat.

In domestic news, an investigation was launched into who tipped their crunchy nut cornflakes into the sink and left them there. While industrial strength cleaner is deployed to unglue the dried-on cornflakes, the investigation has closed in on two suspects. Cherub 2 has denied everything, on the basis that he is a teenager and nothing is ever his fault, and Cherub 2 has firmly pointed the finger back at Cherub 1. The sentence for fly-tipping cornflakes is one week's hard labour and mandatory training on how bins work. Members of the public are advised not to approach the suspects as they may be armed with coco pops.

A source in the treasury has reported that, although the Covid Corner economy bounced back in October, a surge in online shopping has caused a sudden slump towards the end of November. Mrs V, who appears to have bought half the contents of Etsy, claims that she was doing the Christmas shopping. However, the Mr V who thinks he's in charge of the treasury, has demanded an explanation for the box of chocolates and a very nice scarf. Mrs V declined to comment. Possibly because her mouth was full of chocolate at the time.

Finally, the weather. A strong likelihood of storms this evening when Mr V discovers that a bottle of Prosecco has also accidentally fallen into the Christmas shopping. There will be an area of high pressure when Mrs V explains that she has no idea how these things keep happening to her and possibly another lady did it and ran away. Gale force winds are predicted for tomorrow, following chilli night. Wee hairy boys are advised to take cover, lest they get the blame.

26th November

Vegas' View of the World

Hello. Vegas here. My favourite human asked me to tell you all about how we dogs are doing lockdown.

Firstly, I have no idea what lockdown is. Maybe it is something to do with my favourite human being at home all day. Maybe it is why my bottom is so big. My human keeps mentioning my bottom and saying I need more walks. She clearly hasn't looked in the mirror lately. Also my human says that my bottom has expanded since she had my balls chopped off. I assume HER testicles were removed back in March.

I recently considered adopting a new favourite human, the one they call Cherub 1.

- Pros: snuggly blankets, more treats, less farting (the blame culture in this house is ridiculous).
- Cons: the other dog has already claimed her as his favourite human. I'm not keen on the other dog. He's a bit of a twat.

The jury's still out on my allegiances. I will see how the current favourite responds when I pretend to be deaf later.

I really am quite deaf, but some times I am deafer than others. For reasons I can't explain, the word 'sandwich' filters through perfectly, whereas the words 'go out for a pee in the freezing rain' somehow go unheard. Unless it is at night, when my human wants to go to bed. Then I like to go outside for ages and bark at things until she appears in her pyjamas to whisper-shout at me. We have other humans living nearby that my humans call the neighbours, but who are actually the Mortal Enemies. Apparently, it is very rude to bark at the Mortal Enemies and they don't like to be alerted to the presence of imaginary hedgehogs at midnight. Sometimes I hear the whisper-shouts of my human. Sometimes I decide that she must be talking to another Vegas.

Why do humans and cats pee indoors but dogs have to go outside? And why is my human allowed to see me poo, but if I barge into the bathroom to check whether she needs any help, I get yelled at? Just a thought.

Anyway, whatever this lockdown is, I'm happy that I get to spend all day with my favourite human, even if my centre of gravity has shifted so far backwards that I can no longer jump onto the sofa.

Woof woof,

Vegas x

28th November

Mrs V, Problem Solving Genius

I have solved the problem of Mr V never replying to texts:

Me: I've won £14,298 in the lottery?

Mr V (within 3 seconds): Really?!

Me: No, but now that I have your attention, do you know where I put my Prosecco?

Does anyone else use proper punctuation in texts? It really annoys my kids. They interpret a full stop at the end as an angry text. So, I text something helpful like "You left your plate in the living room, you lazy little git." and all of a sudden I'm being told to calm down. Jeeze.

They annoy me when they type kk instead of ok. Is it really too much trouble to move your thumb that extra half centimetre to the o? Although it might explain why those few metres to the dishwasher are an effing mission!

Anyway, I'm off to do my Christmas present wrapping now. I've thoroughly messed with Cherub 2's head by taking delivery of lots of parcels all week and not opening them. He doesn't understand how I can resist. Easy. None of them are for me. Although at least I know how to annoy him in future. Next time we argue, I'll threaten to do online shopping and not open the parcels for a week. Obviously, it will be sheer hell for me, having to do all that shopping, but being a parent means making sacrifices.

29th November

NOT Effing Lilac

I locked horns with my darling son this morning when I told him to use the blue jug. He says it's light purple. Others think it's grey. What colour is it?!

***

Can I recommend that you never post a picture of something and ask people what colour they think it is unless you're prepared for a lot of disagreement. Here's my post from my personal page a couple of days later:

"I made the mistake of putting the jug colour on the blog and spent the weekend with hundreds of people shouting lilac at me. They're still doing it! It's Tuesday, people, I've moved on to a whole new set of trivial problems!"

Furthermore, some people queried why I had "locked horns" with Cherub 2, suggesting it was a bit of a strong reaction. All of those people can come back to me when they've successfully had a calm discussion with their nearest and dearest about whether the milk should go in first.

***

DECEMBER 2021

Ooh, Christmas. Deck the halls with Mariah Careys, falalalala lala la la. The vaccine arrived and the over 80s were shooting up all over the place. My local GP surgery became the geriatric hang-out of choice for the next few months. Nurse Lisa was enjoying sticking needles into someone who wasn't me for a change and her patients were grateful for it. There was some light at the end of the COVID-19 tunnel, even if we didn't realise it yet.

Being in Tier 3, people in my area weren't allowed to do much of anything. There were complex rules about going to pubs if we had a meal and the entire country became obsessed about exactly what constituted a meal. The North watched with envy as the crowds in Tier 2 London shopped, ate and drank their way to a happy Christmas, only sneering slightly when they were all thrown into Tier 3, swiftly followed by a newly invented Tier 4 from the 20th December. The Kent variant was spreading and Christmas plans were cancelled for London and the South East. We didn't sneer at that. It was going to be a very lonely Christmas for some people.

Across the rest of England, despite still being allowed to mix with other households for Christmas, many of us started to have second thoughts. Good old Nicola up in Scotland said, 'Enjoy Christmas Day together, because that's your lot. As of 26th you're all trapped in Scotland and there'll be nae gaun oot.' With the Kent variant being more transmissible, many other countries said, 'And there'll be nae coming here either,' leaving many people unable to fly home to their families. None of this was helped by Westminster making some last-minute Brexit changes and pissing off the EU. France did relent at the last moment, but it was too late for many freight drivers to make their deliveries and be home in time for the big day. Most of England was told they'd be joining the Tier 4 brigade as of Boxing Day, a South African variant of concern was found in the UK and tales of panic buying began to circulate.

The circuit breaker lockdown hadn't worked. "Record" numbers of cases were recorded (I use inverted commas here because the numbers were still far lower than what we would see in the coming months). What a flipping shambles of a month. I think it's fair to say that we all hunkered down, ate our turkey and made the best of it.

To my delight, I discovered that on 4th December 2012, 2013 and 2015 I had posted that I was eating food. I shared a screenshot and reassured my friends that, five years on, I was still eating food. Looking back at my personal posts for December, I think I was struggling a bit. Writing things like "Remember when you could go for a coffee while you were shopping, have a meal out and catch a movie? Welcome to Tier 3, London. It's shit." and "Christmas 2025. London is in Tier 5093, we're all having Christmas dinner alone in our gardens and the SAGE committee has overthrown the government in a bloodless coup. This feels like it will never end!" Nevertheless, I was mightily cheered to discover that on 23rd of December, my Facebook Memories consisted entirely of 12 years of me saying, 'Off to M&S to pick up the turkey.' It was slightly comforting that, despite All The Rules, this year was no different. Bring on the Baileys, pour the wine and eat until you fart pure sprouts.

1st December

Maybe It's Lilac

Thank you for joining in with the jug colour at the weekend. When several hundred people say something is lilac, I have to wonder if maybe...just maybe...it's a tiny hint that I was wrong and Cherub 2 was right.

Today has been surprisingly good for a Tuesday. Here are all the great things that have happened:

1.   The first person to test read my new book came back to say they laughed a lot and they cried twice. And not even because of bad writing! This was a relief.
2.   I mentioned a pain in my shoulder to Mr V and he said he has a pain in the backside. 'That'll be piles,' I told him. Nope. 'Then it must be the children.' Nope. 'Well, it can't be me because I'm a delight!' Oh, how Mr V laughed and laughed. Laughing is a good sign, right? It must be because he agrees it's not me.
3.   I received some important ginformation. Mr V has reminded me that today is the day I get to open my gin advent calendar. Hurrah for gin!
4.   And hurrah for knocking off work early. Which is what I did this afternoon, lest something awful come along and burst my happy bubble.
5.   Cherub 2 has taken up archery in the back garden. He has not accidentally killed any of the neighbours...yet.
6.   The house is vaguely tidy. This house is only ever properly tidy when we have visitors. Every other day, the bar is set at 'vaguely'. However, in reality, some days it barely reaches the standard of "particularly unhygienic bedroom of teenager with hoarding habit". Cherub 1 and I recently agreed that we're actually looking forward to Christmas because Cherub 2 and Mr V

will have to clear out the Lego man-cave that is our living room. Lovely Granny is coming for Christmas dinner and she is man-cave-intolerant.

7.   Mr V is getting the Christmas tree out of the sacred garage today. Most likely along with every box of decorations we have ever owned, just in case I get a sudden yen to hang threadbare tinsel circa 1993. The tree has Bluetooth speakers - slightly naff, I know, but I didn't realise that when I bought it and, to be fair, they are excellent for playing things from afar and scaring the shit out of people. I have plans to record myself singing All The Christmas Songs and play them at random times. Mr V and Cherub 2 will surely thank me for this helpful incentive to clear out the man-cave.

8.   I might have accidentally ordered cute Santa outfits for the dogs. So, now I have something to look forward to. Although if you have the special Mr V Google Translate on your browser, that sentence will read "She has definitely wasted far too much money on completely pointless outfits for the dogs. So now she's going to nag you into getting the fancy camera out to take photos." Tomato, tomayto.

I think I'm mainly happy because it's December 1st and I can now officially get excited for Christmas without people shouting 'TOO SOON' at me.

2nd December

Baubles and Chesticles

This is what I love about being British. We get straight to the heart of the matter. Lockdown ends, new Tier system is introduced, businesses are going bust and the most pressing question for the whole country is "Can I go to the pub if I buy a Scotch egg?" Let's face it, if Greggs ever goes under, there will be a national day of mourning.

Here in Tier 3, I am facing some big dilemmas of my own. I only have enough tonic water left for today's advent calendar gin and Cherub 2 has shown an interest in decorating MY Christmas tree. How to tell Cherub 2 that if he puts a single bauble on my tree, I will stab him in the throat with a plastic icicle, but also could he please go to the shop for some tonic?

In other news, I went for a chest X-ray yesterday. I had one two years ago and seem to recall two women getting quite annoyed with me as I stood there, half naked, trying to line my chest up with a black cross. The trouble was that there were two circles either side of the black cross and, for some weird reason, my brain decided that my nipples had to go in the circles. This is quite difficult to explain to two women who keep squealing, 'You moved again!' We eventually got it on take four.

This time, gravity and barely wearing a bra since March did the job. My nipples took one look at those circles, declared they were never going to reach and asked to be tucked back into my socks. The whole thing was done in one take. Also, they gave me a gown to wear, so I didn't even have to explain that I was a lazy cow who couldn't be bothered shaving her armpits. Yay, go me!

It may be crappy out there, but every day brings its own small triumphs.

***

Back in 2018 I took the day off work and went to the arthritis clinic. Because that's how we middle-aged ladies roll. Day off? Oh, yippee! Rheumatology!

First was the weight and height nurse. I kept my eyes tight shut for the weight bit until she eventually tapped me on the shoulder and said, 'You can go now, you big fat eejit.'

Then there was the doctor. I hadn't really planned ahead for the fact that if you tell a doctor you have sore knees they tend to want a bit of a poke around. I spent much of the appointment apologising for not shaving my legs and explaining that winter was coming, so I needed the extra layer. I also asked lots of questions about wheelchairs until the doctor told me to shut up because I was going to be fine.

After this, it was off to get a chest X-ray. They put me in a cubicle with a gown and a shopping basket for my clothes. The nurse explained how the gown worked and I instantly forgot. Couldn't work out which bits tied to which and eventually emerged, shopping basket in hand, with the top tied in a knot round my neck and the rest flapping about like a big flowery bed sheet. I think the nurse maybe hadn't stayed long enough to explain properly. I definitely didn't listen properly because, as soon as she introduced me to the shopping basket, my head filled with a vision of ninja nurses raiding Tesco. I mistakenly thought she wanted me to strip there and then, so just whipped off my top half. I don't think either of us expected me to be quite so keen to get the girls out and I suspect much of her explanation was done with her eyes closed.

Anyway, I sashayed into the X-ray room, flowery bedsheet threatening exposure at any minute, plonked my shopping basket down and stood while a nurse placed me in front of a plate. She was very particular about where I stood. Unfortunately, the plate had two big circles drawn on it and no matter how she positioned me, my brain wanted to line my boobs up with those circles. After repositioning me three times, we eventually got there.

151

Finally, it was off to the pharmacy. There was a posh coffee shop next door with a flight departure style board which told you when your prescription was ready! Gone are the days of sitting in a grim corridor trying to keep three feet between you and the bloke waiting for his scabies cream. This was a wonderful place of cappuccino and free wifi. By the time I was done my number was off the board and I ended up paying an extra £1 for parking.

Honestly, if you're ever at a loose end, get yourself down to rheumatology for a day out.

***

5th December

Recipe for Baking a Chocolate Cake

Ingredients:

1 enthusiastic yet clueless teenager

1 knackered, middle-aged woman

2 dogs

A large bottle of gin

1 hour of bickering

15,000 questions

Method:

Try to convince the knackered, middle-aged woman to bake a cake with you. She will claim that she's had a long day at work and is far too tired, but don't let that put you off. Add all the questions about cake ingredients, recipes, Vikings and what dogs think about.

Now you have worn the middle-aged woman down, insist that she finds a recipe for your ideal cake. Reject fifty options on the basis that you don't like the colour of the icing. Wonder if extra things would make your cake taste nicer and ignore all warnings from the middle-aged woman that adding weird stuff is unlikely to improve the recipe.

Your middle-aged woman is now on her third gin. Hide the bottle before she starts singing.

Use electric mixer to combine the cake ingredients and spray them all over the kitchen. Under no circumstances clean up the mess - you are a teenager, you definitely didn't make the mess and, logically, it must be the middle-aged woman's fault for owning a kitchen/giving birth to you.

Use dogs to clean floor.

Put cake in oven for half an hour.

Ignore calls from annoying middle-aged woman that oven timer has beeped. You are in the middle of a game and someone else will sort it out.

Be very annoyed that the middle-aged woman has taken your cake out of the oven. How dare she interfere! Tell her how much you hate her, then ask her to please help you make the icing.

Cede control of the mixer to the middle-aged woman because she has tidied up the last mess and is threatening to stab you to death with a wooden spoon if you decorate the walls with buttercream.

Ice cake and lick all the bowls. Wake up middle-aged woman to ask where you should put the cake. Ignore her suggestion. A cake tin is probably a far better place to shove it.

Congratulate yourself on a job well done.

6th December

These Are a Few of My Favourite Things

A Christmas favourite. If you're not singing along by the end of this, are you even human?

Gin drops in glasses

And hold you in knickers

Once they were Marathons and now they're called Snickers

Icing on cupcakes all covered in bling

These are a few of my favourite things.

Shiny glass baubles and page one of note pads

Glitter and shopping

And knickknacks and doodads

True Scots in kilts dancing wild Highland flings

These are a few of my sparkliest things.

Hairy boys dozing in front of log fires

Mr V's collection of cables and wires

Did I mention true Scotsmen and wild Highland flings?

Definitely one of my naughtiest things!

When the dogs bark

And the kids fight

And I'm feeling sad

I picture a large glass of Sauvignon Blanc

And then I don't feel so bad.

7th December

Wrap Battle

Reasons why someone else can do the effing present wrapping this Christmas:

1. I have done the present shopping. Okay, I like shopping, but that is not the point.
2. I can't hold a glass of wine and apply sticky tape at the same time. Something has to give.
3. I am far too busy providing other essential services, such as testing which Christmas chocolates are nicest.
4. Wrapping makes me want to stab myself in the eyes with a fork.
5. I get easily distracted and do things like this to the dog...

***

I posted a picture of the elder wee hairy boy looking rather glum about the tinsel wrapped round his head.

Scout's honour, I did do the wrapping and I hated every minute of it. Next Christmas, I'm going to adopt...hmmm...what shall I adopt?...effing Nigerian donkeys or something. You don't need to wrap them. The charity just gives you a card that says "Congratulations on behalf of the donkeys of West Africa. You've done a Very Good Thing. Now, go away and enjoy your invisible present." I once got the cherubs a well in Africa, thinking they'd be pleased to give part of their Christmas to those less fortunate. Turns out I'd seriously underestimated the selfish little feckers. They had absolutely no interest in doing A Very Good Thing. I found the cards in the bin. And not even the recycle bin! Heck, for the amount I spend on their Christmases, I could probably buy them a donkey and get it flown over first class. 'Merry Christmas. Can you guess what this carefully wrapped present is? You're right. It's a poo shovel and it's all yours. Now, your real present is in the garden...'

***

10ᵗʰ December

The One with the Big Dog Bed

Dear Jeff Bezos,

Please can you impose a lifetime Amazon ban on my son?

Cherub 2 has bought the wee hairy boys a new bed. Unfortunately, the enormous one was much cheaper than the small one and his teenage brain didn't take into account the amount of available floor space. Kind gesture, but now I have a miniature jack russell sprawled out, balls to the wind, in a bed fit for a Great Dane, and the whole family has to leap over it to get to the other side of the room. My boobs are not made for leaping. Gravity and age have taken their toll. I have tried to explain to Cherub 2 that my main objection to the dog bed is that I will have to wear a bra, but he just doesn't seem to get the connection. The only upside I can think of is that any burglars looking in our window will assume we have a big dog and give us a wide berth.

You may be wondering why we can't just walk around the dog bed. Surely our living room floor is wide enough. Well, yes, it would be if Cherub 2 hadn't also bought the world's largest footstool from your store. At least it opens up, so I can probably stash his body in it should he buy any more enormous things.

Nevertheless, I think the courts would look more favourably on me if I take all reasonable steps to avoid twatting him to death with a giant standard-lamp. Therefore, I think it would be best if you just close his Amazon account and we'll say no more about it.

Lots of love,

Mrs V xxx

***

Everyone got sick of leaping over the giant dog bed and it was quietly disappeared into the sacred garage. Then, yesterday, Cherub 2 asked if I could buy a dog bed. No, I definitely could not buy a dog bed! We have approximately 350,426 dog beds scattered through the house and every posh throw I ever bought has been claimed by the wee hairy ones. We even have a cat bed – one of those pyramid ones that they can snuggle inside. Vegas used to love it until his lockdown bottom got so big that he got stuck. I feel his pain. We dealt with this by buying him a new bed and it is so comfy that I have to put on my angry voice to make him get out of it.

I would quite like a new bed myself. The underside of mine is propped up by my shoe drawer. One of those under the bed drawers which is brimming with all the shoes that seemed like a good idea at the time. Mr V says I should throw them out, but he doesn't appreciate the versatility of shoes. You're never too fat for shoes and bags. Except maybe the shoulder bags with little straps that both cut off the circulation and perfectly emphasise the bingo wings. Also, never wear one with a vest top. I bought a new bag for going on holiday once. In all the photos, I have one normal arm and one half-cooked chunky sausage.

Anyway, I'm off on a tangent again. My bed. I sat on it one day and one of the slats underneath gave way. I investigated and discovered that it had almost snapped in two. For years I thought that I'd broken the bed with my hefty backside, so I propped the thing up using the power of shoes and didn't tell Mr V lest he start taking me on long walks and refuse to buy me ice cream. Only recently did Cherub 2 confess that he and his friends broke my bed by using it as a trampoline. This means I can now confess to Mr V that the bed is broken and make a full business case as to why I should have a new one. The only thing holding me back is that he may make a counter-offer – get rid of the shoes. Nooooo!

***

11th December

Samples and Sandwiches

Oh good. Me time. Mr V and Cherub 1 have gone to Costco. Cherub 1 is an excellent influence on Mr V, making him buy all manner of essential items that he wouldn't have otherwise bought. Important things, like Baileys and fancy chocolates.

Cherub 2 appears to have stayed up all last night, eating. There was almost a nuclear explosion this morning when Mr V found an empty box and howled that Cherub 2 had scoffed all his fish fingers. It was a national fish finger emergency! How could he be expected to cope? He might have to eat...gasp...vegetables! Worry ye not. Mrs V to the rescue. I delved so far into the freezer, I was practically in Narnia. A fresh packet was discovered and Mr V went off about his Mr V business, satisfied that his future fish finger sandwich needs have been taken care of.

There was a brief hiccup this morning when Mr V announced he had accidentally won some Lego. For a nanosecond, I thought he meant he'd won a competition. But no. My exact words were, 'You mean you bought some on eBay. What happened? Did your finger accidentally slip on the bid button?' For anyone who hasn't seen previous posts - my living room has been turned into a Lego man-cave. The boys have had the run of the living room for far too long. I'd say I was going to put my foot down, but I'd probably just get speared by a Lego brick. Time for a girl revolution methinks.

Vegas has to go to the vet this evening. I always feel so sorry for him when we take him to the vet. He gets excited that he's going somewhere, then we get to the door and he starts quivering. Anyway, it's nothing drastic. But I do have to use some of my 'me time' running around the back garden with a plastic tub, trying to encourage a reluctant Jack Russell to provide a pee sample. A bit of pre-Christmas entertainment for Old Ivy Next Door. Wish me luck.

12th December

Vegas Makes His Mark

Oh, there were shenanigans and awful goings on at the vet yesterday. Vegas did his usual thing of sitting on the floor and digging his heels in. Mr V dragged him along, not realising the poor thing had decided that a poo was in order. To cut a long story short, Vegas left the world's longest skid mark all the way from the front door to the reception desk.

No dogs were hurt in the making of this skid mark. Vegas has a little harness, instead of a collar and leash, because he's a puller. Although, in this instance, he was a pusher. It was like the song...

"On the third day of Pissmas, my Vegas gave to me,

One doggie skid mark,

Two wees a-pouring,

And a big jobbie on the vet's floor."

All before he even saw the vet. Then a big dog got jealous that Vegas was winning in the dirty protest stakes. So, he got in on the act and produced an enormous jobbie of his own. And, just when everyone thought things couldn't get worse, an effing shih tzu, who'd eaten a bar of chocolate, puked all over the place. With a name like shih tzu you'd think it would have come out the other end!

I feel so sorry for Vegas. I know he was just making a mess because he was scared. My poor wee baby.

Also, I didn't manage to get a pee sample before Vegas went to the vet. No amount of running around the garden in my dressing gown, brandishing a pink tub and trying to sneak up on him from behind like the piss ninja, made any difference. He was happy to widdle on my carpet, the doormat or the bed. But no way was a single drop going in that tub. And, despite his urinal profligacy at the vet, apparently any sample taken from the floor would be tainted.

The vet has given him antibiotics, but we have to try again for a wee sample before he can take them. Well, Old Ivy Next Door can have another laugh at me. Vegas and I are secretly hoping she laughs so hard she pees herself.

13th December

All I want for Christmas

Santa here's my list for Christmas

How about a new left knee

Could you make me one stone lighter?

Maybe two...well okay three

I just want some rhubarb gin

And could you pop a tonic in?

Oh for goodness sake

All I want for Christmas

Is cake

Santa here's my list for Christmas

Can you make my teens behave?

Can you get them out of bed

In time for lunch on Christmas Day?

Would you give the hairy boys

Lots of furry, squeaky toys

Make their dreams come true

All they want for Christmas

Is food

Santa here's my list for Christmas

Can you turn time back a bit?

You don't have to make me twenty

But I'd like to be more fit

Smooth the wrinkles, lose the 'tache

Years away from first hot flash

What more can you do?

All I want for Christmas

Is 32...oooh baby

Give me magic chocolate

You eat and you grow thin

I won't need that pair

Of pants to hold me in

And here's what I'm desiring

What gets my neurones firing

Santa won't you bring forth a new pelvic floor

So I can cough, laugh and sneeze safely!

Oh Santa here's my list for Christmas

Glitter, sequins, shiny things

Dancing like there's no one watching

Never mind the bingo wings

Everyone please join with me

In Growing Old Disgracefully

What more could there be?

All I want for Christmas?

Twattery

***

I should apologise for the sheer amount of poetry and singing in December. I bloody love Christmas and I get carried away. Everyone at work shouts at me for singing in the office.

I once almost joined the carol singers at work. I thought it would be a whizzy idea to go around the building, belting out Christmas songs and cheering folk up, so I went along to the staff canteen at the appointed time to do a bit of rehearsing with my fellow carollers. I thought they'd be people like me and it would all be jolly mince pies and God Rest Ye Merry Gentlemen. Instead, there was a deep discussion about musical arrangements and who was in charge. There was mention, in hushed tones, of last year's carol-mageddon, when Brian had put himself in charge and made everyone sing dreadful things. This year, Douglas, a mild-mannered, earnest type, who was only a couple of elbow patches away from being a geography teacher, sort of put himself in charge and handed out music sheets. Everyone oohed and aahed at his brilliance. I wondered if now would be a good time to mention that I couldn't read music.

I decided that I could definitely wing it. I mean, they were familiar tunes, it was only a few carols, no problemo and all that. As Douglas set up his keyboard, I latched myself onto a matronly woman with a kind face, in the hopes that we could become carol

BFFs and she would keep me right. This was a bad decision. As Douglas began to play, two things became apparent; a) he had started on the wrong note (I was sure it must be the wrong note – I didn't know which note it was, but it was definitely one of the high ones) and b) I was standing next to Dame Kiri Te Kanawa. In fact, the air was filled with trembling sopranos and smooth tenors. Bugger me blind with a candy cane! These were serious singing people. I was more X-Factor reject than Puccini princess.

Douglas stopped playing and told everyone off because SOMEONE was singing out of tune. Not so mild-mannered after all. More like my music teacher at school, who used to throw things in rage and allegedly dangled a pupil out of a fourth-floor window by his ankles. For a moment, I thought it might have been me who was singing out of tune, but then I remembered that I'd been standing next to Dame Kiri, mouthing the words in the firm belief that she was making enough noise for the both of us. Everyone got very flustered and started saying intelligent things about music. I got very bored because I didn't have a clue what they were talking about. I began to imagine that I might have an urgent meeting I'd forgotten about and may have to leave early. These people were lovely people, but they were not my people.

Eventually, the appointed finishing time arrived. Everyone seemed remarkably cheerful despite being shouted at by Douglas. In fact, they were all set to carry on for a bit longer. Nobody minded another half hour. 'Absolutely no problemo, Douglas. Don't put the keyboard away,' they cried. To great rapture, Douglas suddenly produced a guitar and offered it to one of the tenors. Where the heck had he been keeping that?! Also, if he magicked up a flute, then there was only one explanation for where he'd been stashing it. If he offered it around for a blow, no way were my lips going anywhere near the thing. Time to make my excuses and run.

I scuttled back to the office, flumped into my chair and composed a very polite email to Douglas, saying that I wouldn't be back. I tried to think of an excuse but became overly focused on having come down with double pneumonia and, what with him having seen me ten minutes before, I had a tiny suspicion that Douglas wouldn't buy it. So, I just wished him a merry Christmas and good luck with all the singing. Then booked a day off for when the carollers were due to visit my office so that I wouldn't have to face them. I'm an ardent Christmassy person, an enthusiastic warbler and a brazen coward.

***

15th December

Making Best Use of Resources

This post is late today because Mr V has been clearing out the sacred garage. You may wonder how this could possibly impact on me, since I'm lounging around in Covid Corner contemplating a box of After Eights which Mr V has put on a high shelf in the mistaken belief that I can't reach it. He clearly hasn't taken into account my prowess with long kitchen implements. Honestly, if hooking things down from high shelves was an Olympic sport, I'd have the gold medal for Innovative Use of The Big Carving Fork.

I digress. I was in the middle of writing a tale about the post office queue when Mr V came in to tell me all about garage organisation and how, if you clear a space, you no longer have to blah blah blah. Sorry, I didn't listen to the rest. I just nodded politely and wondered whether his feelings would be hurt if I asked him to stop talking. Then I decided to make spag bol for dinner before the mince goes out of date.

I abandoned the tale of the post office because it will take me ages to write. But the good news is that Mr V is back out organising the sacred garage and I'm once more alone with the After Eights. Part of me thinks I should take the opportunity and pinch some now. The other part of me has my mother hissing in my ear, 'If you have some now, you won't have room for dinner.'

Such huge life dilemmas. It isn't easy being me, you know.

18th December

Boob Day

I went for my first breast screening yesterday. It was not a comfortable experience.

Top tip: Men, if you want to relate to the experience of a mammogram, pop your todger in a George Foreman grill and get your partner to slam the lid down. A mannogram, if you will. You're welcome.

The boob nurse, who had clearly funded her degree by operating a mangle in an S&M dungeon, spoke very loudly in a thick Spanish accent. She kept shouting, 'LITTLE SQUEEZE,' at me before pushing one of my precious girls around like it was a lump of play-do. There were also firm instructions to 'RELAX YOUR BODY', as I stood, half-naked, with a stranger touching my boobs. Yep, because this was extremely effing relaxing.

You know, the cervical smear nurse says mad things like 'relax' as well! Although that might be because I once boxed her ears with my knees when she came at me with the speculum.

Anyway, back to the boob nurse. She brought the plate down hard and yelled at me to 'STAY THERE.' I had one boob firmly clamped between two plates attached to a massive machine. Where did she think I was going to go?! I imagined myself dragging the whole thing out the door and through the car park, using only the power of my left breast. By the time I reached the car one boob would be six inches longer than the other. Would the NHS pay for a corrective boob job if I'd just tried to steal their boob machine?

Obviously, it's important to get all these lady checks done, no matter how uncomfortable they are. I hadn't expected all this manhandling and clamping of the girls, though. I thought I'd just pop them both on a machine, someone would take a picture et voila! It wasn't the most pleasant experience but, on the upside, we had a nice chat and I learned that Aldi have a special offer on peas and carrots. So, to anyone hunting out their toastie machine right now, don't forget to give your partner some shopping tips as you slam down the lid.

**

Just to be clear, I was in no way trivialising breast cancer. What was in my head as I wrote this was that I'd had no idea what to expect and the whole thing came as a shock. I really should have done some research before I went. The experience was uncomfortable, but not incredibly painful, and obviously a million times better than the grim alternative. It was clear from the comments that for some ladies it is not uncomfortable at all. When it's your turn to be invited, please go. These checks save lives and we are so privileged to have them.

**

19th December

Colin And His Magic Mail

Here's a little Christmas story for you. There really was a man in the post office who didn't realise you had to put an address on an envelope and Mr V really did come home to have a jolly good rant. There may be some artistic licence with the rest.

Once upon a time last week, a man, whom we shall call Confused Colin, arrived at the post office, letter clutched in his sweaty hand and mask over his mouth (but not his nose, because you definitely can't give anyone coronavirus by breathing through your nose).

Having braved the cold and rain to walk all the way to the post office to buy a stamp for his very important letter, Confused Colin waited in the socially distanced queue, feeling mildly irritated with the pensioner at the front, who couldn't work the chip and pin machine. Behind him stood a rather grumpy chap in a dog haired fleece, whom we shall call Mr V. Mr V was trying not to glower at the old lady, lest it make her even more flustered, but he was definitely saying lots of swear words at her in his head. He was also thinking deep manly thoughts about what he'd like for his dinner and which of his dogs would make a better pirate. There was rather a lot of important stuff going on in his head today.

In contrast, Confused Colin wasn't thinking about much at all. He had one task - post the important letter - and he was going to do it.

Slowly, the queue shuffled forward. Slowly, Mr V became more impatient. By the time he was near the front of the line, Mr V's manly thoughts had turned to exactly how big a diamond he should buy his beautiful wife for Christmas (or at least that's what I imagine he was thinking).

In front of him, Colin approached the counter. Could he have a stamp please? The post person, cheery in his Christmas jumper, got out his big book of stamps which, following the recent price hike, was now worth the GDP of Luxembourg. He passed Colin a first-class stamp.

'That'll be £3950,' he said, or words to that effect. Colin duly dug into his man purse and passed over some coins. The post person looked at him curiously. 'You haven't put an address on the envelope.'

'Why do I need to do that?' asked Colin.

'So they know where to deliver it.'

'Well, I didn't know I had to put an address on it! Can I just put the name?'

'No. You need to write the address on there too.'

Mr V stood behind Colin, mentally Googling "how to commit the perfect murder". As the discussion about the address went on, Mr V could feel his blood pressure rising and wondered what Mrs V had put in the parcel he was posting. If it was a sharp implement then perhaps...

Approximately three years and much arguing of the toss later, Colin opened his letter, got the address from the document inside and borrowed some sticky tape from the post person to seal the envelope again. By this time, a long queue of people had formed, all of whom were sending telepathic death rays in the direction of Colin for being the blithering idiot who was holding up their day.

Eventually, it was Mr V's turn to be served. 'I have no idea what's in this parcel, but I was starting to hope it was a weapon to turn Confused Colin into dust,' he joked.

The post person gave him a hard stare. 'And does the package contain a weapon?'

173

'No, I don't think so. I mean, my wife would hardly be sending her sister an AK47 in the post for Christmas.'

'But you're not sure. Because weapons are prohibited in the post, you know.'

'Look, it's not going to be a weapon. I was just joking,' Mr V protested. He turned around to appeal to the rest of the queue for support. They were all sending him telepathic death rays for being the blithering idiot who was holding up their day.

'I'm sorry. I can't take any parcel that might contain prohibited items,' said the post person, no longer quite so cheery in his Christmas jumper.

Mr V considered arguing some more, but could feel the silent wrath of the crowd behind him. Sighing, he picked up his parcel and headed home.

On arrival, Mr V found Mrs V allegedly working, but actually hiding the box of After Eights he'd bought for Christmas Day in the folds of her dressing gown. She'd been in a very long online meeting. It had required sustenance. The brain runs on glucose and the After Eights box said they contained glucose. 'Ergo,' she had said to herself, 'After Eights are really just brain food.' Mrs V was expecting some minor ructions over the disappearance of the After Eights, but wasn't prepared for the explosion that heralded the arrival of Mr V.

'How can anyone not know that you need to put an address on a letter?!' he expostulated. At least, Mrs V thought he was expostulating. Maybe he was postulating. She'd google it later, just to check. She was vaguely aware of some more ranting going on, but was distracted by doing a check of her brain dictionary for other good words that didn't get used nearly enough. There was bethink, carbuncle, ague, discombobulated ... Mrs V's musings were brought to an abrupt halt as Mr V demanded (nay, entreated...catechized?), 'Are you even listening? What did you put in that parcel anyway?'

'Just a bottle of champagne. I had a notion they might like it with their Christmas dinner.'

Mr V googled the Royal Mail banned items list. 'Banned!' he spluttered. 'You are no better than Confused Colin. You can't be trusted. You just bowl through life, merrily having ideas and notions, without regard for sensible things like lists, the most efficient method for loading dishwashers and reading instructions properly.'

Mrs V thought for a moment. She loved her husband very much and didn't want to cause him stress. He was normally very patient with her notions, but she felt she may have gone one notion too far. How could she fix this? What was the ideal solution that would make life easier for everyone?

'Tell you what,' she said, 'how about, in future, you do the Christmas shopping and the wrapping. That way, you'll always know what's being posted.'

'Yes! Finally, you've said something sensible.' Mr V strode off to stew about post office queues and banned items lists and annoying wives who would be lucky to get so much as a bean for Christmas. Well, now that he was in charge of shopping and wrapping...hang on...he'd just agreed to do all the shopping and wrapping in future...how had that happened?

Downstairs, Mrs V slipped another After Eight from the box and wondered how she could con Lovely Granny into making the Christmas dinner.

In a little house in a little street on the other side of the village, Confused Colin licked an envelope and sealed it. He regarded the neat stack of around fifty Christmas cards before him. He'd take them to the post office in the morning, once he'd arranged a second mortgage to pay for the stamps. Surely, he didn't need to put addresses on these as well?

***

Someone commented on this post, saying "Well that's ten minutes of my life I won't get back." I really wanted to remind him that I'd spent a couple of hours writing this and I put it out there for free. I wanted to ask why he kept on reading if it was so awful. But most of all, I wanted to know if he went to his kids' school parent's evening, flicked through their work and muttered, 'Shit. Shit. More shit,' before going home and telling them to stop wasting his time with their crap pictures. Of course, I didn't say any of those things. I simply ignored him. Yet it's still hurtful when someone is rude about your best efforts, so I try to bear in mind something I once told Cherub 1 – 'Don't put yourself down. There's a whole world out there ready to do it for you. Don't do it to yourself.' Onwards and upwards. Keep buggering on and all that.

***

21st December

Woe is Mrs V

First draft: A very long, depressing ramble that I won't reproduce here because it was just self-indulgent twaddle. #dramaqueen

Second draft: Slightly better but still a bit "woe is me". I'll let you read this version. #dramalesserroyal

I've been feeling quite low over the last few days. Seeing all the new restrictions imposed on people, just a few days before Christmas, really got to me. My mind kept coming back to the people who are suddenly facing Christmas alone and all the people who have spent money they can barely afford on a feast that will go uneaten.

I couldn't put my finger on why this was gnawing at me so much. I always tell my kids to worry about the stuff you can change and just go with the flow on the rest.

I started to write a post a few times, but I wasn't in the right frame of mind to respond to any comments. I know that many of you will be finding this time of year difficult and I decided that the last thing you needed was me unintentionally trampling all over your feelings because I was in a blue funk myself. I even wrote a Cheer Yvonne Up plan. It mainly involved reading the Harry Potter books yet again (am I the only person who finds them therapeutic?) and watching schmaltzy Christmas movies. I tried to buck myself up with the thought that tracking my food intake all month has resulted in me no longer being in danger of having to be cut out of my pre-lockdown tartan lounge pants when I need the loo. Yet, I couldn't kick the feeling of everything being wrong.

177

However, when Lovely Granny and Grandad made the decision yesterday to stay at home for Christmas, I realised that at the heart of things lay concern about us potentially infecting LG & G if they came to our house. Obviously, we're all disappointed, but at the same time I feel like a worry has been lifted. I hope LG & G don't find this insulting. It's coming from a good place. We love them and we want them to be safe. I know many of you will have had difficult decisions to make (or thrust upon you) this Christmas and it's such a personal choice - no judgement here. But (and I never thought I'd say this) I'm quite looking forward to standing in Granny's garden, freezing my tits off, when we deliver their presents on Christmas Day. A quick, socially distant hello. I wouldn't say I'm back to bouncing off the walls, but I am back to the mindset of Christmas 2020 being a reasonable excuse to go completely over the top for Christmas 2021.

However Christmas is panning out for you this year, I hope you still manage to find a little merry in it. I can't solve the problems of the world, but I do send you my warmest wishes and enormous digital hugs xx

Final version: A bit less melodramatic. #dramaminornobility

I've been feeling quite low over the last few days. Seeing all the new restrictions imposed, just a few days before Christmas, really got to me. My mind kept coming back to the people who are suddenly facing Christmas alone and all the people who have spent money they can barely afford on a feast that will go uneaten. This can be a difficult time of year for so many reasons and I'm heartily sorry for each and every one of you whose plans have been disrupted by this effing virus.

Even those of us (my family included) who are allowed to have someone over have had second thoughts. Our plans are to deliver presents to Lovely Granny and Grandad outdoors. I never thought I'd say this, but I'm quite looking forward to standing in their garden, freezing my tits off, while we all shout "social distancing" and dodge LG as her natural inclination to hug everyone kicks in.

With our plans made and the BBC news app consigned to the farthest reaches of my phone (so I can no longer keep picking at the Covid news scab), I'm feeling a bit more resilient today and back to viewing Christmas 2020 as a reasonable excuse to go completely over the top for Christmas 2021.

22nd December

Potato Panic

With the borders being closed and tales of bare supermarket shelves, I was a bit worried that there wouldn't be any vegetables for our Christmas dinner. Why?! They'll all be delighted that I'm not making them eat vegetables! I'll admit to a lingering worry on the potato front. There will be hell on in our house if there are no roast potatoes. I shall have to distract them all by wafting pigs in blankets under their noses. Now that LG & G aren't coming, we have a surplus. Well, I say surplus - it just means Cherub 2 will scoff the lot then wonder why he has indigestion.

All the presents are under the tree and my days of screaming 'don't open that' every time the post arrives are almost over. Work will be finished tomorrow and I can tidy the computer off the table. When I said that to Mr V, he looked at me like I had two heads. Turns out he thought that, now LG & G aren't coming over, he'd be allowed to eat his dinner in front of the telly, the big eejit. Christmas means the good cutlery instead of his favourite fork and proper napkins instead of kitchen roll! He should be grateful that, for once, I'm not nagging him to find the old kitchen chairs in the back of the garage so folk have somewhere to sit for their dinner. I really am the gift that keeps on giving.

Nevertheless, in these strange times, where vegetables are the new toilet roll, I am grateful for what we have. A message I shall reinforce should there be a single protest on the roast potato front.

Thank you for all your comments on yesterday's post. There were a lot of wise words in there and to all the people who are going through a tough time, I hope you are getting loads of love and support. Thank you to everyone who is working through the holiday season, particularly the NHS staff who are under so much pressure right now. My warmest wishes to you and yours for a safe Christmas and may 2020 please eff off (I was going to say something nice about 2021, but quite frankly I don't trust it either. I'll keep my powder dry and wish you a happy New Year when I know that 2021 can behave itself).

24th December

Operation Christmas Dinner

The government of Covid Corner is pleased to announce that Operation Christmas Dinner is complete.

A crack team of troops infiltrated Marks and Spencer last night and located both potatoes and vegetables. There was no turkey gravy to be had and, despite a subsequent recce of Morrison's, the gravy was not located. An anonymous source has suggested that the gravy may be hiding in Tesco. A team of Gravy Seals is being sent in today. In a gravy boat.

Throughout the operation, Commander Mr V did a sterling job of leading from the rear. As troops cleared the shelves, he remained at the top of the aisle, bravely manning the trolley and humming Christmas tunes to himself.

Private Cherub 2 swung into action, selflessly buying all the sugary things so that other people don't have to suffer from post-Christmas large bottoms. The noble sacrifice of his one bottom for the many will earn him salad all January.

Sgt Mrs V was injured in an early engagement with the mince pies. A rogue box of Mr Kiplings broke free of the stack and she broke a nail catching it. Commander Mr V got caught in the crossfire, when he didn't take the nail breaking seriously and Sgt Mrs V was forced to poke him in the belly with a stick of garlic bread.

Despite a number of setbacks and queues, the conquering heroes captured the pigs in blankets, defeated the check-out lady and returned to base with a lot more shopping than they went out for.

Hooray!

27ᵗʰ December

A Happy Christmas

Despite all the strangeness this year, we had a lovely Christmas. World War three broke out between the cherubs over which movie to watch, the dog ate too much turkey and was sick on the carpet and we all got to shout at Grandad when he was in charge of the camera for the present opening FaceTime ('That's the sofa! Point the camera at Granny!'). SOMEBODY drank three glasses of Prosecco before midday and forgot to put the turkey in the oven, so Christmas dinner was more like Christmas supper, and I had far more presents than everyone else because Mr V went a bit mad and bought tons of stuff on the basis that I'd moan if I didn't get loads of presents. Why he'd think that, I don't know. It doesn't sound like me at all! He got two presents from me because he wanted quality stuff. Honestly, I'd have been happy with six whoopee cushions if they'd all been wrapped separately so I had six things to open. They'd have to be different colours though. That's quite important. Oh yes, I forgot to mention that we spent Christmas Eve binge watching Vikings and Cherub 1 mentally scarred me by suggesting that the sexy Viking I fancied looked a bit like grandad #vikingsruinedforever

I'm now covered in expensive body lotion, wearing my new tartan lounge pants and am about to eat a bag of chocolate truffles for breakfast. Hooray for Christmas!

28th December

2020 Vision

Here's one I didn't post. P.S. I saved Eff You 2020 for my New Year message – and I gave it a tune!

"I wrote this on 31/12/2019. Can I just say that if I could kick my own backside, I would? I'm going to write a new version called Eff You 2020. I hope someone sets it to music!

2020 Vision

Last year I swore by now I'd be

A slim and healthy, yummy me

So full of hope and wine and beer

I danced into another year

Now here I am still round and stout

Seeing 2019 out

Still sure that I will drop a size,

Despite my ever-growing thighs

(And my fondness for mince pies)

The evidence somewhat belies

That chances of success will rise

If I continue eating fries!

Well sod the old goals, aim for fun

To see us through to '21

Fly a plane or join a club

See a band or buy a pub

Climb a hill or climb a tree

As long as there is twattery

So make some noise and raise your glass

Let's kick some 2020 ass.

29Th December

2020 Hindsight

This time last year I wrote a wee bit of nonsense called 2020 Vision, looking forward to the year ahead. How little did I know! So, this year I've written its companion piece...

2020 Hindsight

We set out full of hopes and dreams,

A new year to inspire us,

We'd heard the rumours, seen the news,

But it was just some virus.

By February we watched aghast,

From balconies serenaded,

By songs of locked down Italy,

As the enemy invaded.

In March we stopped.

We stripped the shelves,

We clapped for all the nurses.

In silent streets,

The only sound,

The passing of the hearses.

TikTok, TikTok went April's clock,

While somehow time Zoomed by us,

We furloughed, home schooled, shopped online,

As death tolls hit their highest.

(Though, if you were the ruling class,

You didn't need the hassle,

Far simpler just to test your eyes,

And drive to Barnard Castle.)

In May the cracks appeared and our

defence saw wholesale breaches,

First hint of sun, the numpties cried,

"We shall fight it on the beaches!"

As summer woke, the protests broke

out, screaming Black Lives Matter,

Then Antifa and right-wing folk,

Took over all the chatter.

Through June, July, the statues fell,

Old Churchill was defaced,

The message lost amid the cries,

Of "History being replaced!"

August brought some light relief,

We ate out to help out,

Exam results, illegal raves,

Our holidays in doubt.

September came with grimmer news,

The R rate escalated,

The test and trace could not keep up,

Worse - pub hours were truncated!

October, Tiers came in, we yelled,

'You said, 'Eat out,' and then

You opened schools, sent students back,

And shut stuff down again!'

November lockdown 2.0,

We honoured those who died,

Their sacrifice in stark contrast,

To those who strayed outside.

And finally, come Christmas time,

We made do and we mended,

We prayed for vaccines, full of hope,

For all next year portended.

Now open the doors and ring the bells,

To welcome 21,

Big girl pants, chins up, eyes front,

As we all keep buggering on.

31st December

Eff You 2020

Rare video footage of Mrs V singing. Here's my script, which I practiced like mad and only fluffed up a little bit. How TV people do this stuff every day, I'll never know:

Hello you gorgeous people. And hello to the ugly ones as well. As you can see, I'm trying something a bit different today. This is because I wrote a poem to wish you all a happy new year and I decided it doesn't really work unless I sing it to you. Even then it might not work. Before I start, can I just say that this is the one thing I've done that I really don't want to go viral. Still in my dressing gown, no make-up and you could take the curling tongs to my nose hair. Honestly, I'm getting so hairy that when we come out of Tier 4 it'll be like shaving a yeti. This is what happens to you, children, when you stay in the house for months on end. You write daft nonsense and appear on camera wearing a T-shirt that you try to pass off as day wear when really you slept in it last night. Don't be like Mrs V. Get dressed. On the other hand, do be like Mrs V. There's cake and wine. It's great. Cheers. Happy New Year. Here we go with Eff You 2020.

Oh 2020, year from hell

You didn't bring much luck you

Brought plague and made my waistline swell

For that, I will say...For cu..

..riously I'd like to expel

In fact I'd like to chuck off

A cliff what made us so unwell

For headaches, fever, for cough...

...ing 2020 go to hell

You absolutely suck

So cheerio and fare thee well

Goodbye and off you...

JANUARY 2021

After a temporary stay of execution over Christmas, we went into lockdown 3.0 on January 5th. On the same day, we were told that 1.3 million people had received their first dose of the vaccine. Boris promised tens of millions of jabs over the next three months and, for once, the man was right. Nevertheless, at one point, the daily death toll almost reached two thousand and we were back to watching charts and graphs on the daily Downing Street griefing.

The lockdown meant home-schooling. Joe Wicks brought back his online PE lessons and Bez from the Happy Mondays also said he was launching fitness classes – Get Buzzin' with Bez. I was tempted to roll my eyes but, instead, I googled Bez. The man has had an amazing life. Nevertheless, despite Bez's fitness classes being aimed at people my age, he had stiff (or should that be lithe and flexible) competition in the form of the lovely Joe, a man who comes fresh out of the box every morning and oozes avocado smoothie from every pore. Just to be clear, I don't mean Joe is encased in bubble wrap and a revolting shade of 1970s bathroom green. Before I go on, I'd also just like to say that it took me ages to figure out he wasn't someone from Eastenders.

Of course, I can't talk about January without mentioning our withdrawal from the EU. Utter border chaos. We were all going to starve and, even worse, we now had to pay taxes when people posted us gifts from France. I recall reading an article about an ex-pat facing deportation from Spain. He said he'd never have voted for Brexit if he'd known this was going to happen. Given that much of the Brexit argument was around immigration, I couldn't help noting the irony. The newspapers were full of triumphant articles about Brexiteers finally realising what they'd done. I asked my friends, 'For exactly how long is it acceptable to smugly say "well that's what you voted for"?' The answers ranged from "settle down, Mrs V" to "forfuckingever."

January was also the month of the Donald Trump soap opera grand finale. Most of us do jigsaw puzzles or crosswords in our down time. Not Donald. Now that he had a bit less presidenting to do, he was keeping himself busy by challenging election results, being banned from social media and, allegedly, inciting the storming of the Capitol. Quite a few American readers have commented on the blog to the effect that "we're not all like that." We know you're not all like that, any more than every Brit is a person who voted for Brexit on the basis of a blue passport and a message on the side of a bus. We have all learned a lot about the hitherto hidden extremes in our countries over the past year. Sadly, in the US, those extremes led to the deaths of five people in the Capitol. On 20th January, Joe Biden was sworn in as President, with Kamala Harris as Vice President, but more importantly, the Bernie Sanders mitten meme was born and the world fell a little bit in love with knitting. I like to imagine that Donald Trump finally had something constructive to fill his time now he was no longer presidenting.

Back on the home front, what with January and February being dark, cold and approximately three thousand days long, we enjoyed a wee celebration; Cherub 1's twenty-first birthday. We did our best to make it special, but I suggested she be twenty-one again next year so that she could go out and do all the irresponsible things properly. My own twenty-first was a tense family meal out, being criticised by my parents every time I opened my mouth, followed by a grateful escape in a friend's car to go clubbing in the city. Cherub 1's twenty-first was her mother handing her a sparkly tiara and a bottle of Bailey's, followed by a ridiculously expensive cake that, except for the icing, nobody really liked. She should have been out snogging and dancing. I hate that this virus has robbed my kids of a year of being daft young adults. Although, saying that, they've still managed to have their moments. Read on…

193

2nd January

Happy New Year?

First draft: Not posted because too ranty. Also, a risk of Smug Sandras telling me how awful my children are. Don't need Smug Sandras for that. I know they're awful, but they're also wonderful, kind, thoughtful, compassionate and utterly brilliant. Apologies to all the real Sandras out there, for taking your name in vain. I know you're not all smug, just as not all Karens complain to the manager. For a moment there, I wondered why annoying people are always portrayed as women, then I remembered that lots of men are Dicks. Winky face emoji. Okay, here's the post that never made it.

"Here we are. Second day of 2021. We're in Tier 4 now and it's like herding cats. Cherub 1 is confined to her room for forming a social bubble with her mate and a crate of cider on New Year's Eve. Cherub 2 was delighted not to be the one in trouble for a change and diligently went about loading the dishwasher and telling me what a marvellous son he was. Until I caught one of his friends in our back garden and sent them both on a socially distanced walk that neither of them wanted. I hope they stepped in dog shit.

Old Ivy Next Door thinks I've turned into the corona-police ("aw they're only kids, it's much harder on the young ones") and was treated to a ten-minute rant about it being a slap in the face to the NHS.

I'm putting this out there because I know I'm not the only parent in this situation. It's embarrassing to admit your kids have broken the rules, like somehow it's your failure. Local Facebook groups are full of Smug Sandras, blaming the parents for groups of marauding teenagers. You can't reason with Smug Sandras. Their politics are somewhere to the right of Hitler and their own children would never break the rules. Whereas, in reality, the little feckers have had to develop extra sneakiness as a survival skill. Well, sod the Smug Sandras. Short of nailing their feet to the floor or following them everywhere, there's nothing you can do if your young person decides to ignore everything you've said and do their own thing."

Final version: A less ranty start to the new year.

Day 2 of 2021. My children hate me for being the corona-gestapo and Mr V is none too pleased with me. Apparently "Can you come home immediately? I've dropped my phone on the floor, the dog's really comfy and I don't want to disturb him, so I need you to pick it up" is not a good reason to call your husband at work.

Cherub 2 has been trying to get into my good books after I caught his friend in our back garden yesterday and sent them both packing on a socially distanced walk that neither of them wanted. I hope they stepped in dog shit. He's been doing the dishes a lot and we had a lovely conversation while he tried to pull the top off a plastic cup. It went something like this:

Cherub 2: I'm not being sexist or anything, but women are very naive.

Me: Yes, you are being sexist.

Cherub 2 (still tugging the lid): No, I'm being factual. Women *are* more naive.

Me: I'm not being sexist or anything, but that lid screws off, man-idiot.

My family will be glad to hear that my new year's resolution is to continue being a delight.

3rd January

Cold Comfort

The boiler has broken down today. I tried to book a repair online but they want to know ridiculous things like our reference number. I have scoured the house for an old bill but I can't find one. Mr V has stomped off to work, declaring that it is morning, it is probably not the boiler but the stupid thermostat I had installed, that works with a stupid app that he can't understand, and he is unable think of such things before lunchtime. I will have to put a fire on. Then I will run out of logs and make Cherub 2 fetch some. Then I will explain to the cherubs that we have no hot water. And we will all be feral, living like cavemen in a very posh cave with a fridge, and everyone will say it is somehow all my fault. Not that I'm being a drama queen about it, but I think now would be a good time to run away and join the WI. I hear they do a lot of cake.

On the other hand, I should probably stay and tough it out. I have to go back to work and pretend to be a sensible person tomorrow. Outer me will be making important decisions, while inner me will be quietly listing all the reasons why I should have the last mince pie for breakfast.

Despite the trying circumstances, I remain determined to be a delight.

***

The last time we had no hot water, or water at all, was when the new bathroom was fitted. I wrote at the time:

"They're starting work on the new bathroom today and the effing

poo fairy has left a large brown offering which won't flush away. Just as children suspect their parents are the tooth fairy, this parent suspects her children are the poo fairy. Nobody over the age of 25 could possibly have bowels flexible enough to stretch to the truly tardis-like proportions required for the job. Usually, the poo fairy comes in the evening and I discover the offering in time to surreptitiously inspect the members of my family, determine which one looks emptiest and throw a tantrum until someone unblocks the toilet. But the poo fairy has managed to sneak one past me. One last big hurrah for the old toilet. A final deposit in the porcelain bank.

I'm considering asking the builders if they can install an X-ray machine at the door of the new bathroom to act as a deterrent. Maybe employ a sepoority guard. Or play a game of Cluedo - Poodo! - to find the turderer. Was it Colonel Mustard in the en-suite?

I googled 'how to get rid of fairies.' There was no specific mention of poo fairies and now I'm wondering if it's just our house that has one. I'd leave a pound coin under the loo roll but the poo fairy will only spend it on sweets and make a bigger offering next time.

So here I am at 6.30 on a Monday morning trying to get rid of the big brown beastie at the bottom of the bog before the workmen arrive. Maybe I won't have a chocolate croissant for breakfast this morning"

On day three of no water, Biggles decided to take off during his morning walk. What with it being 6am and still dark, I'd tucked my pyjamas and boobs into the top of my wellies, flung a coat over the top, popped his lead on and set off. Of course, I regretted this decision as soon as I started chasing the wee eejit through the long grass, trying not to slip in dog shit and holding my coat together to stop my boobs making a bid for freedom, all the while whisper shouting swear words at a recalcitrant Jack Russell. I eventually caught up with him. He was eating rabbit poo like "ooh

Maltesers!" and he'd rolled in something unmentionable. He was also very, very pleased with himself.

I managed to get the lead back on and get him home. Where I was faced with a problem. He needed a bath. I had no bath and no water.

Now, Biggles had spent the week supervising the bathroom fitters because people being in the bathroom is chief among his crazies. Fireworks are no problem but people in the bathroom require regular checks just in case they're doing bathroom things he ought to be worried about. He had a very worrying week. At one point Mr V found him shut in the laundry room.

'The workmen must have shut the door on him by accident,' said Mr V.

'I suspect it wasn't an accident,' said I.

Anyway, it's lucky that he's a little dog who fits in the kitchen sink. I popped him in and poured bottled water over him. Then I covered the floor in towels so he could roll around and dry off.

By 7am I looked like the winner of a wet T-shirt competition for people with saggy boobs, cellulite and cuddly tummies. The idiot dog had completely ignored the towels and was busy rolling around the living room and I, thinking I'd encourage the dog by setting a good example, was having a bit of a roll around on the towels myself.

Mr V appeared downstairs to find a soaking wet wife on the kitchen floor and a soaking wet dog living it large on the sofa. He told me I should have learned from the time my friend got her head stuck in the cat flap after a bit too much wine - you can't teach an old dog new tricks.

And now you are probably wondering how my friend got her head stuck in the cat flap. I'll happily segue into that one.

Once upon a time, two well-padded ladies, whom we shall call Sue and Mrs V, had rather a lot of wine and thought it would be a wonderful idea to teach the wee hairy boys to use the cat flap. After a brief argument about who had the smallest head, Sue got down on her knees and, backside to the wind, stuck her head through the cat flap.

The two wee hairy boys looked on in wonder, as Mrs V excitedly waved sausages at them and exclaimed, 'Look! This is how you do it!'

Sue kept up a steady stream of encouragement. 'Come on, Biggles, it's easy. Vegas, look at auntie Sue.' However, Mrs V had run out of sausages and the frantic wriggling of auntie Sue's backside was not deemed sufficiently entertaining. The WHBs wandered off, leaving Mrs V to pour another glass of wine and wonder how many views this would get on YouTube. It was, therefore, a couple of minutes before Mrs V realised that Sue's backside was now thrashing wildly, rather than wriggling. It seemed that Sue's head was not as small as she claimed and that it was now firmly wedged in the cat flap.

'Are you okay?' asked Mrs V, for, while she found the sight of her friend with her head stuck in the cat flap quite hilarious, she wasn't an unkind person, mostly. She wondered if she should butter Sue's ears.

'No, I'm not. I'm fu...Oh, hello. Yes, it's very warm for the time of year.'

Mrs V was confused. Why was Sue talking about the weather, instead of doing sensible things like swearing and demanding that Mrs V pass her a glass of wine and a straw? Then Mrs V realised that Sue was having a lovely conversation with Old Ivy Next Door. They agreed that it was lovely drying weather for washing and, yes, Sue was looking forward to a few days camping with the kids. After a splendid, neighbourly chat with a disembodied head, Old Ivy tootled back into her house, leaving Sue free to say all the swear words.

Mrs V buttered Sue's ears and she eventually slid free.

'Now,' said Mrs V, 'what are your thoughts on teaching the dogs to use a litter tray?'

***

4ᵗʰ January

Ah, Bridgerton, Happy Days

I started putting the Christmas tree away yesterday. I say 'started' because I found a bottle of Baileys under the tree. How could I have failed to notice it before now?! I immediately went about rectifying my mistake and by the time Mr V got home from work, I was lying on the sofa, three sheets to the wind, watching a rumpy-pumpy costume drama on Netflix. The kitchen was a hovel, there was a pile of washing to the ceiling and a boiler that still hadn't been fixed. But I assured Mr V that, yesh, my prioritiesh were correct. Should we get takeaway for dinner? Also, I lurved him very very mush and could he pleashe get me a glash of water.

Mr V wanted to know why I got the baubles off but didn't take the tree down. I told him that he's sooooo mush taller than me and he'd do a mush, mush better job of it. I used the same flattery with Cherub 2 when I convinced him to take the baubles off. But we won't mention that to Mr V. Let the drunk lady take the credit.

I'm back at work today and, with the boiler broken, Covid Corner has been temporarily rechristened Cold Corner.

5th January

Boilers and Biscuits

The boiler repairman is here. Is it late enough in the day to get away with claiming I've only just changed into my pyjamas? As opposed to sleeping in my pjs, dressing gown and coat then wailing that it was too cold to get undressed this morning.

Mr V is busy buttering up the boiler man with a steady supply of posh coffee, in an attempt to make him ignore the fact that our boiler is about 100 million years old. The moment the boiler man opens his mouth to tell us it really needs to be replaced, Mr V will be there with a latte and a packet of Jaffa Cakes, using his Jedi mind powers to say, 'Go on, you know you can fix it.' I wish I was the boiler repairman. When I asked Mr V to make me a cup of posh coffee, he used his Jedi mind powers to tell me to eff off.

The wee fat hairy boy is having the time of his life. He has no idea that it's cold. As far as he's concerned, a nice stranger is visiting and his third favourite human is wafting around packets of biscuits that really belong in his mouth.

6th January

Bunny Boiler

First draft: Am debating whether to even include this in the book. I didn't post it originally because I had a sneaky suspicion that I sounded like a mad pervert. I ran it past my sister, who agreed that I did indeed sound like a mad pervert. Also, Mr V was worried about offending lepers. Or was that leopards?

" The boiler man went off to order a part yesterday, saying he'd be back today. I overheard Mr V telling him, 'My wife will be in all day. Don't worry if she treats you like a leper.' Then he did a quick rewind in case he'd offended any people with leprosy. Or anyone who knows anyone with leprosy. Or anyone else who just fancies being offended. Such are the times in which we live. 'Sorry,' he said, 'I mean she'll treat you like a leopard. She was shielding in the last lockdown so isn't going near anyone.'

Now, the boiler man was quite good-looking, and I'd actually been wondering if I should wear a nice top and something that wasn't pyjamas. My imagination took a turn. You know, husband at work, workman comes round etc etc. But minus the big moustache. His, of course. I'm keeping mine - it has taken me months of lockdowns to grow this beauty. I mean, I wasn't planning on rubbing myself all over him because well, Covid, and am not a complete pervert. And any thoughts about handsome repairman aren't real. As Mr V says, it's fine to window shop, but don't get your credit card out. However, if he dropped his screwdriver, maybe I could pick it up all sexy like.

Anyway, none of that is possible now. Mr V has ruined everything by saying I'm going to treat the lovely boiler man like a leopard. And now the lovely boiler man probably thinks I'm going to try to change his spots or turn him into a rug."

Final version: Made myself sound less like a stalker of boiler men and posted this.

The boiler repairman came back with a part today and we once more have heat and water. Now, I'm not normally a big fan of moustaches (except my own, of course. It has taken me months of lockdowns to grow this beauty), but his is particularly luxuriant. I couldn't help but imagine all the uses for such a moustache.

1. Hiding snacks for later.
2. Emergency shoe polishing (perhaps if you suddenly had to join the army or something).
3. Pretending to be a 1970s porn star or Magnum PI at fancy dress parties.
4. Ventriloquism or at the very least pretending it wasn't you who said the rude thing. That's my personal favourite.
5. Face mask. Just tape a layer up over your nose et voila, you need never again have to fish out a manky old mask from your car bin (or is that just me?)

I thought Lockdown 3.0 was going to make me feel depressed, but its tache growing potential is awesome. Brings a whole new meaning to personal growth. You lot may be in lockdown. I'm in face down.

9th January

Smart Lady

In the space of a week I've managed to clutter up Covid Corner to the extent that I bought one of those lightbulb jobbies that you can switch on and off with Alexa because I can't reach the light switch past the piles of books and posh gin.

I'd quite like a smart home. I don't mean a tidy place that you can invite visitors to without worrying that the dog left a skid mark on the carpet when he did the crawly itchy bum thing last night. I mean a nice modern place, full of technology that runs off apps and Alexas and Siris. Where you can confuse your husband by learning the morse code for 'make me a cup of tea' and lie in bed switching the living room light on and off until he appears with a mug of Earl Grey. I had visions of Mr V learning the morse code for "Sexy shenanigans? Yes?" but realised he'll never be able to learn how to remotely switch my bedroom lamp on and off. We've had a smart thermostat for two years and he still can't switch the heating on. Well, at least I won't need to learn the morse code for "bugger off."

I hope you're having a lovely More Wineday. I'm off to sort out this lightbulb thingy. They sent me three and I only need one for Covid Corner. I'll have to find somewhere to put the other two. Definitely not the living room or the bedroom - Mr V really isn't ready for that level of technology yet. However, if you hear a minor explosion in the north of England, it'll probably be Mr V suddenly having a shower in the dark

10th January

The Piddler on the Hoof

Vegas is getting quite confused and doddery, which is worrying me. At first, I thought he had a wee infection, but now I think he's just forgetting that he has to go outside. He got up yesterday, peed next to his bed, then went back to bed again. I wish I could do that. How handy would that be?! Although I suspect Mr V wouldn't be nearly as kind to me as we are all being to Vegas. I'd definitely give him the same unrepentant look, though. Nevertheless, the laundry basket is full of socks where people have stepped in Vegas puddles.

Really, if the government want everyone to get very good at washing their hands to prevent spreading the virus, they should consider lending Vegas to people for a day. A Doggy Wee Programme! Or DWP for short.

I realise that there's already a government department called DWP, but mine offers more benefits. A day spent making the dog go out every two hours or cleaning up the consequences would soon instil some discipline. He's quite prodigious in the wee department, so I could probably give the government some spare wee to spray around a bit. Maybe over all the anti-lockdown protestors and conspiracy theorists (sorry not sorry if you're one of those people).

Before I go, thank you NHS staff and carers. You're all under horrific pressure just now and words really aren't enough. Deeds are better. Stay safe everyone, to support the people who are looking after our loved ones and delivering the jabs. Also, teachers - how you have managed to pull it out of the bag this past week I don't know. You are just bloody brilliant.

***

I am normally very careful to stay away from anything controversial because I want people to visit Growing Old Disgracefully for a giggle, not an argument. Someone did get quite offended that I had suggested spraying wee on anti-lockdown protestors. I cheerfully ignored them and let other people point out that it was a joke. 'But she said she was sorry not sorry,' huffed the offended person. So I did and so I remain. People are dying alone and families are unable to say a proper goodbye to their loved ones. The people of the NHS have had to deal with more death in a year than they'd have expected in their entire careers and they've done so at great cost to their own well-being. I am not sorry for offending anyone who is intent on damaging the efforts to get us out of this mess. My view is that they are welcome to disagree with lockdowns, vaccines etc, but they are not welcome to interfere.

***

12th January

My Celebrity Influences

Do you ever do something technological then spend the rest of the day strutting around like you're Bill Gates? That was me this weekend. Smart lights are up and running. I've tidied Covid Corner as well, so not only did I feel like Bill Gates, but my inner Marie Kondo gave me a high five and told me to take care of the last of Mr V's Jaffa Cakes, which were cluttering up the place.

Sadly, Mr V is not very understanding when it comes to imaginary ladies making me do things, so I left him a clear note to explain. He was less than impressed and told me that scrawling "I have accidentally tidied up your Jaffa Cakes with my mouth" in my tiniest handwriting on something the size of a postage stamp does not constitute telling someone. Good grief, next he'll be claiming it doesn't count when I tell him stuff when he's asleep! He's so unreasonable and I have no idea how I put up with him.

13th January

Top Mummy

My second new year's resolution this year was to get dressed every day. It's fair to say that I've had varying degrees of success and, when I take my bra off at the end of another long day of having breasts, I wonder whether it's too late to make a different resolution. One that's more achievable than putting all my clothes on. Maybe if I started small, with slippers, say, and worked my way up the body over time? Set a goal for clean knickers by March.

In other news, Cherub 2 asked for a slice of pizza. Here was my reply:

'Knock yourself out. Actually, don't knock yourself out because you'll have to go to hospital and I won't be able to visit you, which from your point of view is a good thing, but believe me when I say that from a mother's point of view it's a bad thing. Then you'll catch Covid in hospital and have to self-isolate and I'll have to deliver meals to your room and clean everything. It'll be a lot of effort. So, no.'

That's top parenting right there.

And finally...it is coming up to Cherub 1's birthday and she has ordered a unicorn cake for a ridiculous price. It better be made of unicorn shit and rainbows or I want my money back! To be fair, she'd normally be spending the money on a night out with friends, so I don't really begrudge her blowing it on cake (at least she's inherited my extra cake chromosome). Mr V is feeling deeply curmudgeonly over the whole thing, but he came out of the womb with the words "stop spending money" on his lips, so we are taking his views into account then politely ignoring him. Some more excellent parenting and some great wifing too.

There you go. I'm achieving lots of things today. And my other new year's resolution of continuing to be a delight is clearly working out perfectly.

14th January

She Who Has a Ladle

Six o' clock this morning found me running around the garden waving a ladle around under the dog's gentleman's area to collect some wee. As I was quite literally aiming in the dark, I was surprised to catch any at all. He was delighted to have company for his doggy business and didn't mind a metal implement in proximity to his nether regions. Something to which, as a lady, I am entirely averse.

Old Ivy Next Door appeared, just to check what weird things her neighbours were up to now. For once, she was wearing the dressing gown and I was properly dressed. I thought about pointing this out, but feel I've disgraced myself far too often to consider this one instance as evening the score. I just contented myself with shouting, 'Wee collection!' at her. She said, 'No thanks, dear,' and headed back indoors. Hopefully to call off the Neighbourhood Watch.

Later on, Cherub 2 came down for breakfast and I issued a warning that anything in the fridge which appeared to be apple juice could not be trusted. There was some cherubic discontent that the sealed container was in the vicinity of the milk and butter. Like some sort of weird osmosis had occurred and I was expecting him to spread dog wee on his toast.

Mr V hit peak curmudgeon because he was in charge of taking the dog to the vet. I would tell you all about it, but I don't think he's ready to laugh at himself yet. Matters weren't helped by the allegedly sealed cup leaking on the journey. Possibly the cherub's osmosis fears weren't, after all, entirely unfounded. Long story short, everyone except me agrees that I'm the worst wife and mother in the world. I tried to point out that someone called me a national treasure the other day, but apparently this particular treasure deserves to be buried in the garden, in a six-foot hole.

Normally today is Almost Wineday. However, I'm declaring it Extra Wineday and pouring myself a large one. Now, would Cherub 1 be upset if I had one more teensy big slice of her birthday cake?

P.S. Vegas is fine. As I suspected, a bit of dementia. Which is obviously not great, but better than kidney failure. We'll just give him loads of love and kindness in his doggy dotage.

17th January

Totally Heysexy

My email address seems to have become very popular with the spammers and scammers. I could make my fortune in Bitcoin, get a Tesco voucher if I hand over all my bank details and enlarge my penis with one simple trick. I decided against internet shenanigans with a very nice lady who called me hey sexy. I don't know how she knew I was hey sexy and I was almost tempted to go on her website to find out. She'd be there on a bed with her bum swaying, trying to hypnotise some sweaty dude into paying £50 if she takes her knickers off and, instead, she gets me saying, 'How did you know I'm sexy? Ooh, lovely knickers by the way. Marksies?' Finally, I did not give $200 to a cash-starved prince, but I did forward him the link to enlarge his penis. My random act of kindness for the day.

22nd January

Breaking news...

Residents of Covid Corner would like to thank Tesco for getting rid of the paper under mince (that's ground beef in American). Millions of Brits will no longer have sleepless nights wondering about its purpose. Mrs V, a vaguely loyal customer unless they've run out of her favourite ice cream, was overheard saying, 'Yay, there will be no more tipping mince into a pan then trying to hook the bloody paper off in one piece with a fork before it accidentally gets cooked on.' Nevertheless, the thrilling egg-and-spoon-like dash to get the paper to the bin without it dripping on the floor has been mercilessly stripped from the culinary experience and Mr V is worried that he will have to get used to spaghetti bolognese without stray bits of paper. Covid Corner news has contacted the CEO of Tesco for comment, but suspects that paperless husbands may not be a priority for the supermarket chain right now.

In canine news, the Wee Hairy Boys have reported concerns about their human, who has recently taken to loudly singing Bringing In The Sheaves. They staged an intervention, where they cried pitifully and requested treats, yet no treats were forthcoming. Instead, their human appeared delighted that 'we're all having such a good time.' They have written to the Prime Minister and Mrs V's old Sunday School teacher, requesting that lockdown be lifted before she starts on All Things Bright And Beautiful.

Old Ivy Next Door is getting new blinds in her conservatory and has taken her old ones down in preparation. Nose picking and being naked in Covid Corner is now confined to after dark and lights off. There was an accidental mooning at 6am on Wednesday, when Mrs V forgot and came downstairs to get a clean pair of knickers off the radiator. However, Old Ivy is now fully recovered and members of the Neighbourhood Watch can rest assured that Mrs V's bottom will remain firmly under wraps for the foreseeable.

And finally, the Wineday weather. A hard frost will descend on Covid Corner when Mr V finds out how much Mrs V has spent on new curtains. Expect howling gales and a torrent of swear words. A glimmer of sunshine will break through when Mrs V ignores him, drinks a large glass of Sauvignon and browses for new cushions to match the curtains.

23rd January

The One Where Karma Bit Me on the Bum

Top tip. Never scratch your bum after rubbing Deep Heat into your husband's back.

Mr V has been deconstructing Cherub 1's bedroom shelves and my peace was shattered by cries from upstairs. 'How rude,' I thought to myself. However, the cries were followed by much groaning and, eventually, I abandoned my highly important game of Angry Birds to find out what the chuffing hell was going on.

'Are you okay?' I shouted from my comfy chair, unwilling to stray too far from my glass of wine lest it unexpectedly evaporate into a teenager's mouth the minute my back was turned.

'No,' came the reply.

Oh bugger. This might mean actually getting off my arse and helping him.

'Do you need any help?'

'Yes!' Once more, oh bugger. 'Ooh. Aaaargh. Actually no, it's just my back.' Phew, I could do helping by shouting sympathetic words. And still play Angry Birds. I'm a woman. I can multi-task.

Mr V appeared at Covid Corner door, bent over and clutching what he calls muscle but what we both know is muffin top. 'Can you rub some Deep Heat in?'

Really? I was already very busy. Reluctantly, I peeled myself off the comfy chair, accompanied him to the kitchen and entered into negotiations over exactly which bit was the sore bit.

'Up a bit, down a bit. Left a bit. No! Right a bit. Ah, that's the bit. Yes right there.' Honestly, I've had sexy shenanigans with better aim and fewer bits.

This was when karma decided to give me an itchy bum. I had a good rummage down the back of the old pjs, as you do when you've been married for decades and anything sacred went out the window when he watched babies turn your lady parts into a pound of mince. I came away gasping. I mean, I hadn't hit the bullseye or anything, but even there at the top there was a deeply unwelcome warmth. Suddenly, my comfy chair didn't look so comfy.

The long and short of it is that neither of us could sit down and Old Ivy Next Door, she of the conservatory with no blinds, was treated to the sight of me frantically shoving a damp dishcloth down the back of my knickers. I am fairly sure she must call us The Perverts Next Door.

24th January

Mrs V is Given the Yellow Card

I wrote a lovely wee post last night, updating everyone on book things and thanking everyone for the reviews and stars for The Big Blue Jobbie. The post didn't go out on Facebook because it apparently violated community standards. Facebook told me, 'Any more of that nonsense, Mrs V, and you'll be kicked out.' Or words to that effect.

Now, given that I posted yesterday about deep heating my own bum, I wasn't sure how a post with absolutely no rudity, nudity or swear-a-lot crudity could possibly be violating anything. As you can imagine, I was cross, vexed and downright hopping.

I told Mr V all about it. 'What you need to do,' said my wise husband, 'is play it safe for a couple of weeks...'

'Too late for that,' I interrupted, my voice rising. 'They told me I couldn't appeal, so I made my own appeal process. I reported their abuse of me to their abuse reporty thingy. I asked them how an innocent post could possibly...'

It was Mr V's turn to interrupt. 'Hang on, did you put something in at the beginning saying *to be read in a high, squeaky voice*?'

'Ooh, that's an idea. Maybe I should have signed it "Outraged of the North"'

Mr V, who has been diligently binge-watching the Game of Thrones box set I bought him for Christmas, immediately decided that everything should be signed with "of the North". I suggested that he could sign his things "Cock O' The North" and he, in turn, suggested I might like to sleep in the spare room tonight. I happily agreed because no annoying snoring. 'Anyway,' he said, 'be

218

careful what you write over the next couple of...'

'Too late for that,' I interrupted, waving my phone at him. 'Outraged of the North has won. Well, common sense has won. Facebook has agreed that my post is okay and cancelled the warning, so I can even say f...'

'No! You can't say that!' interjected my darling husband.

'...acebook was wrong and I was right. Jeez, what's with everyone today? You'd think I have no filter or something!' I exclaimed.

Mr V wondered if this would be a good moment to remind me that I posted about deep heating my own bum, but decided that I'd only threaten to sleep with him and he was quite looking forward to a night with no annoying snoring.

25th January

Wanted. One Life Back Please.

Another Monday. Doesn't time fly when you're stuck indoors instead of having mocha-frappe-latte-chinos in coffee shops and trying to find your way out of House of Fraser?

I only go into House of Fraser to mentally lick the handbags and swan around pretending I can afford stuff. If I ever owned a Mulberry handbag, I'd be checking to make sure I was carrying it with the logo on the outside at all times, just so all the other ladies would think I was posh. I would still be using that handbag (logo out and proud) when I'm 95 because it's the poshest thing I ever owned. I would ask them to pop my ashes inside and bury me in that bag. Dream big, Mrs V.

By the way, I once thought all the other ladies were staring at my new boots because they were impressed. Turned out I'd accidentally left the 'real leather' tag on and all the other ladies thought I was a bit of a twat.

I don't really miss shops so much as the event of going to the shops. Nice coffees and lovely lunches and buying things on a whim and walking miles because Mr V's idea of convenient parking is the furthest away space in the furthest away car park. Moaning that my feet hurt and only the purchase of shiny things will make them better. Drinking an unplanned cocktail or three and chatting with a homeless person about their dog while Mr V spends approximately 300 hours in the camera shop, then texting him to remind him my feet are sore and we haven't bought any shiny things yet. Realising that there's something good on at the theatre or cinema and throwing all our plans out the window so we can spend a few hours being entertained. Or, as I once did, abandoning shopping altogether and going on a rollercoaster instead. By myself. For absolutely no reason at all.

Covid may have made our worlds very small and left devastation in its wake, but there really will be an end to it. And I really will appreciate all the things I took for granted before. Keep buggering on, my lovelies. We'll get there x

28th January

Clever Alexa

Mr V thought he'd be clever last night and switch the light off on me, now that I have a smart bulb in Covid Corner. He strode into the kitchen and said, 'Alexa, switch the dining room light off.' Alexa said, 'Do you mean Covid Corner?' I thought he was going to explode with outrage. He's now convinced Alexa knows far too much about us and has told her to switch herself off forever.

I offered Alexa a glass of wine, as she is clearly on my side, and pointed out to Mr V that the good ship Privacy sailed a long time ago. If anyone had told me in 1990 that there would be giant corporations based in other countries who knew more about me than my own mother, I'd have said, 'Well I better be bloody boring then!'

I recently checked to see how much google knows about me. I had no idea just how successfully boring I'd been! Apparently, I'm interested in property (well, when your neighbours put their houses up for sale you have to take a look!), business news and coffee & tea. Not even cake and wine! Probably because I don't buy them online - I just send Mr V to Costco with a list and maybe text him "don't forget the cake and wine" a few times.

Look yourself up on adssettings.google.com if you want to see how boring you are. I thought about checking on Mr V but it's just going to say camera shops and stopping my wife spending money.

29ᵗʰ January

If It Wasn't for the Pesky Wife...

Mr V told me today that he felt it was high time for a DCI Mr V story.

'But you haven't investigated anything recently,' I told him. 'I can't write a story if you haven't investigated anything!'

'Ah,' said he, 'I have been doing crime prevention.'

'What do you mean?'

'Well, you know the smart water the insurance company sent me to put on the campervan? I put it on the Jaffa Cakes.'

'What Jaffa Cakes?'

DCI Mr V checked the cupboard. All his Jaffa Cakes appeared to have accidentally fallen into someone else's mouth. I have no idea whose.

'How was smart water going to protect your Jaffa Cakes? Were you going to check everyone's poo with a UV light? See if the serial number lit up and tell the owner of poo number RX456893Z to step forward?' I asked.

DCI Mr V admitted that there was a tiny possibility he hadn't thought this one through properly. He needs a proper mystery to investigate. Keep his skills sharp. Hone his interrogation techniques.

Fortunately, he hasn't checked the secret place where he stashed his Christmas chocolates yet...

31ˢᵗ January

Stools, Stockings and the Sabbath

Finally! It's the 99th of January at last. What I need is one of those SAD lamps. A massive eff off one that I can shove my whole family under. Well, a SAD lamp or a bus. Either will do.

Mr V took his breakfast on a tray in the living room yesterday, allegedly so he wouldn't have to talk to anyone. But I know what was really going on. I was sitting in his spot at the kitchen counter. There are three other stools, but his brain gremlins said only this one would do.

On the subject of stools, Cherub 2 thinks I'm the worst mother in the world because I failed to enquire after the state of his bowels. I know the state of his bowels. I had to use the bathroom after him. Never mind lighting a match, a box of TNT and giant can of Glade was required. In fact, I have a suggestion as to where he can shove the can of Glade. Cut out the middleman, as it were, and go straight to the heart of the problem.

Cherub 1 is the only nice one, even if she did say, 'Are you going to wear them outside the house?' when I showed her my new tights. To be fair, they are not sophisticated lady tights. They are the sort of tights you buy in a fit of malaise to cheer yourself up, then realise that you're many, maaaaany decades too old to be wearing them. However, I defiantly assured her that, harumph yes, I would be wearing them outside, so now I'm stuck with bloody things. If you spot a middle-aged woman tootling around on neon pink legs decorated with love hearts, that'll be me and my mid-life crisis tights.

Maybe that's what Mr V needs. A good mid-life crisis to cheer him up and get him through the winter months. Do you remember back in the eighties when teens used to sew patches on denim jackets? I'm thinking a nice, big Black Sabbath patch on the back of his fleece. Oh, he will be pleased. Clever me.

FEBRUARY 2021

The darkest month, yet with a glimmer of light this year. The vaccine programme was in full swing and "where are you on the list?" was the hottest topic. Looking back, January was the peak of the second wave. February was the month where there were signs of improvement. The people around me were feeling ground down by the winter months and the seemingly endless lockdown. Home-schooling was taking its toll. At work, a colleague described his ten-year-old's maths homework. The online team meeting went slightly off-topic as nine adults, with degrees in things like accounting, scratched their heads in bewilderment. An interesting meeting, although not quite as educational as one where the sole topic was "which is the best vacuum cleaner." I was looking for a new vacuum cleaner at the time and I do like my meetings to stick to the important points.

Let's remind ourselves of the important points in February. Topshop was rescued from insolvency. Quite important for Cherub 1, less so for me. I once bought Cherub 1 a pair of size 4 skinny jeans in there. The assistant looked at me with pity, like she was thinking, 'You poor, deluded cow. You'll never fit a toenail in those.' I smiled and breezily told her they were for my niece, a very famous actress *whispers the name of some skinny woman I saw in a gratuitous bikini shot, being bitched at by the newspaper for having a hint of cellulite, right next to an article on women's rights*. I have no idea why the assistant suddenly became so helpful!

The best bit of February was the snow. Seeing pictures of happy families out sledging was wonderful. It was so cold that my fluffy, pink dressing gown stopped working and I had to wear a jumper on top of my pyjamas to work.

The saddest bit of February was the death of Captain Sir Tom Moore. The nation lost a good man and some bloke got into a spot of bother for saying horrible things about him on social media. For those of us who grew up in a world where there was no such thing as social media, the discovery that there are so many twats in the world has come as a shock. You go through life thinking that most people are like you; decent, honest and cleaning their bathroom at least once a week. Which is why it comes as a bucket of cold water each time a new twat crawls out of the woodwork and waves it's little twat flag, shouting, 'Pay attention world, I'm lowering the stupid bar.' What must it be like for our children, who are growing up in a world where this stuff is normal? They must assume that twats rule the earth and they are the odd ones out.

By mid-February, fifteen million people in the UK had had their first dose of the vaccine. How immense is that?! There was a sense of national pride in the achievement. Also, the amount of baking done for Valentine's Day was stupendous. My social media was wall to wall love heart cakes. At this point, I was going to write things about lots of warming of the cockles of my heart, but I got slightly distracted by Googling "what are heart cockles".

Towards the end of February, Boris revealed his roadmap out of lockdown and the Scottish Government revealed their "cautious" approach. One country frantically checking Google maps for a way out, the other with a headmistress-in-chief casting a beady eye over her unruly citizens. It's worth pointing out that in March, Northern Ireland went one better when they unveiled their "cautious and hopeful" plan. And somewhere in the mix, a meteorite fell, Harry and Meghan said they weren't coming back and a politician got a smacked bum from the High Court for being less than transparent about Covid contracts.

1st February

Caulking with Craig

Some Mrs V DIY is on the cards. I've watched a manly YouTube video and have prepared all the materials I'll need to replace the seal round the shower. This includes a tube of silicone, some masking tape and a set of noise cancelling headphones to muffle out the protests of the Cherubs when I tell them no showers for twenty-four hours while it dries.

Why can't I have normal young people who are averse to showers? Most teenagers I've come across have to be thrown under running water when they start sticking to the walls.

Also, what is the deal with them wanting to spend quality time with us? I've trained them over time to accept a certain level of parental cringe-worthiness, but lockdown has completely removed the usual ultimate deterrents of threatening to wear matching jumpers and snog in public. They've become so used to having us around that they regard us as...gasp...human beings with...bigger gasp...feelings, who they actually...mini-stroke...love!

On the other hand, Mr V is so sick of the sight of us all that the sacred garage is the most organised it has ever been. Which is just as well because I need him to find the gun thingy for the tube of silicone.

P.S. he is also sick of me because I have a serious case of Craig-worship. I watched a few manly DIY YouTube videos presented by Craig off of Big Brother 2000 and have spent the last two days saying, 'But Craig says...'.

***

DIY disasters are an ongoing theme in our house. I probably give the impression in the blog that I rely on Mr V to do most of the jobs around the house. I certainly get the odd comment along the lines of "Well, I'm perfectly capable of doing things myself, without having to rely on a man to do them for me." I tend not to reply, mainly because I can't be bothered to explain or justify myself. The thought of repeatedly telling people that this is a humorous snapshot of a particular day in my life, and I too am perfectly capable of doing things for myself, is exhausting.

I don't aim to be a "strong woman". I just aim to be half of the team that puts a roof over my family's head and sends a couple of decent young citizens out into the world. You're unlikely to find me at the front line of feminism, fighting for the important issues of the day. You'll find me at the back, proud that I've raised a son who puts the toilet seat down and muttering darkly that maybe it's about time he learned how to put a loo roll on the effing holder.

I do my fair share of jobs. Although, I once built a shoe rack and made such a mess of it that Mr V grumpily asked if I was deliberately cocking it up so he'd do it. I was quite miffed with him that he asked and quite miffed with myself that, for once, the thought never entered my mind!

There was also the Day of Hattery Twattery, when I triggered a top rant by committing the heinous crime of moving Mr V's hat. I'd made him a special little hattery in the cupboard under the stairs, where he could hang all his hats. He didn't appreciate my genius and pretended that the hattery didn't exist. To this day, he hasn't used it. He much prefers to stride around the house, being outraged and telling me about all the annoying people who have touched his stuff, ever. My little hooks are wasted on him.

I was looking back through all my old scribblings, thinking I might regale you with a tale or two of our DIY disasters, when I came across this one, which I think represents how we all do our bit (I'd just recovered from a chest infection at the time):

"I've stopped coughing and can breathe again. Finally, things have perked up in the chest department. Sadly, not my boobs. Did anyone do the pencil test at school? Me, my friend Karen and an unfortunate lad called Keith all passed. The idea was to put a pencil under your boobs. If it dropped, great. If was trapped, you had a saggy pair. I could fit an entire pencil case under there these days and it wouldn't budge. I don't mind. They don't make women's clothes with pockets, so the extra storage space comes in handy.

Mr V has big plans this weekend. Fixing Lovely Granny's curtain rail. He has given me a list of all the things 'we' need. I don't know why I'm involved in this. I'm in charge of fixing Lovely Granny's computer when she breaks the internet. Mr V is in charge of fixing everything else. As it's almost my birthday, I'm entertaining fantasies that this is all a big ruse and he's actually going to whisk me off somewhere swanky. Now that I've stopped violently coughing, we could even go somewhere with a swimming pool without the risk of me accidentally turning the water dark blue and creating an impromptu jacuzzi.

If we really are going to fix Lovely Granny's curtain rail then the air will be blue this weekend, as Mr V swears his way through another DIY job. Also, I'd like to point out that the service level agreement for fixing Granny's stuff is two weeks but in our own house it's six months. I would like to know what Lovely Granny has on Mr V to get such favourable terms! I asked Google. No answers. I shall add cake to the list of things we need to take and hope that granny is susceptible to bribes in exchange for family secrets."

***

2ⁿᵈ February

A Sad Goodbye

Such sad news about Captain Sir Tom Moore. He was a true inspiration. We all make a difference in our lifetimes, in hundreds of small ways; a smile for a stranger, a call to a friend who is having a bad day. Captain Sir Tom set out to make a small difference, yet made a big difference and had a grateful nation behind him. He would say "Tomorrow is going to be a good day." Thanks to the money he raised, so many people will have a tomorrow to look forward to. What a legacy! RIP Captain Sir Tom Moore.

5th February

I Love My Children But...

List of things I'm going to do in my children's houses (assuming they ever leave home):

1. Open a fresh carton of milk, even though one is already open (ditto bread);
2. Put empty cereal boxes in their cupboards;
3. Collect all my empty loo rolls and scatter them on bathroom floors;
4. Open the fridge door and wail "there is no food in this house" every hour, on the hour;
5. Hide their plates, glasses and cutlery under their beds;
6. Deny all knowledge of whereabouts of plates, glasses and cutlery;
7. Retrieve all plates, glasses and cutlery from under beds when they've given in and bought some new stuff (this to include quietly placing said items next to sink, denying it was me who did it and blaming Mr V);
8. Only do 7 immediately after they've put the dishwasher on;
9. Tell them I'm popping out for biscuits and come back six hours later, having ignored increasingly frantic texts;
10. Spray their mirrors with suspicious substances, help myself to their keys and forget to give them back, leave my post lying around, scatter dirty knickers on their bathroom floors, place boxes of eggs on top of the egg holder instead of decanting the eggs etc etc etc.

I love the little buggers, but sometimes I want to murder them in their sleep.

7ᵗʰ February

Back in the Good Old Days

I didn't post this one because it was too niche, yet I expect some of it will ring a bell, even if you didn't grow up in Scotland.

"Things I look back on fondly about growing up in Scotland in the 1980s:

1. Scottish country dancing was considered PE for the entire month of December;
2. When the TV and video recorder was rolled into the classroom;
3. School bus hierarchy;
4. Knowing the interior decor of everyone's houses by the covers of their school books. We had the same kitchen wallpaper as Mrs Mangle in Neighbours;
5. High tea;
6. Feeling like international jetsetters when we visited my auntie in Berwick (just over the border in England);
7. Shoe-horning mum, dad, four kids, a cat, two dogs and my granny into our Lada for a twelve hour drive around the Highlands of a Saturday...just because;
8. Always having bowls in the car for when my mum spotted wild raspberry bushes by the side of the road;
9. Taking in my jeans. The most popular girl was the one whose mum owned a sewing machine. I was briefly she;
10. Imagining what I would buy if I had (gasp) £100 to spend on clothes."

8th February

Just Be Yourself, They Said!

I wondered how my personal statement on a job application would look if I wrote it Mrs V stylee:

Hmmm. What do I bring to this job? Oodles of enthusiasm and a big old dollop of initiative. I am a great team player (note that I have not even once murdered my family in their sleep), although I sometimes annoy people when I accidentally steal their Jaffa cakes. However, it takes foresight and planning to accidentally steal Jaffa cakes. You have to wait until you know the Jaffa owner is out of the room to do the thievery, then put your work headphones on and pretend to be in a meeting so they can't interrupt you when they catch you eating said Jaffa cakes. You can see how well I've thought this through. That's skills, that is.

Now, you said you're looking for someone with experience of managing change. This morning I put a bra on for the first time in six months and my husband thought I'd had a boob job on the sly, so perky were the girls. I had to prevent him checking our bank account for large withdrawals (lest he see how much I spent on makeup to go absolutely nowhere during a pandemic). Instead, I sat him down with a nice cup of tea and showed him my tits. Mr V is now happy that my boobs are as droopy as ever, but also a bit sad that my boobs are as droopy as ever. He gave excellent feedback on the cup of tea, though.

I know that communication skills are important to you. I'm very good at being nice to people about whom I have mean thoughts, if that helps (see above re murdering family in sleep). I also do very good shouting, particularly at people who fail to flush. Many a time, my cries of 'IF IT'S YELLOW LET IT MELLOW.

IF IT'S BROWN FLUSH IT DOWN, YOU BIG TWAT' have rung through the neighbourhood. The fact that this has had no effect could be misconstrued as poor communication, when in fact it is poor hand-bottom coordination on the part of my family.

You also want someone who is strong on dealing with HR issues. I have lots of experience of dealing with poor attendance. Cherub 1 will testify that when she doesn't respond to texts and phone calls, I relentlessly hunt her down by finding her friends on Facebook and messaging them. I'm a persistent bugger. I'm also a delight at dealing with misconduct (see above re flushing it down). I prefer the screaming approach, but there is also threatening silence, changing the Wi-Fi password, no dinner and (the ultimate weapon) being very, very disappointed. Sometimes I even talk to people to find out what the problem is! Finally, I'm great with performance issues. My ex totally believed me when I said, 'It's okay. It happens to lots of men.' In hindsight, maybe it wasn't the best time to do impressions of his mother.

In my spare time, I do animal husbandry. I have no idea what that is, but I have two dogs and a very grumpy husband, all of whom pretend to be deaf when I talk to them and need fed at regular intervals.

As you can see, I would be brilliant at this job. Please, please, pretty please can I have it?

Tinkety tonk,

Mrs V x

10th February

Emergency Biscuits

Yesterday, I was not in a good place. My ability to keep buggering on had temporarily buggered off. I'm allowed a bit of angst once in a while and the best thing to do under the circumstances was to have a good moan. A good moan is always better than a bad place.

It doesn't really matter what the problem was. What matters is that I texted an entire essay to a good friend and she did a bit of cheerleading. Then I read a comment on one of my posts and, oddly, knowing that I made somebody else feel better made me feel better. My point is that these weird times can magnify feelings, so it's important to shout up if you're not okay.

Also, chocolate biscuits. Try to keep emergency chocolate biscuits. They really are the most versatile of all the food groups (with the possible exception of cake). I recently managed to score a brilliant own goal with a chocolate biscuit during a meeting about the important role of exercise in good mental health. I was in the middle of lying to all and sundry about how much I exercise, when I dropped my chocolate biscuit on the keyboard and accidentally cut the call. The irony cheered me up so much that I didn't bother dialling back in.

If you are having a bad day, fancy screaming at the world or just want a good moan, shout up. We probably can't solve things for you, no matter how much we want to, but it does feel good to share a grumble. On this blog you and I are surrounded by the loveliest bunch of people we've never met.

If it's a bit more than a bad day, my heart goes out to you and I really hope you are getting the help you need. https://www.samaritans.org

11th February

Extra Wineday

Lordy, I poured myself a large glass of whine yesterday, didn't I?! Thank you for all your supportive comments. Mr V appeared with a ton of chocolate and a large tub of ice cream. I was feeling much better by then, but told myself that my brain could do with the glucose anyway and chomped my way through my afternoon meetings.

This sudden chocolatey munificence on the part of Mr V was most unexpected. Last week, as he does around this time every year, he bought a big box of creme eggs which he claims belongs to him, but which the rest of us view as communal property. As usual, he has been demanding we account for each egg eaten. I fear I may once more have to batter him to death with a giant toblerone. In fact, I suspect he didn't even notice I was feeling blue and just bought me some goodies so I'd keep my mucky little hands off his precious eggs. Pardon the double entendre but...I wish I'd known sooner that chocolate was a reward for steering clear of his precious eggs - I'd have kept my mucky little hands off 'em years ago and saved us a fortune in childcare!

Anyway, I'm back on top of the mountain, cheerfully screaming, 'Bugger off world unless you have something good to throw at me.' I've booked myself a week off at the end of March, which will no doubt be spent in Costa Del Covid Corner, unless Boris gets his skates on and decides that enough of us are vaccinated to be allowed out again. In which case it'll be Playa Del Scotland. Don't worry, I'll send a flare up beforehand, just to warn all the men in kilts I'm on my way.

If yesterday was Whineday, today must be Wineday (yes, I know it's officially Almost Wineday, but I'm declaring an extra Wineday this week). Bottoms up.

13th February

Romance Is Not Dead

Valentine's Day tomorrow. What romantic treat does Mr V have in store for me? We are talking about the man who takes his socks off in bed to signal that sexy shenanigans are long overdue. What with his fungal toenail being out and all, he imagines I simply cannot resist. I'm being very rude. The Night of The Living Toenail was many moons ago and his big toe is currently fine.

For my part, I spent this morning baking some heart shaped biscuits. Actually, I'm still mid-attempt. The recipe said, "beat the butter smooth." I looked at the hardened lump I'd just extracted from the fridge and wondered how on earth I'd do that. So, I gave it a bit of a prod with a spoon and hoped for the best. Then I was supposed to beat in some icing sugar. Well, what with the butter still being hard, the spoon was slipping all over the place and, to cut a long story short, I currently look like a snowman who's been on the cooking sherry.

I really have been on the cooking sherry! I discovered it at the back of the cupboard when I was hunting down vanilla essence and it seemed rude not to check that it was still okay to drink. Although...the vanilla essence expired in 2018 and, strangely, I don't feel compelled to take a swig of that. Just chuck it in the bowl and hope Mr V survives.

I think that, after twenty-five years of marriage, not poisoning one's husband is the ultimate romantic gesture. Maybe I'll leave out the vanilla essence and go break the good news to Mr V that I've decided to let him live.

14th February

Romance Is Definitely Dead

I had to confess to Mr V that he was getting a broken heart for Valentine's Day. I made a big heart shaped cookie and was a tad clumsy when moving it onto the cooling rack. Nevertheless, I glued it back together with chocolate, then I spent ages covering the whole thing in more chocolate and sprinkles and a big icing 'I love you'. Like a proud child, I presented my efforts to Mr V. 'You know I don't have much of a sweet tooth,' said the light of my life, love of my heart, mate of my soul and utter, utter big twat whom I would divorce at the earliest opportunity if we didn't have an endless well of love and forgiveness for each other. 'There's a reason why I like dogs more than people,' I replied.

Romance is officially dead in our house and I'm off to mend my broken heart with some more chocolate.

16ᵗʰ February

Screwing Up

I've taken possession of the tools and am fixing stuff. Mr V is hovering anxiously, like his screwdrivers are going to develop Stockholm syndrome and start being nice to me. Like the big Phillips might pop its crossed head up and suggest a smaller one will do. Like the cute little bent one in the corner will tell me his name is Allen. Allen Key.

There are all sorts of things in the tool collection and I have no idea what they're for. Mr V did try to tell me, but I kept slapping the side of his head and telling him the reception was a bit dodgy. All I could hear was white noise.

Anyway, I only need to fix a hook in the bathroom but, while I'm at it, I may put batteries in all the things you have to unscrew to put batteries in. Why do they do that? Make changing batteries require screwdrivers? It turns a quick job into a six-month battle of wills to see who will give in and find the teeny tiny screwdriver that is the only handy thing anyone ever won in a Christmas cracker. It has made me into a person who asks questions on Amazon – "Does this need the Christmas cracker screwdriver to change the batteries?" Then Mr J from Suffolk regards this as an opportunity to display his in-depth knowledge of the history of screwdrivers and Mr V has to stop me posting another question, asking if Mr J from Suffolk is a bit of a tool himself. You see how tricky this is?! If, thousands of years from now, archaeologists wonder what brought down our civilisation, the answer will be screwdrivers to change effing batteries!

Phew. I don't know where that came from, but it was quite cathartic. Maybe I'll have a glass of wine before fixing stuff. And maybe another wine before explaining to Mr V that I've thrown out his dressing gown (which has hung untouched in our bathroom for 20 years) on the basis that the weight of its mankiness was what broke the hook in the first place. In my DIY expert opinion.

Cheers and happy Pancake Day.

17th February

The Modern Man

The smart thermostat went through a 3 week 'learning your winter schedule' phase in January, which coincided with Cherub 2's nocturnal phase. Now we're freezing all bloody day and nobody is getting any decent sleep. Although, to my delight, I can truthfully say I'm hot in the bedroom. However, I can't tell Mr V because he already thinks the thermostat is Satan, with its app and Alexa thingy sent to befuddle him. How am I supposed to make him enthusiastic about joining the 21st century now?!

Honestly, when he finally figured out how to switch off Covid Corner light using Alexa, you'd have thought he'd pulled a unicorn out of his bum. He immediately demanded smart lights for the living room. Admittedly, I did buy the plain white ones because I was concerned that if I bought him the ones that do fancy colours, he'd get permanently stuck in a red-light zone with not a clue how to change it back. I simply couldn't take that level of curmudgeon. My 'Things You Must Know How To Do After I Die' list already contains 1) switch the heating on by yourself instructions; 2) detailed diagrams of how to change a duvet cover and 3) directives that clean skirting boards and windows is an actual thing. Adding "work the lights" is just too much hassle. Of course, he immediately tried to change his new lights to fancy colours, demanding to know why the effing app wasn't working, so we had the conversation about how it was better for everyone's sanity if he didn't have fancy colours.

Now the heating muddle is going to destroy all my hard work. He's going to declare all smart things unsmart and demand we go back to the old ways. If anyone wants me, I'll be in the garage getting the horse and cart ready.

***

Switching the heating on is the top reason for Mr V using his 'only phone me at work in an emergency' emergency phone call. Other reasons for my family using their emergency phone call are:

1. *I went for a wee in the woods and squatted on a nettle (Cherub 1);*
2. *Can you lend me £5 (both Cherubs, frequently);*
3. *SOMEONE has eaten the chocolate out of my advent calendar (Cherub 1);*
4. *My brother is being mean to me (Cherub 1 – the entire office went silent as I asked her to put her brother on the phone and roared, 'Stop calling your sister a buffoon.');*
5. *What ingredients do I need to bake a chocolate cake? (Cherub 2);*
6. *I've learned to use the heating app and buggered up all the settings (Mr V);*
7. *Can you fix the heating? Dad has learned how to use the heating app and buggered up all the settings (Cherub 2);*
8. *Where are my trainers? (all of them);*
9. *Cherub 1 has pitched a tent and ruined my lawn! (Mr V);*
10. *The painter* (Mr V);*
11. *I'm locked out of the house. Can you phone a locksmith?** (Mr V);*
12. *Do you think cavemen found farts funny?*** (Mr V);*
13. *There are no clean bowls (Cherub 2);*
14. *I have no foundation left (Cherub 1);*
15. *There's a spider. You deal with spiders (all of them).*

My confusion at being expected to magically sort these problems when I'm not there is only matched by their utter incomprehension that I can't!

* Mr V used up a month's worth of 'only phone me at work in an emergency' emergency phone calls in a day to moan at me about the painter, Glen, making him do jobs and make tea. When I got home from work, I cheerfully asked if he was Glen's bitch now. Not

realising that Glen was painting the other side of the kitchen door.

** *Re Mr V's reluctance to call a locksmith, I should explain that Mr V objects to anything which involves a) having to talk to other human beings he doesn't know on the phone unless absolutely necessary and b) having to use the internet on his phone (particularly if he has to download an app, join anything or create a password). Over the past 23 years this has resulted in stern words – 'I'm at work! Just phone them! You always have chicken chow mein with soft noodles.' It should, therefore, come as no surprise that there was a wee hopeful note in Mr V's voice that I would use the internet, explain to a locksmith that my husband was locked out of the house and tell them that, even though I wasn't actually there, if they drove to my house, they would meet a grown man who required access to his Xbox and who was only willing to talk to them face to face.*

*** *My response to the caveman question was, 'Of course, they found farts funny! Why would you waste your only phone me at work in an emergency emergency phone call to ask that? Surely a better emergency question is if you were a shoe what shoe would you be?' Mr V said he would be a hiking boot because it's useful and tough. I don't know what he was on. I had him down as a pair of sensible loafers with surprise winklepicker toes. We both thought I'd be a glittery pump. Then, with all the important issues of the day resolved, we went back to work.*

***

18th February

Mow Me

I'm so overall hairy right now that it would be a blessing if I was run over by a lawnmower. My head hair is just awful. I don't mind the greys or the roots. It's the lack of shape. Somehow, I've managed to grow a style that perfectly emphasises my double chin, whilst having no volume or shape whatsoever. The worst thing is that you just have to take one look at Boris to know that his roadmap out of lockdown definitely doesn't go anywhere near a hairdresser.

As for the legs. I could win a hairy legs competition between me and the dogs. Chin? Today I discovered three sterling examples of what happens when you only bother looking in the mirror about once a month. And we won't even discuss the amount of lady gardening that needs to be done. It would make your eyes water. Let's just say something is keeping my knees warm and it isn't leg hair.

Honestly, the first thing I'll be doing when we get out of lockdown is trying to remember where I put my self-respect back in March 2020.

20th February

Covid Corner News Again

There was widespread alarm yesterday when a Covid Corner resident disappeared. A search party consisting of her family and a wee hairy boy found her watching telly in the kitchen. The leader of the search party, a certain DCI Mr V, roared at her, 'You're not in your chair. Why are you not in your chair? Why are you watching telly in here? You're just confusing everyone.' The WHB, who had no idea whose feet he was supposed to sleep on in the event of his human sitting Somewhere Unexpected, told Covid Corner News that, to prevent further incidents, he intended to teach his human some basic commands, with priority being given to sit and stay.

In technology news, on Thursday a woman switched her phone torch on while hunting for gin at the back of the cupboard, then spent two days wondering why her phone battery kept dying. She is now wondering whether the dog's dementia tablets work on humans.

The Neighbourhood Watch attended an emergency call yesterday. Old Ivy Next Door reported a man going through her neighbour's bins. The man in question, 19-year-old Mr Cherub 2, explained that he had recently been made aware of the existence of bins when his mother screamed, 'The effing bin fairy is not like the effing tooth fairy - she doesn't magic away effing bags of rubbish from outside your bedroom door and leave money under the pair of manky socks that seem permanently glued to the effing carpet!' Recognising the level of eff words as a warning sign, Cherub 2 had used his newly discovered knowledge of bins immediately, lest he be made to do more chores.

In other bin news, Covid Corner government suffered a setback this week when its policy of no alcohol on a school night was threatened by the arrival of some delicious strawberry and lime cider. Prime Minister Mrs V told Covid Corner News, 'Am totally shticking to the polishy and rilly don't shee what the pwob...prom...problem is...hic.' Deputy Prime Minister Mr V was later heard grumbling that the recycle bin was very full this week. Prime Minister Mrs V says she has no idea how that happened.

Finally, the weather. A hard frost is expected to settle in today when Mr V sleeps in, comes downstairs, demands to know why nobody told him to get up and finds out that he had an entire conversation with Mrs V on the subject of getting his arse out of bed, but that he chose to ignore her and go back to sleep. There may be some thunder as Mr V adjusts to the idea that sleeping in was his own fault. A thaw will occur post-coffee and cornflakes, with the air turning blue later when Mrs V asks him to fix broken things. This weather pattern is fairly common at weekends.

22nd February

Meadow Muffins

Celebrity recipes we have tried and hated - discuss! I made a dozen breakfast muffins from a celebrity recipe at the weekend and can only conclude that the man in question must like the taste of feet. Also, they so closely resembled something I saw on the path on my walk on Sunday that I'm considering calling my next book 'The Twelve Big Horse Jobbies.'

Cherub 2 asked what Mr V and I talk about when we're out on walks. I think he expected an interesting answer like "You, darling. We talk about you whenever you're not there because you're so important to us." Instead, I told him the truth. There was a weir with fish pools to help eels swim upriver and I insisted on reading the information board out loud in BBC newsreader fashion to Mr V and all the other people there (I may have added a few made-up bits of my own). Then I called Biggles a very rude swear word for growling at a dog. Fortunately, by that stage, most of the other people had become bored of my extended eel news report and had left. Then Mr V and I sat on a bench and he pontificated about rocks. I smiled inwardly because just that morning I'd written a story for the new book about a man who wanted a garden full of rocks he could pontificate about. I'd been a bit worried that perhaps I was imagining the ability of men to pontificate about rocks, but Mr V unknowingly put my mind at rest. I told Cherub 2 all of the above and he said, 'Okay, you've been found innocent.' Phew. Quite glad I didn't mention that I've sometimes called him a few worse names than I've ever called Biggles!

So how are you doing today? Have you had a productive afternoon being a marvellous human being or have you spent it like the rest of us, trying to use your Jedi mind powers to make Boris open the pubs?

23rd February

It's Important to Have Hobbies

I have a new hobby. It is standing at the front door yelling, 'AND DON'T COME BACK!' at Mr V every time he leaves the house. Just to mess with Old Ivy Next Door. Mr V has tried to think of an embarrassing riposte, but this is quite difficult when your wife bemoaned the state of her lady garden to the whole of the internet last week. There really isn't anywhere left to go.

I'm in trouble today for texting Mr V when he's asleep. Normally, if I think he's going to be annoyed with me, I tell him things when he's asleep. That way, he can't say he hasn't been told that we are about to become the new owners of something very expensive. However, recently, I've also taken to texting him important reminders when he's asleep. Things like "We need bread" and "As you're going to the shop for bread, can you get me some wine?" That way he has a to do list ready for when he wakes up. You'd think he would appreciate having such a helpful wife! But no. Apparently, I am Being A Nuisance and It Must Stop.

Once more, I am forced to remind him that I'm a delight.

26th February

Hard Work and Sausages

I'm like Tigger at the moment, bouncing around all over the place. After weeks of pain, my arthritis has eased off and I can finally wash my bum without feeling like I've done ten rounds with Muhammad Ali. I messaged my lovely boss to tell her I am once more ready to Be A Nuisance. I left out the bit about my bum. Also, the bit about Tigger. Best not compare myself to Disney characters at work, especially as my lockdown belly is approaching a state of Pooh-like rotundity. Cameras-on meetings are getting increasingly difficult as I have to shuffle further away to make myself look smaller. Any day now, I'm expecting a pop up from Zoom to say they don't do wide screen.

Her Lovely Bossiness was suitably impressed (and possibly surprised) by my enthusiasm to do some actual work. Particularly after I dialled into a mindfulness workshop on Wednesday, fell asleep while concentrating on my breathing and woke up to find I was the only one left on the call. Today, I duly churned out fifty thousand emails and Her Lovely Bossiness' sigh of relief was barely audible when I told her I'd be finishing early to observe Wineday.

Mr V is less impressed with me. I was in a very, veeeeery long meeting earlier and I may have mistaken his ice cream for a healthy apple. Apparently "All the extra thinking had depleted my brain's glucose levels and I became confused" is not an acceptable excuse. Jeez. Mistakes do happen!

Mr V is currently engaged in a battle with a tree. He is resolved to move the enemy to a new location in the garden "before it gets too big." I suspect it might already be too big. We are on day three of digging and I fear that if the battle drags on any longer, there will be an off-battlefield fatal injury when the spade slips and accidentally batters him to death. Admittedly, there may be a well-padded Scotswoman on the other end screaming, 'Three effing days of moaning about your back!'

In other news, Vegas has registered a complaint about the 50% reduction in surprise treats. This has coincided with the opening of his new tablets, which are once a day rather than twice a day. The new tablets are massive, so I've been hiding them in cocktail sausages. Mr V tried to convince me the tablets were pessaries and I said no way was I shoving cocktail sausages up a dog's bum. I told him when he gets old and doddery, I'm going to convince him his tablets are pessaries. See how he likes a sausage up the bum. All these tablets have made absolutely no difference to Vegas' dementia. He still assumes I must be talking to another Vegas and he still pees on the carpet, but his deafness has improved to the point where he can hear a fridge door opening at a hundred yards.

27th February

Hair Comes Trouble

Remember that time when you were a teenager and cut your own fringe? This was the conversation in our house last night:

Cherub 2: Oh my god, come here!

Me [sympathetic mum]: What? What's happened? Oh, my word. Your head looks like a cube. *Laughs like a drain* Hang on. I'm going to have to sit down. I think I'm going to pee myself. Where's my phone? I need a picture.

A few minutes later...

Knock knock

Me: Who's there?

Cherub 2: What are you doing in there?

Me: Having a pee and reading the news.

Cherub 2: Are you going to be long?

Me: Why?

Cherub 2: So you can cut my hair!

Me [again, sympathetic mum]: Oh, I'm far too tired to be cutting hair.

Cherub 2: We can't leave it like this!

Ten minutes later...

Mr V: What's been going on here? Why is there hair everywhere?

Me: There was an accident.

Cherub 2 [sporting a fresh buzz cut courtesy of his sympathetic mammy]: Well, my hair was getting a bit long and...

Me: He accidentally made himself look like a twat.

All credit to Cherub 2. He laughed at himself as much as we did.

MARCH 2021

Ooh, March was an exciting month. Everyone became very upset when the government gave NHS workers a 1% pay rise. To most, it seemed an extraordinary decision in the circumstances. I'm not entirely sure how or if it was resolved because, a couple of days later, the Sussexes gave *that* explosive interview and Piers Morgan went off like he had a stick of dynamite up his bum. There may have also been some news about Covid and a budget, but we were all far too busy hotly debating the royals to pay proper attention.

We soon started listening again when the police found the remains of a missing woman, Sarah Everard, and a Met Police officer was arrested for her kidnap and murder. The conversation turned to how women feel unsafe quite a lot of the time. I told Mr V that I too feel unsafe walking alone at night. Mr V said that he also feels unsafe and is hyper-aware of people around him. 'Yes,' I said, 'but you've never had to walk with your keys between your fingers or pretend to be on the phone.' It was good to have these conversations because it made me realise that the things I have automatically done to protect myself for the past thirty-five years and think are normal, don't apply to half the adult population. They really shouldn't be normal and it's simply horrific that Sarah died in circumstances that are every woman's worst nightmare. Sadly, a vigil for her ended with the arrest of four people and swift criticism of the actions of the police. Shortly afterwards, a report found that the police had done a sterling job, but politicians declared that women's confidence in the system had taken a knock and "something must be done about this." What was done about it?

Covid vaccinations continued apace and towards the end of March, a minute's silence took place across the UK, to remember the 126,172 people who had died from Covid since the first lockdown was introduced on 23rd March 2020. A year before, I don't think any of us could have imagined how much our lives would change and that this virus would go on to wipe out millions. Even though lockdowns, masks, restrictions etc have become normalised, I am still occasionally struck by that sense of almost disbelief that I'm living through these times.

The month ended with glorious sunshine and riots in Northern Ireland. Oh yes, and there was a lot of press about whether Nicola Sturgeon misled the Scottish Parliament over her actions in relation to the allegations of sexual assault against Alex Salmond. I lost track of what was going on, but I do hope that if I ever do something terribly wrong, there will be similar levels of obfuscation. In the end, someone important said that women's confidence in the system had taken a knock and everyone agreed that "something must be done about this."

One of my favourite Facebook memories popped up in March. Ah, the day Mr V got banned from going to the shopping mall on his own. It makes me smile every year:

"Conversation with Cherub 2 today about when he would be mature enough to go to the shopping mall on his own -

Me: you'll be mature enough when you can walk past a naked shop mannequin without noticing.

C2: well, when dad and me went to KFC there was a woman and she was definitely wearing a push up bra. Dad noticed and he's allowed to go to the shopping mall on his own!"

Some nice weather in March gave Mr V a yen for cider. He bought my favourite kind, prompting me to comment that if strawberry and lime cider was the vaccine, I'd be so immune right now. It distracted me from my arthritis. Lordy, I hate having arthritis. It makes me sound so old! Lumbago would be worse in the 'sounding old' department, and I suppose I should be thankful that I don't have bunions. My granny had terrible trouble with her bunions and I seem to recall an awful lot of lumbago in the Broons books. Most people outside of Scotland won't know much about the Broons or, the other favourite, Oor Wullie. They were Scottish Christmas staples. One year you'd get the Broons book and the next year you'd get the Oor Wullie book. You're a grown up, you can google the rest for yourself. Suffice to say that Grandpa Broon had awful lumbago.

March was also the month I got addicted to true crime documentaries. Specifically, any murders with forensics or cold cases. I felt ghoulish watching them, so I didn't mention them on the blog in case anyone thought I was trying to get top tips in relation to Mr V's life expectancy. I found that some documentaries were very good, and some were awful. I watched one where the narrator was clearly catering for the lowest common denominator. 'Officer Stuart gets in his vehicle and drives off.' Cut to a gripping scene where the police officer gets in his vehicle and drives off. At one point, the narrator told me, for absolutely no reason at all, 'An officer is on the telephone.' I had to switch off. I just couldn't take the tension anymore. The one take away from all the documentaries is that American CCTV is rubbish.

Righty-ho, enough rambling from me. Let's get on with March.

1ˢᵗ March

Playing Musical Dogs

Now that Vegas is a bit old and doddery, I have to remind him to go for a pee. Several times a day myself and the wee hairy boys go through the same ritual:

Me: *pauses work* Do you want out for a wee?

Vegas: Hmmm let me think about it. Maybe if I walk very slowly in the direction of the back door, it will give her time to forget about this 'out for a wee' business.

Biggles: Yes, yes, yes, I need a wee, ooh cold outside, no, I'm fine, no wees to be had here.

Vegas: Okay, I'll go out for a wee, if I really must.

A few minutes later...

Vegas: Woof, let me in. Woof let me in. I neeeed to come in right now.

Me: *pauses work in Pavlovian response to woofing at back door - dogs have me very well trained*

Biggles: Ooh you've opened the back door. I think I'll go out for a wee.

Vegas: Well, if he's coming out, I'm staying out too.

A few minutes later...

Biggles: Woof, let me in. Woof let me in. I neeeed to come in right now.

Me: *pauses work again* Where's Vegas? *screams for him to come in - the only response is the twitching of Old Ivy Next Door's new conservatory blinds*

Vegas: I'll just ignore her. She must be shouting at another Vegas.

Biggles: Thanks for letting me in. I'm off to find Cherub 1 because she's a bit less shouty than you.

A few minutes later...

Vegas: Woof, let me in. Woof let me in. I neeeed to come in right now.

Me: *pauses work yet again* FFS!!! Am I ever going to get a moment's peace?!

Vegas: I don't know what you're swearing about. You were the one who suggested I go for a wee. Now, seeing as I'm such a good boy, I'd like a treat.

A few minutes later...

Cherub 1: I've just let Biggles out for a wee. Can you let him in when he barks please?

Working from home isn't really working. It's just an endless round of catering to the bladders of my dogs interspersed with sending emails!

4th March

Five Star Mr V

I do like a good online review. I once booked a campsite on the basis of a review of the music piped into the toilet blocks. I hoped for a pitch near block 2 - 80s pop, but sadly got block 4 - modern jazz. The thought 'can you return husbands because this one's broken?' made me wonder what I'd write if I did an online review of Mr V.

Review of The Husband (verified purchase) by Mrs V.

I originally purchased the new boyfriend model, which lived up to its promise of surprise gifts, romance and sexy shenanigans. However, when I installed the husband update, I noticed an increase in the number of pop ups saying, "Stop spending money". This corresponded with a decrease in surprise gifts and romance. The delivery of two small attachments in the early noughties also resulted in a decrease in sexy shenanigans. Those annoying pop ups happened more regularly, as the small attachments depleted our finances and deprived us of sleep. I can only assume that the pop ups are a system error, so I have ignored them. Since the installation of the middle-aged dad upgrade, The Husband has taken a liking to sheds and insists on buying all his underpants in Marks and Spencer. Although worn around the edges and sporting a Lurpak where once there was a six-pack, The Husband continues to function well. Five stars!

5th March

Wonder Why I Didn't Get the Job

I had a job interview today and issued strict instructions to all cherubs and wee hairy boys that they must behave themselves, be quiet and STAY OUT OF THE ROOM. So, of course, there was barking at threatening leaves on the drive, Vegas peed on the carpet and Cherub 2 wandered in halfway through. I suppose I should just be thankful that he was wearing underpants. There was an almighty row between Cherub 1 (lifelong follower of the rules) and Cherub 2 (ignorer of all rules since the age of four) when C1 gave C2 a telling off for breaching my inner sanctum. This row was conducted in silence through the medium of hand gestures, hard stares and the mouthing of swear words. With Cherub 2 standing behind me the whole time. I carried on regardless and expect to collect my KBO (Keep Buggering On) from Buckingham Palace after lockdown. I shall post something proper tomorrow. I don't have time today because I'm too busy screaming at the twats I live with. Pass me the wine.

6th March

Five Star Mrs V

Review of The Wife

***** "Nice Hills"

Mr V, The Living Room, United Kingdom

When I first visited The Wife in 1993 there were a couple of gentle hills and I quite enjoyed a dip in the lake. The nightlife was bouncing and I rarely got denied entry. By 2002, the arrival of a couple of small marauders had rendered the hills and lake off limits to all but the most intrepid of travellers. Which was a shame because the hills had grown bigger and looked very interesting. There were sporadic attempts at conservation, but unpredictable nighttime incursions by tiny, feral insomniacs made the area unsafe. As the years passed, I found myself making hefty contributions to beautifying The Wife and her surroundings. Somehow, inexplicable things like false nails, reed diffusers, fancy face creams and cushions appeared. My favourite armchair was replaced with a modern sofa and I wasn't sure how I felt about that. Despite the changes wrought by time, I keep coming back to The Wife. The quality of the food varies, with far too much emphasis on vegetables and too few chicken nuggets imho, but there's always lots to do and fun to be had. Also, five stars for looking like a twat when she tries to pout in selfies.

7th March

Reflecting on a Year of Lockdowns

Have you braced yourselves for a round of 'One Year Since We Went Into Lockdown' this month? There will be no doubt be retrospectives in the news and we'll all be thinking about what we were thinking about this time last year. At least there is some light at the end of the lockdown tunnel now.

Lockdowns are like children. With the first, you're precious about everything. You make your other half strip when they get home from work (to be honest, I'm still doing that, but only coz I like it), you're zooming everyone you know and the Mission Impossible tune plays in your head every time you walk through Tesco. By number three, you've relaxed a bit. You're half-heartedly waving a wet wipe in the vague direction of the shopping and you're back to texting "still here" once a week to assure your family you're alive. Cross fingers we never get to lockdown four. I'll be drunk-posting naked pictures of myself on the family WhatsApp group and wearing a bra again just for the novelty factor. Probably just as well I stopped at two children. Number three might have scraped through but number four would have been feral. However, I digress.

A year on, with Boris' roadmap clutched in their sweaty little hands, a lot of people with very bad hair are about to be released into the wild. I wonder what history will say about us. Or, like the Spanish Flu, will it all be forgotten, only to pop up a hundred years from now when something else happens?

It has been a tough year for so many people. Frightening, stressful, depressing. It has also been a year where we have seen deep divisions in our society. The situation we are in has often been compared to World War 2. There were probably selfish feckers around then too, but they are gone from our collective memory. We are left with an impression of a nation of good people pulling together. I hope history remembers the many thousands of little kindnesses of 2020-2021, because the nurse who lived in a caravan to keep her family safe, the man who did his neighbour's shopping for a whole year, the people who worked long and hard to keep a nation healthy, fed and safe, the people we lost and the people who cared about us - they're the ones worth remembering.

Whatever your thoughts about the past year, I hope there are some positives in there. Now, eyes on the prize, my Lovelies. Keep buggering on and keep staying safe until we get ourselves over the line.

8th March

The Queen of Computers

I'm quite technologically minded, but Mr V is king of the cables. Our worlds collided at the weekend when I needed cables to do something technological.

I researched the cables then made the mistake of telling Mr V what cables I needed. His eyes lit up, like I'd given him a special man-project. Mr V didn't have those cables in his collection. I'd handed him a challenge. Was I sure those were the correct cables? Had I tried this cable? What about that cable? He set about plugging things into my computer and making me double-check the number of ports. All two of them. Thank fuck I took GCSE maths or we'd have been stuffed. Had I checked this website? What about that website? I assured him I had checked and only these two cables would do the job.

Mr V went off and researched cables. He came back and told me all about his research. What the different websites said. What the different cables did. There was lots of talk about backwards compatibility and male to male/male to female. I was starting to wonder whether we were still talking about cables or if he'd become a wee bit diverted by the sexy shenanigans part of the internet during his research. Finally, having delivered the most boring lecture known to womankind (with the possible exception of yesterday's monologue on fences), Mr V made his pronouncement on which cables I'd need. Exactly the same ones I had told him about an hour ago.

I ordered the cables and they should arrive on Wednesday. Mr V is quite disconcerted by my willingness to wait for *his* new cables rather than pay extra for next day delivery.

Happy International Women's Day. In our house, the struggle is real.

9th March

The Cleverest of Clogs

I went to the loo this morning and couldn't get out again. The handle wouldn't twist and the door wouldn't budge. I pushed and pulled and fiddled with the lock, all to no avail. 'Oh bugger,' I thought. 'How am I going to explain getting locked in the loo again to Mr V?'

The last time this happened, he kicked the door in, emerging triumphant in his underpants and one gardening shoe (the other shoe having sailed into the bathroom ahead of him). We'd had to suffer weeks of no handle on the loo door as Mr V has an SLA that all DIY will be done within six months. Eventually, he patched the door back together and attached a new handle. I could at last stop worrying about Cherub 2 seeing me pee.

This time, relieved that I'd taken my phone with me, I decided to bite the bullet and confess that I was once more stuck in the loo. I called Mr V. 'That's weird,' I thought. I could hear his phone ringing outside the bathroom door. Why would his phone be there? Where was Mr V? The penny did not drop. It took a few more tugs on the door before I heard snickering from the other side.

Eventually Mr V let go of the handle and let me out. He has spent the rest of the day thinking he's the cleverest of clogs. Watch this space. I will have my revenge!

***

Settle in, dear reader, for the story of the first time Mrs V got locked in the loo.

Once upon a time a slightly rotund, yet suprisingly attractive, princess got stuck in the downstairs loo and was late for work. She had to phone her dashing knight, let's call him Sir Mr V, to get out of bed and rescue her. He duly arrived and slid a ruler of the finest steel under the door.

'Use it to jiggle stuff,' cried Sir Mr V.

The princess duly jiggled stuff, but it didn't work. Oddly, no amount of manly instruction as to the correct jiggling technique made any difference either!

Sir Mr V then slid the window key under the door so he could pass the princess a trusty screwdriver through the window. When the princess got the key stuck in the window lock, he asked, 'Have you tried putting the key in the other way round?'

After the princess stopped shouting at him that she was not a blithering idiot and that she knew how to work an effing key, he suggested she take the door handle off. Strangely, this proved impossible without a trusty screwdriver.

It was at this point that Sir Mr V realised he might have given her the wrong window key. To her delight, the princess learned that there are no limits to the number of eff words she could fit into one sentence.

Approximately one hundred years passed, and the duo finally got the window open, the screwdriver delivered and the door handle off. Sir Mr V extracted all the insidey bits, but a piece of metal was still jamming the door. The princess was trapped.

Now, I'm fairly sure Sir Mr V's whole life had been building up to this next bit. He had to break down the door. He actually said, 'Stand back. I'm going to break down the door.' Then, when his first attempt failed, he got to say it again! It really was like in the movies.

Finally, our action hero came bursting through the loo

door in a hail of splinters, wearing one gardening shoe and a pair of boxers.

Hooray! The princess was free!

To reward his valour, that night the princess gifted Sir Mr V some of his favourite movies, which just happen to be a bit girly. Okay, the princess rewarded Sir Mr V with some of her favourite movies. But the thought was there.

And they lived happily bickering ever after.

***

13th March

Those Two Little Words

Mr V is having a slight meltdown because last night I said, 'Have you sent your mum a Mother's Day card?'

'It's not Mother's Day yet,' he assured me.

'It's on Sunday,' I assured him. 'I could have said nothing and watched you panic on Sunday, but I decided to give you a fighting chance.'

'Oh, bugger. Hang on, are you winding me up to get back at me for shutting you in the loo?'

'Nope. That's not my revenge.'

'Oh, bugger. I haven't got you a present. You can have anything you like provided it's available on Amazon Prime. What do you want?'

'Surprise me.'

Those are possibly the worst two words I could ever toss in Mr V's direction. Guaranteed to both confuse and torture. He has no clue, no direction. And dire consequences if he gets it wrong.

He hung around for a moment to see if any more information was forthcoming, before declaring, 'Well, that's not helpful,' and sloping off to spend an agonising hour on Amazon.

Now, that's my revenge.

P.S. I did take pity on him after a while.

14th March

To My Mum

Happy Mother's Day to all the amazing women, past and present, who have done their best to turn us into vaguely sensible human beings, kept us on the straight and narrow and been there for us when we needed them.

My own mum was a woman who quietly made an impact. If you google her, you'll find no trace. She deserved recognition, but she'd have been horrified at the thought of it. Over the years, she fostered dozens of children. They came to her damaged yet, with kindness, patience and sometimes a healthy dose of tough love, they left her whole. She ran a playgroup, two gymnastics clubs and a church kids' group. Over her life, she gave far more than she took. Yet mum had appalling taste in decor and was incredibly untidy. She'd lift the mess, vacuum and put it all back again, and I have her to thank for my high clutter-tolerance. In short, she was rubbish at the things that don't matter and brilliant at the things that do. Which I think is something we could all aspire to.

That is why I'm raising my cup of tea to all the women who have made a difference in our lives. Cheers.

15th March

Who Needs a Perineum Anyway?

Is anyone else out there suffering a lockdown knicker shortage? Honestly, I'm almost reduced to my episiotomy pants. The sexy, lacy ones that only come out on special occasions on account of their ability to ride up and slice you in two. Mr V isn't as keen for a return to big, comfy knickers, because a) they are big, comfy knickers and b) knickers are surprisingly expensive. However, I find that mentioning the words 'gusset' and 'yeast' tend to discourage most enquiries regarding the underwear budget.

I'm also long overdue a visit to the scaffolding department. My rare forays into the world of bra wearing during lockdown have led to the sacrifice of two bras. I can only suppose that lack of use had weakened the stitching. It was definitely not expansion of Mrs V.

I did a job interview this afternoon in posh top, full make-up, no bra and pyjama bottoms. An hour later I am frantically trying to recall if I removed my dressing gown.

Really, I think the best thing for me is a return to normality as soon as possible.

***

Knickers are a perennial (perineal?) problem for me. Over the years, I have successfully brainwashed Mr V into believing that slightly greying granny pants and a T-shirt bra are the sexiest thing on earth. Therefore, I'm wary of sexy knickers. They might raise his expectations and undo all that hard work. I prefer to save my posh knickers for parties. That's how he knows it's Christmas. If he's a very good boy, I might do a spot of lady gardening as well.

The other annoying thing about knickers is when you find yesterday's pair balled up inside your trouser leg. Or, if you don't notice in time, on the office floor. That definitely happened to a friend and not me.

In other embarrassing knicker-related lore, I once went for a job interview in Leeds. It was a long train journey and by the time I arrived, I was desperate for a wee. I'd held it in for so long that I did one of those wees where you think you're finished, but you're not. Long story short, I stood up before the final encore and ended up doing the job interview in a lovely dress and no knickers. My mum once sent me to Sunday School with no knickers, on the very week that I decided to stand on the special 'show and tell chair', so I could tell the class about my grandad dying. Let's just say that there was more showing than telling, and the trauma lives with me to this day. So, turning up to a job interview knickerless was my childhood nightmare. And I didn't even get the job!

Somebody once asked if I'd ever been offered free stuff when I mentioned brands in my blog. I said no, my mentions of Marks and Spencer were merely a form of worship at the altar of comfy knickers. 'In fact,' I told them, 'I think I might be the world's first social media unfluencer.' I must have been quite taken by the thought of being an unfluencer because I scribbled down some ideas on what I would post on Instagram:

No make-up days are the best. The no lipstick and no blusher are from my 'I Don't Care' collection.

Feeling feminine and powerful today. Hair by no one.

Black pumps and cankles are getting me through those hot days at work.

Trousers. Because legs don't shave themselves.

So blessed to have these two girls in my life. Love releasing them at the end of the day. (my boobs)

Completing the look today with a light moustache.

Just loving toenails. They're so ... toenaily.

So grateful for this amazing world planet Earth and all its knickers.

One final thought. Why not use the power of your pants for good? Send them to smallsforall.org, who send knickers to adults and children in Africa and those in dire straits nearer home. Or at least take a peek at their website. You'd be amazed at the dignity a pair of knickers can bring.

***

17th March

Vaccination Day

I had my vaccination today and I feel so privileged. I don't believe any of the fake news guff around vaccines but, if they really have microchipped me, someone at GCHQ is now wondering how it is possible to make so many trips to the fridge. Honestly folks, please know it was quick and virtually painless. It's just a little prick and, let's face it, we've all dealt with a few of those in our time.

Of course, I immediately developed the recognised side effect of having to eat a packet of Jaffa cakes. I rushed home just in time to grab a packet and dial into a meeting. I was so busy trying beat my own record for how many I could fit into my mouth at once that I only realised, when I got the minutes a couple of hours later, that I'd 'volunteered' for an action point. I feel my delicate condition was taken advantage of. I wonder if I could go back to the chair and say, 'Sorry, I'm on leave the day this action point must be done. What do you mean a date wasn't set? I think you'll find I'm on leave on any of the days this action point must be done.'

I know there are some worries around about side effects at the moment and stuff in the news about blood clots. All I can say is that given a choice between vaccine and Covid, I'll take the vaccine, thank you very much.

When I was being guided through various queues by volunteer stewards, I thought about the scale of the operation to get us all vaccinated and felt a huge sense pride in our country and all the people who have mobilised to get this done. I guess that's why I feel so privileged to get the vaccine, so keen to do my bit to protect my fellow humans and so relieved that I have some measure of protection for myself.

This page isn't a place for political debate, but if you are on the fence about getting the vaccine, please please make sure you're getting your facts from legitimate sources (not Nelly Next Door who was a hospital cleaner in 1992 and has a PhD in curtain twitching and complaining that the cat from down the road keeps shitting on her lawn). Please consider the good you'll be doing for everyone. It really is a quick and simple thing that will make an enormous difference.

19th March

Mum's the Word

As a parent it is your job to wind up your kids. This popped up in my Facebook memories yesterday. It's one of my favourites (along with trying to convince him last year that you get 'up the bum' paracetamols and his was the 'up the bum' kind. Ooh, and maybe the time I put a fake dog poo next to his chair, refused to believe the dog had done a poo and picked it up and licked it just to check. And then there was the time...well, you get the picture:

Me - you've never found our secret room have you?

Cherub 2 - what! Do you have a secret room?

Me - I can neither confirm nor deny because it's a secret

Cherub 2 - do you have one, yes or no? You have to say yes or no.

Me - I'll say...erm...no

Cherub 2 - I don't believe you. Do you have a secret room or are you just winding me up?

Me - no

Cherub 2 - so do you not have a secret room or are you not winding me up?

This went on for a while

20th March

Hippocrite

Pass me my angry trousers and saddle up my high horse, for I can feel a moan coming on. Mr V owns approximately 3,496 coats and only wears one of them. Yet I want to buy one teeny, tiny six-foot hippopotamus for the garden and suddenly I'm "wasting money." I reported him to the management, but his mother says she has more important things to worry about. I cannot imagine what could be more important than this!

Then, to top it all off, he seems to have developed side effects from *my* vaccine. I've been absolutely fine. He has fatigue and a headache. He's due to get his own jab next week and will no doubt suffer from horrendous man-jab-flu, requiring round the clock sympathy. Well, my sympathy costs rather a lot of money and it's currently sitting in a garden centre in Essex. Nurse Mrs V gets paid in iron hippos.

I'm fairly sure I'm not being unreasonable.

21st March

Peri-What?

I recently had a day of menopausal brain-farts. At least, I'm assuming they were menopausal and not just me paying no attention as usual.

Nobody ever talks about the menopause and it's only recently that I've become aware that the big M is not simply ten years of hot flushes, periods stop and Roberta's your auntie, job done, now on your way you dried up old husk. It has taken me a long time to work out that my itchy skin, dry eyes and inability to think in a straight line are probably down to (and I'm imagining my mum whispering here) The Change. I'd never even heard of perimenopause until my doctor, the old charmer, described me as a perimenopausal woman a couple of years ago!

Why don't we talk about the menopause more? Why are women quietly getting on with it? Why didn't I know much about it? I'm not suggesting we scream from the rooftops that our fandangos are drier than a mouthful of cinnamon, but I do think we need to be more open. After all, drought in the garden of ladies is only a small part of it. It's about hormones wreaking havoc in the bodies of 50% of the population. We talk about puberty - why not menopause? Have you spoken with your kids about it? I haven't. Would you tell your boss about it? Would your boss even understand?

Last year I asked people in a meeting if we could have the window open because I was too hot. I'd noticed I'd been feeling hot quite a lot, and not even the sexy kind of hot. It being winter, everyone looked at me like I'd just asked them to shit in their hands and clap. 'Sorry, menopause!' I gaily announced. There was an awkward silence. I'd plonked an extremely large elephant in the room and nobody knew quite how to shift it.

So, today I'm inviting you to talk about it. How are you

feeling? How are you coping? How are you sleeping? Do you have fifty fans placed at strategic points around the bedroom and a partner who's terrified to mention that it's minus 10 outside and could we please shut the window? Let's demystify it for the peri-menopausal women of the future - may they never have to go home, ask Google and feel like they've just been given a rather depressing label.

***

I was struck by the responses to this post, perhaps more than any other I've written. Many ladies, like me, felt completely unprepared and wished that someone had told us about this stuff at school. Afterwards, I tried to talk to Cherub 1 about it, but she really didn't want to know. Presumably because she thought I was going to talk about my lady bits (I wasn't!) and hearing that your mum possesses such a thing is just eeeeeewwwww. Which seems rather unfair because both my children regard me as the go to person for all their intimate woes and I have to listen to their moans. Perhaps in future I should offer to take a look. That'll put paid to it.

Back to perimenopause. One of the stand-out things for me was that women had been prescribed anti-depressants rather than their GP twigging that it might be menopause related. It's terrible to think what they and other ladies in a similar situation have gone through. Believing they were losing their minds, when all along it was nature.

People described uncontrollable rage and mood swings, which was incredibly distressing for them and left them feeling guilty about the impact they'd had on their families. There were sore breasts, hot and cold flushes, night sweats, lack of confidence, loss of identity, early menopause, late menopause. The list went on. One lady said that her doctor glossed over it, as if it was a non-event, so she doesn't talk about it to anyone. She was not alone in that. Hundreds of people came on to share their experiences and it was apparent that, right here in the 21st Century, women are simply not getting the education or the healthcare they need around menopause.

22nd March

Being a Nuisance

Mr V was doing technical wizardry last night and kept interrupting my programme to ask me things. To be fair, he was doing the technical wizardry for me because my brain would have exploded if I tried it, but really, he was being most annoying. He kept making me hang around to check I was happy with stuff. I kept digging escape tunnels and disappearing off to do unimportant things, like pee, and important things, like find biscuits. Eventually, he threw his hands in the air and pronounced me "very difficult to work with." I worry that he may have overlooked my delightfulness.

Anyway, the long and short of it is that The Big Blue Jobbie is now available in hardback.

I suggested we quote some of the reviews on the cover, to let people know how brilliant it is. Mr V, who had just spent two hours fiddling with the cover, looked at me with murderous intent, so I decided that now was not the time to mention my delightfulness.

23rd March

Oh Aye?

Itching to cut my own hair and dye it but knowing we're so close to hairdressers being open that I really shouldn't touch it. Then a wee voice in my head pipes up, 'But what if you can't get an appointment for weeks? What'll you do then? Hmm?'

The voice in my head is actually a wee Scottish wifie called Elsie, standing there with hands on hips and headscarf firmly in place over her rollers. Sometimes, when I think I've had a marvellous idea, Elsie gives me a sideways glance and says, 'Oh aye?' Which is Scottish shorthand for anything from "That's interesting" to "This plan is doomed, you big twat." She's a good, strong woman, Elsie. The kind of woman who irons her tea towels and roams the high street, clipping the heels of unsuspecting passers-by with her tartan shopping trolley. She takes no prisoners and sometimes pops out of my mouth to offend everyone in earshot.

She gave me some good advice today, when I was reflecting on a year of lockdowns (lockieversary) at midday. I was thinking about all we've lost in the past year and feeling a bit sad until Elsie hit me across the knuckles with her wooden spoon and said, 'Think about what's been achieved. Vaccines, a whole new appreciation of the NHS, your nearest and dearest are safe and pyjamas are official work uniform. Stop being an old misery. And as for dying your hair pink...oh aye?'

24th March

Catfeckers

A twat has been commenting on yesterday's post, trying to get ladies to message him. Please don't - it'll be a romance scammer who wants your life savings. I've blocked him so hopefully his comments have now disappeared.

We middle aged folk are prime targets for romance scammers using fake social media profiles (catfishing). They assume we're all lonely, well off and a wee bit daft. Every time I read a report in the news about someone being conned like this, I want to give them a big hug. Admittedly, part of me thinks 'do they not read the magazines and newspapers?!', but you really can't judge someone for falling for it. After all, the fraudster's entire job is to psychologically manipulate people, so I imagine they'd be quite good at it.

When I see a "hello lady please message me" comment, I usually check the person's profile and find that it was set up recently. Often there are incongruities, for example their friends are all from a different country and, despite allegedly being men in their sixties, they follow an awful lot of pages about menopausal women. Sometimes stock photos are used or photos are pinched from elsewhere.

Catfishers' profiles (certainly the ones I've seen on G.O.D.) are usually men, although I did get a message from a woman on Instagram recently. When I ignored it, she followed up with a slightly threatening message that I should reply for my own good. Delete!

I always report the fake accounts to Facebook, although they often don't take any action. I always block suspected catfishers from G.O.D. as soon as I spot them. If you spot one or have concerns about any of the comments made, please get in touch with me or report the person to Facebook. Don't reply to their comments.

Age UK has some good information on spotting and dealing with catfishing.

27th March

List of Important Things to Do

Woo hoo! I'm on leave for a week. I'm going to get loads done. I have goals.

1. Apple's "how much time you've wasted playing Words With Friends and googling obscure medical symptoms" weekly usage report will show a 500% increase by Friday.
2. Convince Mr V that the caterpillar toilet roll holder I bought is the thing that has been missing from his life.
3. Reward myself with ice cream when I have dusted the lamp in Covid Corner because that counts as light dusting.
4. Accept my fate and go to the well-known DIY store that rhymes with Wee & Poo to look at gardening equipment with Mr V. Be a supportive wife and do not suggest I wait in the car. However, pick up some paint charts and wallpaper samples. Discuss them at length so that he can a) empathise with my feelings on the subject of lawn scarifiers and b) sh*t himself in case I make him wallpaper the spare room.
5. Poison my children by making them eat wholesome home-cooked meals that are not pot noodles.

That's enough to be getting on with.

28th March

Doomed to Life with Brad

My day so far has not gone to plan. This morning I did exactly the kind of thing my mum would have done. The kind of thing that made teenage me scared to take anyone back to my house. My pyjama trousers kept falling down, so I pinned them to my pyjama top with a clothes peg and happily went about my day. After all, I reasoned, we're not allowed visitors, so it's not like anyone would see me.

The lack of visitors thing has also meant that tidiness has been less of a priority. Where, once upon a time, downstairs was kept tidy even if upstairs was Armageddon, nowadays downstairs is like...edge of Armageddon. Not quite there, but regularly teetering, only to be pulled back when one of us yells at the Cherubs that "this place is like an effing student flat!" My hallway is currently full of the rejects from Cherub 1's bedroom spring clean. Mr V will play garage tetris with them in due course and do lots of moaning about how every time he creates a space big enough for a car, other people fill it up with their junk. We will all look dumbfounded because it has never occurred to any of us that cars go in garages.

So, you see the state of play here. Me, the great unwashed, with my pyjama trousers held up by a clothes peg and my hall serving as the Cherub dumping ground. No visitors expected. Except I hadn't factored in the Amazon man. The Amazon man is a frequent visitor and has taken to popping into the house and leaving my parcels in the hall. He is also very cheerful and quite good looking, and I have toyed with the idea of marrying the Amazon man if Mr V ever divorces me for treating his sacred garage like a tardis. I toy no more. As of this morning, the Amazon man thinks I'm a bag lady who lives in a shithole. The wedding plans are off and we're back to Brad Pitt or Ryan Reynolds as my back-up Mr Vs.

It's disappointing that I now have to marry Ryan or Brad, but somehow, I will struggle on.

31st March

The Last One

Day 6004 of writing. Well, day 2, but my skin is already rebelling due to lack of daylight and the chair keeps cutting off the circulation to my legs. Every time I get up for a coffee, I stagger into the kitchen like Anne Widdicombe on a bender. So far, I've written 11,000 words, watched two episodes of Top Gear and eaten an entire cheesecake. I'm both hungry and easily distracted.

Nevertheless, I have to maintain some perspective. It's a special day today. All the people shielding in England and Wales have been released. I was set free last summer, but some people with serious conditions have been pretty much stuck in self-isolation for a year. A whole year! How are you all feeling? I imagine it will be quite weird to be back out among people again. Some of you will no doubt be anxious about the risks to your health or simply not feeling very confident. After four months of being mothballed, I found the idea of shops, with their queues, masks and one-way systems, quite daunting. Which seems odd now, because if there's one thing I'm good at, it's shops. However you feel, I hope you have some good people around for support as you get used to another new normal.

THE LAST BIT

I'm going to leave things here. I'm writing this ending on 31st March, although it will take me a bit longer to edit the book. It seems a good place to stop.

Across two books, I've covered just over a year of lockdown life and we're now, fingers crossed, on the cusp of some sort of normality. We have vaccines, and the restrictions have changed to allow us to meet up to six people outdoors, including gardens. Mr V and I have plans to see Lovely Granny and Grandad for the first time since we dropped their Christmas presents off and had a shouted conversation from the bottom of their drive. The Cherubs have already visited LG and G, although I suspect that Easter eggs played a part in their haste.

Over the next couple of months, fingers crossed, we can expect a gradual slackening of the rules and things will start to open up. Europe is going through a third wave of the virus, but the UK has so far vaccinated half its population and I fervently hope that our head start is enough to keep all things pandemic on an even keel.

Perhaps future generations will wonder what living through the pandemic was like. Wall to wall Netflix and social media, my darlings. We were glued to our devices and hooked on sharing. We got very annoyed with rule breakers yet none of us would grass up Old Ivy Next Door when she had the grandkids over. Even though Old Ivy would probably grass us up to the entire street in a heartbeat. Old Ivy is great. She'll always be there for you in a crisis, yet she is also the type of person who objects to planning permission just because she can. Mr V once had a nightmare about a boundary dispute with Old Ivy. He woke me up, shouting, 'Okay, I'll move the fence.' Clearly, he lost the dispute.

Here I will leave you with a short story to counterbalance the beginning of this book.

THE ENDING

Once upon a time three friends, whom we shall call War, Pestilence and Death, sat at a small wooden table and gazed anxiously around the Dead Lion.

'Where's Famine?' asked Pestilence, anxiously.

'I don't know, but if he's late for the pub quiz, I'll kill him,' said War.

'Well, that's just great,' harumphed Death. 'Give me extra work on my night off, why don't you?!'

'Sorry,' said War. 'I'll go out to the car park and see if his horse is there.'

War squeezed out from behind the table, trying not to scratch the wood with his armour, and wandered off to find Famine. He returned a few minutes later with his friend in tow.

'Sorry, sorry, sorry,' said Famine. 'I bumped into one of our old teachers by the fruit machine. Do you remember old Morbid Obesity?'

'Oh yes! He was brilliant. Remember that time we hired a choir of angels to follow Mr Obesity around, singing at him all day?' asked Death.

'Yeah, but he got his own back. Took me ages to the pink dye out of my horse,' said War.

'I hated school,' said Pestilence, glumly. 'You guys were the only ones who would sit with me.'

'Because we didn't mind the flies. School dinners were a nightmare, though, mate. We had to wolf everything down before you turned it putrid. It wasn't until I left school that I realised custard doesn't taste like old socks,' War said, matter-of-factly.

'But you do have the putrid thing under control now?' Famine asked. He had just ordered seventeen portions of chips and, although the flies thing didn't bother him, finding worms in your chips was just not on.

Pestilence assured Famine that he only lost control when he was drunk. War mused that he often had a similar problem. He recalled a time when, after a few too many pints, he started a bar fight then went home and mistook his mother's walk-in closet for the bathroom. Not such a huge deal if it had just been a number one. War had wanted to keep that one quiet, but his mum posted something on Gracebook and soon everyone in heaven was calling him Mr Drobe.

The conversation moved on to picking their pub quiz team name.

'How about the Four Horsemen of the Apocalypse?' suggested Death.

Everyone rolled their eyes. Death was not known for his imagination. Things were pretty much black or white in his world.

'Nah, too obvious mate,' said Pestilence. 'How about the Lords of the Flies?'

'Yeah, like that's not creepy,' said Famine. 'Maybe the Lords of the Pies?'

'Do you ever think of anything other than food?' asked War. 'Look. Your chips are here. All seventeen bowls of 'em. How do you eat so much and stay so skinny?'

'Dunno. My mum says I'm just a growing boy.'

'You're four thousand years old! You have your own

chariot, and you even once had a girlfriend. You're not a growing boy.'

Famine looked slightly depressed at the mention of his ex-girlfriend. He knew he'd been punching above his weight with Ruby Nesque and that it wouldn't last forever. She was so gorgeous, though. All those curves and boobs. He mostly liked the boobs. The problem was that Ruby was super-sensitive about her weight and Famine made the mistake of entering them both into a hotdog eating competition. He thought it would be a fun day out. She thought he was taking the piss. Things culminated in a huge argument, where he became so angry that he accidentally wiped out the crops in Belgium. Shortly after they broke up, Ruby died. She dreamt she was eating a marshmallow, woke up and her pillow was gone. What a shame, thought Famine, that her tricky relationship with food should have such repercussions. She never believed that she was beautiful just as she was. Death had broken the news to him the next morning and his first thought had been…hang on just a second. Famine was struck by a brainwave.

'Reapercussions! Geddit? We should be the Reaper-cussions,' he declared.

'Brilliant,' said War.

'Awww, well done mate. Perfect,' said Pestilence.

'Pick on the Death guy, why don't you,' said Death, gloomily running a finger down his scythe. His mum had brought him back a new Scythe from her River Styx cruise last month. She and his uncle Charon had done the Titan tour and found the cutest little weapon shop, tucked away on the great marsh. Uncle Charon earned a fortune on the ferries, so had loaned Death's mum the money for the scythe. 'Don't worry,' he later told Death, 'I think of it as an investment in my future. Now, off you go and bring more people my way.'

Death reflected that he may be on the wrong end of the expiration business. Also, he wasn't too keen on the new scythe. It was a bit bling for his taste. He'd recently started seeing

Pestilence's sister, Disease, and she loved the scythe, possibly a bit too much. She kept making him do this weird role-playing thing where...Death halted his thoughts right there. He fiddled with the zip on his hoodie and felt a pang of longing for his old scythe and his cloak. The hoodie was another Disease thing. She'd dragged him to the Top Man closing down sale and forced him to try it on. 'OMG. Makes you look sooo 21st Century, like,' she'd declared, before pulling him to the counter to pay. Death wasn't sure that Disease was The One, but what with her being Pestilence's sister and all, breaking up with her would have serious repercussions.

Death sighed. 'Okay,' he said. 'Reaper-cussions it is.'

War scribbled their team name on the answer sheet. The Reaper Cushions.

'It's supposed to be Reaper-cussions. Geddit?' Famine pointed out.

War looked at him blankly.

'You don't get it, do you?'

'No,' said War, 'but I'll tell you what I am getting. Another round. Anyone want one?'

War charged off to the bar and Famine, Death and Pestilence gazed after him, their expressions troubled.

'He's my best mate, but he can be dead thick sometimes,' said Famine.

'We're going to lose again. It'll put him in a bad temper all week and I'll have to go around clearing up his mess,' said Death.

'Come on lads. There's three of us. We can carry War. No man left behind and all that jazz,' said Pestilence, ever the optimist. He quite enjoyed the aftermath of one of War's tantrums because there tended to be a lot of people in hospital. And Pestilence really liked hospitals.

A loud squawk and a tap came from the overhead speakers.

293

A few seconds later, a deep voice boomed, 'Good evening, laaaaadies and gentledeities. Are you ready for some questions?'

A half-hearted mutter rippled through the crowd of drinkers.

'I said ARE YOU READY?' shouted the quizmaster, in a vain attempt to whip up a frenzy of enthusiasm.

'I AM READY. I WILL WIN THIS QUIZ AND WOE BETIDE ANY WHO CROSS ME!' bellowed a voice from the bar.

The pub went silent. Famine, Pestilence and Death slunk lower in their seats. Death pulled his hood over his head and tightened the cords. Maybe this hoodie thing wasn't so bad after all, he thought, as his face disappeared into the depths of the soft cotton. War had that confident aggression thing going on. The one that signalled he was only a few beers away from offering to fight anyone who disagreed with him. Oh dear, this really did not bode well when he got all the answers wrong.

War returned to the table and plonked down a tray of beers. Three for him and one each for everyone else. 'It's going to be a good night, lads. I can feel it in my bones.'

'Question one,' came the disembodied voice above their heads. 'For how many years did the Hundred Years War last?'

'Ooh, ooh, I know this one,' said War, grabbing the pen and scribbling 116 on the answer sheet.

'Question two,' came the disembodied voice again. 'What is a spatha?'

'Ooh, ooh, I know this one,' said War, grabbing the pen and scribbling Sword on the answer sheet.

The others looked on in astonishment. After a few more battle-related questions, the quizmaster moved onto round two, music.

'In which year did ABBA win the Eurovision Song

Contest? And an extra point if you can name the winning song.'

'Ooh, ooh, I know this one,' said War, grabbing the pen and scribbling 1974 Waterloo on the answer sheet.

And so it went on, until they got to, 'Which song, released as a single by the Plastic Ono Band in July 1969, reached number two in the UK singles chart?'

Everyone looked expectantly at War. War looked blank. 'I don't know this one,' he said, crestfallen.

'Give Peace A Chance,' muttered Famine.

'Why would anyone want to do that?' chorused the others, incredulous that people were singing about such terrible things.

Before Famine could shrug his shoulders in complete bafflement, the voice boomed once more from the speakers and the quiz continued. Finally, they reached the tie-breaker question.

'In the event of a tie, the team which gets this question right wins. It's a doozie! Add the total number of people infected by Typhoid Mary to pi rounded to three decimal places.'

War turned to Famine. 'Come on, mate. You know about pies.'

Pestilence threw War a pitying look. 'I got this one. Typhoid Mary – definitely fifty-three. And pi...' Pestilence scratched his head. All those years of maths detention couldn't be for nothing.

'3.142,' interjected Death.

'How did you know that?' asked Pestilence, impressed.

Death unzipped his hoodie to reveal a t-shirt covered in numbers. 'Your sister finds maths a big turn on. Listen mate, I really need to talk to you about her. She's making me do stuff--'

'Not now,' interrupted Pestilence. He leaned over to the

next table to swap answer sheets. 'Ha, look at their team name. The Arkivists. Good one, Noah and Mrs Noah.'

The speaker crackled into life and the quizmaster's voice broke through the hubbub. 'Angels and gentledemons, lend me your ears. Are you all ready to mark your neighbours' answers? Here we go. Question one...'

Eventually, the answer sheets were marked and returned. The Reaper-cussions gazed in awe at their score. Every answer was correct. They'd won!

Several hours and many, many pints later, Famine, Pestilence and War stumbled out of the Dead Lion, reeling as the fresh air hit them.

'It's been a great night,' said War. 'I haven't started any fights and I can't believe I knew the answers.'

'Great night, lads. We can't believe you knew the answers either, but good on you, mate.' Pestilence patted War on the back.

'Yeah, good one,' said Famine. 'Are we still on for the Apocalypse on Tuesday?'

'No can do, Famine.' War grinned and levered himself awkwardly onto his horse. 'They have a good quiz at the World's End on Wednesdays. No way am I missing that. I'm on a roll!' With that, he slumped over the neck of his horse and slurred, 'Take me home, Giddyup.'

Famine and Pestilence gazed after him fondly then went back into the pub to find Death. He was deep in conversation with the quizmaster at the bar. As they approached, Death looked up, a smile on his normally gloomy face. 'Alright, lads. Have you met my Uncle Charon?'

'Awww, Death, tell me you didn't fix the quiz,' groaned Pestilence.

'Yeah, well, things have been really busy this past year and what with the Apocalypse next week, I could really do with a lie in instead of dealing with the results of one of War's rampages. So, I asked Uncle Charon here to stand in for the regular quizmaster. What's the problem?'

Famine extracted his hand from the bowl of peanuts on the bar, wiped it on his tunic and held it out to Uncle Charon. 'Pleased to meet you, Uncle Charon. What are you up to next Wednesday?'

And that, ladies and gentlereaders, is why the Apocalypse didn't happen.

THE END

ABOUT THE AUTHOR

As a child, I loved reading. I spent my life with my nose in a book and, when finally forced back into the real world, I wrote poetry and stories. My hero was Pam Ayres and all I wanted to be when I grew up was a librarian, so that I could be around books all the time.

Of course, life takes you on different paths. Somehow, writing poems and stories got lost along the way. I was too busy partying in London through my twenties then being a mum through my thirties and forties. But on an August morning in 2018, at the tender age of forty-eight, I woke up and decided to create a blog on Facebook. Ten minutes later, Growing Old Disgracefully was born and the love of writing came flooding back. Encouraged by my lovely readers, I finally got off my lazy behind, put fingers to keyboard and wrote my first book, The Big Blue Jobbie. Well, first book if you exclude the anthology of truly dreadful poems by Yvonne, age eight, which my parents pretended to love. Bless my own wee cotton socks, there was even an index and I coloured all the edges of the pages purple to make it look posh.

With book number one under my belt, it was onwards and upwards to The Big Blue Jobbie #2 and my first novel, Frock In Hell. Next up will probably be Finding Freddie, the tale of a missing hamster on an island off the coast of Aberdeen. The story is in my head and I can't wait to tell it to you.